sphere

A CIP catalogue record for this book
is available from the British Library.

ISBN 978-0-7515-4251-6

Typeset in Bembo by Palimpsest Book Production Limited, .
Falkirk, Stirlingshire
Printed and bound in Great Britain by
Clays Ltd, St Ives plc

Papers used by Sphere are from well-managed forests
and other responsible sources.

MIX
Paper from
responsible sources
FSC® C104740

Sphere
An imprint of
Little, Brown Book Group
100 Victoria Embankment
London EC4Y 0DY

An Hachette UK Company
www.hachette.co.uk

www.littlebrown.co.uk

Acknowledgements

I would like to thank Steve Gerrard for his invaluable help. It will be clear to all cave divers that I followed his expert advice only as far as suited the plot. Martyn Farr's excellent book *The Darkness Beckons* was also a useful resource.

I am very grateful to Gayle Adam for advising me on the practicalities of finding a loved one lost abroad.

Thanks as ever to Sarah Ballard for her tireless support and editorial input and Joanne Dickinson for her guidance. I am very grateful to Manpreet Grewal and the team at Sphere for their work and enthusiasm. I also appreciate the support of all at

United Agents including Jessica Craig, Zoe Ross and Lara Hughes-Young.

I would not have finished this book without the generous help of my mother, sister and husband, and the rest of my family. Thank you to my friends for their support too – especially Em and Ness.

Finally, thank you to Leigh Roberts, hairdressing guru, for telling me what *he* did on his holidays and getting me thinking about cave diving . . .

We took risks. We knew we took them. Things have come out against us. We have no cause for complaint.

Robert Falcon Scott

Prologue

As the truck bounces and lurches over the uneven track, throwing me rather suddenly to one side, he turns to me and apologises.

'It's OK,' I call over the noise of the engine. 'Don't worry about it!'

He looks relieved, and we lapse back into silence. With the windows wide open it's a bit dusty and pretty hot, but it feels really, really good to be outside. I have one winter-pale elbow resting in the direct sunlight, and instinctively hold my hand up so the breeze can play through my fingers. I close my eyes briefly, too, indulging in my body waking up to the warmth, like stretching after a deep, long hibernation.

I think gleefully of everyone else back in cold snowy England. I hate January in the UK. Who doesn't? Christmas is over for another year, everything feels flat, the decorations have to be taken down. The house looks bleak without them, there's nothing in particular to look forward to and all you want is for it to start getting warmer and lighter – for spring to arrive – but nope, instead it just becomes colder. Surely Christmas is at the wrong time of year in fact? It would be better if it came at the end of January, really, or even February. The idle thought slips away as I glance at the car clock; it's just gone three in the afternoon. So back at home – I have to pause for a moment, maths is not my strong point – it's nine in the evening. Their Sunday is already over. They'll all be shivering, with the heating on. But not me! I can't help grinning. That's when I remember I forgot to phone Kate back yesterday.

I almost reach for my bag, which is slipping around in the footwell, to get my mobile, but hesitate. Phoning at this time of night won't go down well if they've just got my tiny nephew off to sleep. And Kate's probably been in bed for a good hour or so already. Over Christmas she was like Bagpuss, poor thing. I'd turn round because I'd said something to her about what we were watching on TV and she hadn't answered, only to see her head lolled back, eyes closed and mouth open, hand still clutching a tilting cup of tea balanced on her lap, because she'd fallen asleep from sheer exhaustion.

I'll give her a call her time tomorrow, or once I'm back at the hotel. Then I'll be able to tell her I'm coming home on Friday, that I'm going to be back before she knows it, which will be good because once she's asked me where I am, and what I'm up to – as you do in any idle conversation – she's not going to be happy.

I couldn't tell her I was coming away for a week or two in the sun. It would have been too mean. She'll think I've kept it quiet because Mum gave me the money to fund this trip, but it wasn't that. How could I brightly say, having witnessed her practically translucent with tiredness, 'Thanks for a nice Christmas, sis, and by the way, I know you're on your knees at the moment and I really ought to be staying and helping you out, but I'm just off on a little jaunt.' At best it would have seemed like thoughtlessly rubbing it in, and at worst, as if I was abandoning her, because I'm pretty sure Kate would quite like to be hopping on a plane right now.

That's not what I'm doing, though. My smile fades slightly. I'm not escaping. I'm having some me time. Which I'm absolutely entitled to do. I think of Will, standing in the hall of his flat just before Christmas, and our argument about avoiding responsibility, my needing to grow up. He would do very well to remember that he's my best friend, not my father. I feel my mood darken and shift in my seat.

I don't want to think about Will any more.

Turning to my travel companion instead, I shout, 'Are we nearly there?' and he nods cheerily.

'Twenty more minutes.'

'You said that twenty minutes ago!' I tease, and he shrugs, then adds cheekily: 'You British are all the same, rush, rush, rush. You're on Mexican time here. Slow down, smell the flowers, look at the sky, y'know?' He gestures around him. 'It's a beautiful world.'

I roll my eyes and he laughs. 'OK. I think I missed the turning a little while back, but there is another way there, and,' he lowers his voice theatrically, 'it's worth the wait . . . I promise you.'

Even though I know he's saying it purely for my benefit, my insides squirm delightedly and then the rest of me shivers with the anticipation of what I know lies ahead.

This is exactly what I *love* about coming to new places – exploring, getting to see sights you would never see otherwise. THIS is what life is about, Will, I'm getting out there, experiencing things – living. What are you going to be doing with your Monday morning? Getting on the tube? Coffee at your desk? Emails to send, calls to make? Fine – if that's what you want, you do that. Me? I've got other plans. I *am* facing up to things. I am doing quite the opposite of running away, in fact. Getting out of your comfort zone is a good thing; it's necessary.

I can do whatever I want, and I'm about to do something amazing. My muscles tighten and I feel the prickle of nerves needle across my skin at the mere thought of it . . . it's as if the hatch of a plane is opening and I am teetering on the edge, suddenly seeing the spread of space below. I swallow, slightly nauseous; I can almost *feel* the wind rushing, the last fleeting knife-stab of incredulous doubt that I'm actually going to do this . . . wavering for a hair's breadth more and then something just snapping within – before leaping.

When I actually did my first jump, the feeling of

flying through the air, strapped to my instructor, was amazing. There was nothing I could do to control anything. I was free of it all . . .

. . . and when we landed, I burst out laughing with a euphoric rush of endorphins and even whooped aloud because I'd got away with it; I felt like I'd *kicked* it – but it was more than that, not just the adrenalin – it was the relief that life hadn't become so small and boxed in after all.

I felt alive, for the first time in a very long while, in an unremarkable field in Kent. And I knew I'd want to repeat it.

So tell me again, Will, that I can't avoid being a grown-up for ever. If you mean I can't dodge moving forward, I'm not trying to – I'm just not doing it your way. I've certainly no intention of standing still. Who would want to do that? What would it offer apart from . . . *nothingness*?

And that's what you should be afraid of. That's what you should *really* run from.

'Anya? You are OK?'

I turn back quickly. 'Yes! Absolutely!'

'It's just, you suddenly went quiet, you know?' He looks at me curiously. 'You looked a bit – frightened.'

'Did I?' I try to look nonchalant. 'Nope – I'm fine.'

'You are worried about what we are going to do?'

That makes me want to laugh – I'd be mad if I wasn't. I pause for a moment and think about how to explain why this particular . . . *mission*, for want of a less Tom Cruise-esque description, is different and yes, if I'm honest, *is* setting me on edge, without alarming him into saying we'd better not do it then.

I clearly take too long to answer because he ventures, 'Or is it me? You're thinking, "I'm in a car, with a strange man, on a track in the middle of nowhere."'

He throws me a look of concern, suddenly serious, and when he's being genuine it makes him look much younger – a sweet boy in his mid-twenties.

My face breaks into a smile. Bless.

'Of course not!' I insist, to reassure him. 'Not at all!' And I mean it. I've done a lot of travelling over the years, met a lot of people and pretty much all of them simply want you to enjoy their country. They're proud of it, and want to extend a bit of hospitality – in exchange for cash, of course. Rafa's not doing this for the good of his health – but that's all there is to it. Look for the bad, and you can expect to find it. Look for the good and . . . I glance at Rafa . . . or the *very* good, in his case.

Any woman would have noticed. He's got the kind of naturally balanced body tone that comes from a life spent outside doing things, rather than the odd attempt at a gym routine. His t-shirt wraps around strong arms but skims a flat stomach, and when I sneak a glance at the way he is gripping the steering wheel while negotiating the potholes, lumps and bumps in our path, then move my eyes up over the tight chest, I more than happily wind up at his very passable face. Does he know how much money he could probably make lying half naked in a boat for some aftershave campaign? I demurely drop my eyes, suppressing a smile as I consider the fact that perhaps he ought to be the one worried about being in the middle of nowhere with me.

But that's not what this trip is about.

I still cannot believe Will said what he did.

I look out of the window, feeling the itchy sting of his words.

It's easy to make the mistake of thinking that being such good friends entitles either party to say anything to each other – like you might with family. But it doesn't work like that. If you shout something you later regret at your mother or father, they're still your mum and dad. Neither you nor they can alter that, even if they were to walk away from you, or stop speaking to you for ever because of what you'd said. There would always be that bond they can do nothing about. But that's not true with friends. With even the best friendship there is always a line. It is always conditional, even if you both insist otherwise.

'Hey! That's enough all so serious, OK?'

I snap back to see Rafa looking at me curiously.

'We're nearly there now. We're going to have some fun! And Anya . . .' He gives me what he probably thinks is an unafraid, confident stare, accompanied by what I am amused to see is a definite smirk. 'I *promise* I'm going to take care of you.'

Chapter One

Just as I'm beginning to wonder if anyone has actually noticed that this dog I've been charged with looking after is inexplicably shrinking to the size of a mouse — so small it could now drown in a saucer — it starts to *buzz* in some sort of warning alarm. The game is up! They're on to me. Its owners are going to be furious! I start to look around. I should do something, but am not entirely sure what . . . Someone grabs my arm and starts to shake me. 'Kate . . .'

I turn my head towards the voice.

'Kate, your phone . . .' Rob's blurry words are

hushed but urgent. 'You left it on vibrate. Quick! Before he wakes up . . .'

I somehow prop myself up on an elbow, which digs into the saggy mattress as I clumsily scrabble for my mobile. 'Hello?' I croak on autopilot, eyes still closed, voice thick. I have barely been asleep a few minutes, surely.

'Kate Palmer?' says a tense, heavily accented male voice.

My brain is working hard to wrench my faculties into action, even though the rest of my body hasn't realised it yet. Trying to speak is like forcing a loose bundle of cotton wool balls out of my mouth. A befuddled 'Yup?' is the best I can manage.

The man starts to talk, but I can't focus on what he's saying. All I can think is *Wake up, someone is on the phone* and it's – I squint at the clock – one a.m. On what is now Wednesday morning. That is not right. I swallow, try to rub my face with a hand and attempt to concentrate. The man is babbling away—

'—nightfall now, but when they arrive we will start to look for your sister again. I am sorry to have to be saying this to you.'

Look for my sister. The phrase slices heavily through the fog like a blunt knife and jerks me into an upright position. 'Emily?' I blurt, forgetting for a second to whisper. 'You're looking for Emily?' I can hear the sudden fear in the tremble of my voice. 'Who is this?'

Rob turns over and half sits up, hand resting on the bedside lamp switch although he doesn't turn it on yet, just peers worriedly at me. We are both now very much awake.

'Emily?' Now it's the man's turn to sound confused. 'I am talking about Anya Manning. Her passport in her room, in the back it says, "Next of kin: Kate Palmer, sister". That's you? Telephone number 077—'

Uggghh. I relax a little, feeling slightly sick. Anya. Of course, Anya, not Emily . . . 'Yes, that's me, and I *am* her sister.' She's on holiday? She never said a word to me about going away. But then why does that not surprise me? And apparently she's also lost her passport. I sigh, although mostly with relief. 'Sorry,' I am now more worried about keeping my voice low, 'you said you found it left behind in her room? Where did you say you were calling from?'

At that, Rob rolls his eyes and collapses back irritably to make his point, before turning to face the wall. I throw a slightly defensive glance at the back of my husband's head. He's right, of course, this is annoying of her, but then she's hardly done it deliberately.

A snuffling begins, followed by a whimper and then a thin, low wail from our little boy's crib. He's woken up.

'Terrific,' mutters Rob, exhaling heavily. 'Nice one, Anya.'

'I am calling from Mexico,' the voice on the phone cuts back in. 'Her passport was found, and—'

'I'll do my best to help,' I practically breathe, even though it's too late and there's no chance he's going to go back to sleep, 'but I've no idea where she is. I can try her mobile but she rarely answers calls when she's away.' I swing my legs out of the warm bed, shivering as I start to rock the crib hopefully with my foot. I only fed him three-quarters of an hour ago. Please, please, please . . . I am *so* tired. 'Can you give me your details, and when I get hold of her I'll tell her to call you?' Peering at the jumble on my side of the bed, I spy my Christmas card from Rob and flip it over as something to scribble on before grabbing a pen.

There is a confused pause. Just for a moment everything falls silent – and then the stranger drops the bomb.

'Ms Palmer, please,' he urges, with some frustration. 'There has been an incident. We go through her belongings in her hotel room because we need her details and now we are calling you. No one at the hotel has seen her since Sunday, but they are not worried because she says she is going out for a night, maybe more. But now something is wrong. A truck was reported, it's been by the side of the road near the cenote for . . . I don't know . . . one, maybe two days? That is not regular for here. It's very remote. Your sister's bag is in the trunk – and all the gear for sleeping. There is food as well.'

I'm completely confused by all of that. 'Sorry – she left a car near a what?'

'Cenote,' he says patiently. 'A freshwater pool. It looks like a dive trip might have been planned – there are spare tanks – and then there are their clothes at the side of the water . . .'

I'm struggling to absorb what he's saying. '*Their* clothes? So she's not on her own, then? She's with someone?'

Rob tries to shush me but this time I ignore him.

'Yes,' says the man patiently. 'She is with a local man.'

My heart skips a beat but I try to ignore it. 'Well

. . .' I say slowly, 'my sister is a very experienced diver, she's not ever—'

'Ms Palmer, they have been gone from the hotel since Sunday. They have not come back. There is a problem. Rescue divers are coming so we can search in the water.'

'*Rescue divers?*' I repeat foolishly.

I am suddenly aware of Rob reaching for one of my hands, gripping it tightly. The tips of my fingers begin to turn white.

'The authorities have been notified. Emergency teams, the federal police . . . We are all here at the water, which is why I am ringing you because, Ms Palmer, I urgently need to ask you something – could you tell me if—'

But I don't hear the rest of what he says because the bed starts to roll from side to side, like a boat starting to lift on a rising swell, my book and Rob's discarded jeans are small islands on the sea of carpet, the horizon of bedroom curtains blurs ahead, the sound of the man's voice in my ear becomes distant, squished out by the thump of my pumping blood. Over the top of it all, I realise Mathias is beginning to cry properly, as if he can sense something is suddenly very, very wrong. The phone slips from my grasp, plops onto the duvet in front of me and both hands fly to my mouth. Rob grabs it and I hear him say, 'This is Rob Palmer. Can you please tell me what's happened? My wife is very shocked, she's . . .'

My little sister . . .

'There has been an incident . . .'

This can't be happening.

Not again.

Chapter Two

'Kate please.' Rob tries to keep his voice even as he soothes a scarlet-faced Mathias, who doesn't appreciate being jiggled up and down so absently by his father. 'Don't panic, OK? He said they're going to call us back as soon as the dive team arrives. I expect then . . .' He trails off, not sure how to finish the sentence. Mathias has actual tears streaming down his tiny cheeks and his tight little fists wave around frantically. Then his particular cry, that he does when he's *really* unhappy, starts up – the one that pierces straight through every nerve and sinew in my body straight to my core, making me need to stop everything immediately, for him. I take him numbly into my rigid arms and attempt to make soothing noises, while also staring dead ahead.

Anya was last seen on Sunday. It is now Tuesday evening there . . .

But I only called her on Saturday. It didn't ring, just went straight to answer phone. I remember leaving her a message saying I was calling for a chat, but it never occurred to me when she didn't ring back that there might be a problem. Anya never returns calls.

And how can she be in *Mexico*? Sometimes – OK, quite a lot recently, to be honest – I fantasise about upping and going somewhere on the spur of the moment, just booking a plane ticket, but I don't actually *do* it. No one does! I've certainly never been to Mexico, my entire knowledge about it as a place is based on what I've seen in films and snippets I've read in newspapers; essentially lawless, very significant drug problems . . . In short, not safe. Not safe at all. I have to swallow down a hot surge of frightened anger. So why go somewhere like that, Anya? *Why*?

Closing my eyes briefly, I try to stay on my feet as an icy wave of panic crashes over me. A picture appears in my head of Anya smiling, casually walking out of a hotel foyer dressed in denim shorts, vest top, toned legs climbing into the passenger seat of a beaten-up car, slinging her bag onto the floor. The car roaring off, and . . .

I feel very, very cold. This man thinks she's had a diving accident, and no one has seen her for, potentially, two whole days? That's what he said, isn't it? Or did he? I can't remember – I can't remember exactly what he said, apart from *rescue divers are on their way* to search in the water.

'I didn't even know she was out of the country.' Hearing myself speak the words out loud, my voice sounds very strange, like I am saying lines in a film, or a TV drama; as if this is not actually happening. Even more oddly, I'm somehow detached enough from my body to know what I look like, standing here holding my little boy, trying to absorb this news, almost watching it happen to someone else.

'I really think we should stay calm. Remember, this is Anya we're talking about,' Rob reminds me. 'This isn't exactly your first middle of the night phone call.'

That's true. In the past I've arranged and paid for a whole new set of travel documents to be issued in Tanzania (her backpack got stolen), scanned copies

21

of travel insurance documents and sent them to France (she broke her ankle snowboarding), and there have been plenty of other comparatively minor events involving wiring money that Rob doesn't actually know about. I try to take an even breath. Somehow my fatigue has miraculously flicked off like a switch. My body is now wired, every muscle tight and ready for action – it's just my mind that, frustratingly, isn't keeping up.

'It's not that she doesn't know how to take care of herself,' Rob adds quickly, 'she just . . .' he scrabbles around for a diplomatic phrase, 'needs a little administrative back-up now and then. This is going to be another of her scrapes.'

'But they said a rescue team was . . .'

He shakes his head firmly. 'No – that must be a mistake. Anya's a really good diver, you know she is. You said so yourself. Some pool isn't going to faze her. She was good enough to *teach* diving for a while when she worked in Bali, remember—'

—before she got bored or sacked, I never entirely worked out which. Anya has a very short attention span, always has done, since she was tiny. I can see her now, starting to bob a fat and gurgling Emily, sat placidly in her baby bouncer, up and down, Anya's smile turning into slightly gritted teeth as she sped up, Mum then having to intervene with a kind but firm, 'Let's be gentle, Anya.'

An wasn't being mean, it was just a much-needed outlet for the intensity of her energy. When she was about six, a doctor told our increasingly desperate parents Anya was allergic to food colouring, that it was responsible for her inexhaustible stamina. We stopped the food colouring. Anya, however, did not stop.

'There are any number of reasons why she might not have gone back to her hotel yet.' Rob sinks down on the bed. 'It'd be just like her to decide at the last minute that she doesn't fancy a dive after all – let's go on an overnight trek instead!'

But the man said all of the camping gear was still in the back of the truck, didn't he? Who goes trekking without any equipment? Anya might be impulsive, but she's not stupid.

Except then I remember her passing me a photo to look at, her dark blonde curls dancing around all over the place, green eyes glittering merrily as she laughed at the shock on my face. 'You should try it,' she'd urged eagerly as I'd stared at the image of her, tumbling through the air at God knows how many thousand feet, grinning insanely at the camera, parachute straps just visible in the shot. 'It's perfectly safe. People do it all the time – closest thing to flying.'

Oh, God. I close my eyes and sway slightly; she is an idiot. An idiot who *thinks* she can do these things, thinks she's different, when in fact she's like the rest of us . . . human. I swallow and breathe out raggedly. Mathias, having quietened temporarily, explodes the silence with a sudden squawk, arching his small back in my arms, demanding to be fed.

'I'm just going to call her,' I say, dazed, beginning to rock him automatically. 'I'll call her now – this will all be explainable.'

Rob stands to take Mathias and, having passed him over, I grab for my mobile. Scrolling quickly as I sit down heavily on the bed, Anya's name slides onto the screen in front of me. It rings with a foreign dialling tone . . . and rings and rings, eventually going to voicemail.

'I can't take your call right now.' Her voice is light and breezy. 'Leave me a message.'

I try again.

'I can't take your call right now . . .'

And again.

'I can't take your call right now . . .'

24

'Her not answering doesn't mean anything,' Rob says quickly.

But it does. Three rings back to back is our emergency code. She wouldn't ignore it. She knows what that would do to me. She ought to be ringing me back *right now*. And she isn't.

'Shouldn't you keep the line free, anyway? In case that man calls again, I mean,' Rob ventures. 'He said he was going to.'

Sleep-deprived though I am, and as hard as it would be anyway to make sense of something so scarily abnormal as receiving a phone call like this in the middle of the night, my confused and frightened brain is nonetheless starting to question what the hell has just happened. 'Did he say who he was? The man on the phone?'

'No,' Rob says. 'But he sounded official, seemed to know what he was talking about. Should we ring someone, do you think?' He sticks his little finger in Mathias's mouth and he falls immediately silent, beginning to suck furiously, looking up at Rob reproachfully, eyelashes still wet with tears.

'Yes,' I feel dazed, 'I think we should.' I glance down at my mobile. The last call shows up as *number withheld*, so I can't phone whoever *he* was back. 'Who, though? Who are you supposed to ring when something like this happens? Is it the police? She's abroad. I don't know . . .'

'Oh. I meant your family, actually,' Rob says. 'They should be told, shouldn't they?'

'What?' I jerk my head up in shock and then automatically shake it. 'No! Dad'll spin out – assuming he even registers what I'm talking about – and Mum will just . . .' I take a deep breath and see in my mind my youngest sister Emily looking steadily back at me, her pale, calm face full of trust. So like Mathias – they could be twins. No: I need to get some actual information before I ring them. They are going to be terrified.

'We don't actually have anything to tell them yet, Rob. Why did that man withhold his number? How am I supposed to reach him now?' I stare at the handset, trying to think. 'I have no idea who he is, he could be anyone.'

'Well, he had your details. He said he's going to call back.'

I look up at him incredulously. 'I can't just sit here and wait. There must be someone else, someone official here who can help us.' I jump to my feet.

Mathias, realising he's being fobbed off, starts to

wriggle and pull away from Rob's finger. I look at our son anxiously. 'Could you just take him down and do the feed?'

'Of course,' Rob says. 'I'll just change him quickly.'

'But if you're about to give him something to eat—' I begin. Rob always does this. Changes him first, then Mathias gets all wound up and won't take the bottle properly, whereas if Rob just did it the other way round and fed him before anything else – which of course makes Mathias poo again anyway – he'd stay all nice and calm . . . But Rob is already reaching for a clean nappy. At the door, I can't help turning back. 'Can you at least not use the wipes on him, though? That rash is—'

'Kate,' Rob says quietly. 'Go downstairs. I'll be right there.'

Chastened, I close my mouth, tighten my dressing-gown cord and flick the hall light on before hurrying downstairs. Rob's right; he'll be fine, he's always fine.

Crashing down in front of the computer in the chilly study, the start-up screen illuminates the room with a cold and clinical white light as I switch it on.

God, I didn't even ask that man *who* last saw Anya. I need to start thinking more clearly.

Rapidly tapping 'Missing or injured persons in

27

Mexico' into Google merely brings up numerous links to various news articles about a recent mudslide. I try again with just 'Missing persons in Mexico', which offers me the American embassy page – it looks very helpful, but is completely useless given we're British. Another option provides a UK web address and the promise that 'we can tell you how to file a missing persons report'. It turns out to be the UK in Mexico, Foreign and Commonwealth Office website.

It can be very distressing when someone goes missing abroad.

Quickly, I begin to read on.

You can file a report with your local police so Interpol enquiries can begin—

I reach for my phone, continuing to scan the page anxiously.

—but you should be aware that responsibility for conducting searches overseas rests with the local police force abroad. Only occasionally do UK forces become more actively involved in the investigation, and at the invitation only of the local police force, which will be arranged by Interpol who do not take enquiries from the public. Please note that we cannot conduct physical searches on your behalf, even where the local investigating authority is not considered effective—

My heart begins to speed up. What? Does this mean the man who rang me probably *is* the person I should be speaking to? How am I supposed to reach him? I've got no way of contacting him back!

—we cannot use public funds to finance rescue operations for people missing in remote areas—

But Anya's in a remote area – that man said so. She's in *Mexico*. Oh, Jesus . . .

—nor pay for the recovery or repatriation of the body in the unfortunate circumstances where this may be necessary. Costs should be met by relatives or the insurance company.

And that is when it hits, when I read *repatriation of the body*.

My muscles lock, like a million elastic bands simultaneously contracting down into a painfully tight, immobile knot. My breath starts to come in short little gasps as if my lungs are in a wire cage and can't expand, while my eyes flit straight to the two picture frames that sit next to each other on the desk. Em's is a school photo, taken when she was about seven. She's set against one of those roll-down blue sky, white cloud backgrounds. The photographer must have been bored out of his brain having to snap the entire school individually in one day, so I don't think he can take credit for catching Em at precisely

29

the right moment – it must have been luck – but it is a luminously beautiful shot; photographic evidence of fairies at the bottom of the garden. Quite unwittingly, he's captured the very essence of her. Her smile is shyly happy, her huge eyes brimming with sweet trust. Her almost white–blonde hair is escaping in wayward wisps from the neat ponytail my mother would have attempted to coax it into that morning, and the slightly too big for her orange jumper – obviously once belonging to me or Anya – only makes her look more heartbreakingly vulnerable and innocent.

The photo of Anya is an altogether different affair. She's sitting by a window at Holly Lodge in one of the upstairs bedrooms, the one our grandparents used when they came to stay with us in the holidays, so it was probably my grandfather who took the photo. The room in the background is oppressively dark, and Anya – aged no more than about five – is staring bleakly through the leaded panes of glass into the garden below, like a poor little workhouse urchin that longs to be allowed out to play. Even knowing that seconds afterwards, Granny would have said something like, 'Oh, Anya, you looked *lovely*, poppet!' or something equally indulgent, at which An probably gave a 'yeah, I know' smirk, jumped off the window seat and happily ran off to do something naughty, it still feels incredibly poignant.

In contrast to Em, she is wearing a slightly too small for her stripy jumper and – surprise, surprise – *my* trousers, even though they are much too long for her, which only adds to the waif-and-stray effect. I know full well that she would have chosen that outfit herself. She bullishly insisted on choosing her own clothes from eighteen months, and if Anya wanted to wear it, no matter how outlandish the selection, or if any of it was mine – which it often was – Mum seemed to find it easier just to let her.

I stare at the picture so hard it blurs as I try and calm my panic, but I'm aware I'm starting to tremble violently.

My sister's clothes are by the side of the pool, he said that, the man said that—

Repatriation of the body

And her camping stuff is in some abandoned car.

Repatriation of the body

Her bag was there too. Was that where her phone was, then? The one I've just rung? I imagine it out there somewhere, just ringing, ringing, ringing on the other side of the world.

Rob doesn't think she'd have had a diving accident, that she's too good for that.

My head begins to whirl with confused questions. So what *has* happened?

Her clothes, her clothes were lying on the ground . . .

I start to feel sick, like I'm clutching onto the centre of a roundabout that someone is deliberately spinning too fast. I grip the edge of the desk as bile rises in my throat.

Rob appears in the doorway. 'Matty's actually gone back down . . .' I lift my head – he's what? – and Rob catches sight of me. 'Hey! Hey, sweetheart!' He hastens over, twists our office chair so I'm facing him and tries to hug me to his body, but I'm starting to hyperventilate, attempting to gulp air, eyes wide and wet with terrified tears.

'Mathias didn't feed? He needs . . .'

'He's fine,' he says. 'Kate, talk to me.'

'I can't think straight,' I gasp. 'I can't – I don't understand. She can't be in Mexico – there's a mistake. Someone has made a mistake. It's not her. I should call Will – he'll know where Anya is. I mean, you don't always tell your *family* what's going on, but she'll have told him, right?' I scrabble frantically for my phone.

'Don't!' Rob firmly takes the mobile from me and sets it down on the desk. 'It's the middle of the night, it'll just make him feel like you are now. We should hang on. Kate look at me, *look at me*,' he instructs, and takes both my hands. 'Calm down.'

'Someone must have made a mistake!' I repeat frantically.

'Don't talk, just focus on breathing.' He takes a few deep inhalations along with me. 'You're in shock. That's it – just breathe.' He tries to make some soothing *shhhh* noises and finally pulls me to him. 'She's going to be OK,' he whispers, kissing the top of my head furiously. 'I promise you. She's going to be OK.'

But his words have exactly the opposite effect that he intends. They are not warm and comforting, something I can wrap myself securely in; instead their lifeless familiarity drapes damply over me, and begins to cling. 'She'll be OK,' he says again.

Except sometimes people are not OK; no matter how much you would give for it to be otherwise. He doesn't know that Anya is going to be all right; he doesn't know it at all. I have to lean my head on his tummy so he can't see my eyes fill up with tears. I feel unbearably alone, even though he is holding me – how is that possible? 'Soft pillow for you,' he tries to joke as he strokes my hair.

I attempt to focus on the repetition of his fingers moving. It's not his fault – not even slightly his fault – but Rob doesn't understand how dangerous it is to make promises like that. You believe what you are being told because you so, so want it to be true . . . and only later do you realise that they are just words people say when they want more than anything to help, but that actually, they can't control outcomes any more than you can.

'She'll be OK,' he insistently repeats.

Which is when my phone begins to ring again.

Chapter Three

We both lunge for it at the same time.

'Let me,' Rob says quickly, and for once, I do.

'Hello? Yes it is . . . OK. Right . . . So you've got . . . that's great.' My heart jolts with hope, even though to my frustration he doesn't say anything else, just listens. 'So, two?' he says after a pause. Two what? Two a.m.? When's that? How far ahead or behind us are they? Didn't that man say it was night there? 'OK, yes, please do. Thanks . . . Yes, I will. Thank you.'

He hangs up and I wait, not daring to say a thing. 'Right,' he exhales. 'Two divers are definitely on their way. They'll be searching the water very soon.' He smiles encouragingly at me.

I stare at him. Rob is a good person – a very good person with the gentlest soul. At school he was the fit fifth-former everyone fancied, and I was a lowly second-year who wordlessly handed him 10p when he was short for a can of Coke in the queue at the Spar, holding my breath because I was *actually standing right behind Rob Palmer*. 'Thanks!' He'd taken it and grinned. 'I might just marry you when you grow up!'

He swears he doesn't remember saying it – but those nine words were enough to fuel years of fantasising, even though he left before sixth form and I eventually went off to university. I'd been living back at home for a few months when, to my surprise, he came up to me in one of the local pubs, cleared his throat and said kindly, 'It's Kate, isn't it? Can I buy you a drink?'

He did, and that night he walked me home before hesitantly kissing me and asking if he could see me again. Rob Palmer wanted to see me. And at what was then the worst time of my life, he was just what I needed. Eight on-and-off years later, true to his word, I married my childhood sweetheart.

Which is exactly what he is – a sweetheart – but Rob, you cannot possibly think that two divers arriving to search the water is in any way heartening news. I don't want there to be any divers! *None*. I want Anya to ring me right this second!

There must be something in the look on my face, or a lack of colour; maybe I sway, I don't know, but Rob says quickly, 'Don't move, OK? I'm going to get you a drink,' and he hurries from the room.

Divers in the water. This can't be right. They really are sending a team in to look for my sister. How is this happening?

He reappears and places a whisky-chilled hand on my arm.

'Drink this, please, it'll help. We have to wait for them to call us back. I know it's hard. I understand, but—'

Feeling tears building, I'm already shaking my head. No you don't, actually.

He insistently holds the glass in front of me, thinking I'm declining the alcohol. 'I know you don't want it, but please, for me . . . turns out not breast-feeding has benefits after all, hey? Shit – not that I'm saying you gave up too soon,' he adds hastily. 'You really tried . . . Kate. I'm sorry. I shouldn't have said anything.' He starts to deflate. 'I wasn't making a point, I was—'

'It's OK,' I say automatically. 'I know you weren't.'

He looks so thrown and confused that I take the glass and have a small sip, to make him feel better. 'Who was it? On the phone?'

Rob looks at me blankly. 'The same man we spoke to before, I think. He *sounded* the same. He said his name was Augusto.'

'But did he say *who* he was? What capacity he was calling in? It's just I didn't hear you ask.'

'He didn't actually, no.' Rob trails off anxiously and I feel my gut tighten in disbelief. It must be written all over my face, because Rob hurriedly continues: 'But Kate, he must be official. You don't just call someone in the middle of the night and—'

'This website says we need to inform our local police so they can raise an Interpol report, which is what they do when someone is missing, and they'll want to know who we spoke to,' I cut across him. 'How can we now? We have no idea – what are we meant to tell them?'

I turn and bring the document up again so he can see. Rob scans it and says doubtfully, 'But it says you *can* file a report, not you should . . . here, look:

"*Responsibility for conducting searches overseas rests with the local police force.*" And I think this is more for missing persons, as in, they haven't called when they said they would, who do we contact? That's not our situation. We know where she is.'

We have a situation. An hour ago I was asleep. I was in bed, like normal. Now this; a situation. And no, I *don't* know where she is, and five seconds ago, Rob, *you* were saying you couldn't see how she could have had a diving accident. All we actually know for sure is that she was last seen with a local man and their abandoned clothes have been found . . . although presumably they would have taken them off if they were going diving, wouldn't they? That man did say *their* clothes, didn't he? Not just hers?

Why can't I remember exactly what he said?

'Rob,' I try to keep the mounting panic from my voice as I recall something else, 'when I spoke to him he said there was something he wanted to ask me, but that's when I dropped the phone. What was it? Did he ask you?'

'No.' Rob shakes his head. 'I think we have to wait, and—'

Wait? I can't *wait*. I should have answered the phone myself! Spinning back to my computer, this time I hurriedly type 'Foreign Office advice', and as I'm tapping it in, the search engine helpfully offers suggestions – Egypt, Sri Lanka, India, Madeira – so I add 'Mexico' at the end.

It takes me to a travel summary page.

I begin to scroll down through a bit about the hurricane season being June to November, how most visits to Mexico are trouble-free . . .

But then I pause. '. . . *Crime*,' I turn cold and begin to read aloud, '*and kidnappings continue*—'

'Well, Anya hasn't been kidnapped,' Rob says firmly.

'*You should be alert when dealing with real or purported policemen*,' I continue slowly. Which is when a hideous thought occurs to me. 'The man on the phone.' I grab Rob's arm urgently. 'What *exactly* did he say to you?'

'Kate—'

I begin to scroll faster through the information:

```
. . . Street crime on the increase . . .
dress down . . . theft on buses is common,
travel on first-class buses if possible
. . . passengers have been robbed and/
or assaulted by unlicensed taxi drivers,
particularly in Mexico City . . . women
```

```
travelling alone should be particularly
alert. A number of serious sexual offences
have also occurred in tourist areas in
Cancún. Care should be taken, even in
areas close to hotels . . .
```

Oh Anya. You *chose* to go somewhere like this? What the hell were you thinking?

```
. . . vigilant when leaving a bureau de
change . . . incidents of people being
followed and attacked . . .
```

'Sweetheart, I know that it's almost impossible to—'

'Rob, will you shut up a moment!' I say desperately, because I've just reached a bit entitled 'Longer-Term Kidnapping for Financial Gain.'

I begin to trace my finger along the words. 'There have been allegations of complicity by police officers in kidnappings. Anyone approaching you requesting personal information or financial help should be treated with caution.'

Oh my God. I cannot believe what Rob and I might already have been naive enough to have done. 'What did I say to him when he first rang?' I look at Rob frantically. 'Did I tell him anything that could put Anya at risk? I just gave him my name didn't I? What did I say to him? Help me think, Rob!'

Rob is staring at me incredulously, like I am going mad in front of his very eyes. 'You can't seriously think Anya might have been kidnapped?'

Said out loud in the otherwise dark study of our small house, in the middle of a cold January night in Kent, it *does* sound risible. But then Anya is not here, in the safety of a place where such a scenario would be ludicrous. She is somewhere in which the rules we live by simply don't apply. A country unfamiliar to me, and seemingly dangerous enough that I might see it on the news and shake my head in horror at the reports of the heinous crimes people there are committing against each other, before thanking my lucky stars that I live in a comparatively safe corner of the world.

'It says here you should always ask for the officer's name, badge number and patrol-car number.' I am reading on. 'We didn't do that. We should have done that, Rob!'

More terrifying words and phrases slide past . . . Fought over by rival drug gangs . . . shootings of high-ranking security officials in Mexico City . . . attacks aimed at prominent citizens and journalists, caution after dark, tensions, keep car doors locked at all times . . . aware of surroundings . . . And then I get to the bit that says Sea Travel: be aware that sports and aquatic equipment may not meet UK safety standards, and may not be covered with any accident insurance.

'So even if she simply has gone in the water . . .' I point to the words before covering my face with my hands and pushing my fingers into my brow, trying to force an end to the torrent of atrocious possibilities pouring into my head.

'Kate, all countries sound dreadful when you look at the travel advice for them,' Rob reasons. 'If you read what it says about America it would probably tell you to keep your car doors shut all the time, but you'd still go there, wouldn't you? As for this equipment issue – so, there are places that hire out dodgy kit. Anya's not a newbie, she'd know how to spot something that wasn't right. I think we should—'

'—call someone *now*. That's what we should do. A man has contacted us randomly in the middle of the night, he says he's been through her stuff, he has *all* of her stuff . . .'

Rob hesitates, and I see him glance at the photos of my sisters.

'We have to call someone,' I reiterate. 'This isn't how something like this happens. Police would come here, we'd be notified, they'd be—'

'But he said they were mobilising divers. Kate, why would he say that if—'

'Well if that's true, my contacting someone *official* isn't going to make anything worse, is it? Maybe they'll be able to do something to help.'

I start to hunt on the page for a number, a contact – anything that might . . . and there it is. A link that says, 'If things go wrong overseas, then this is how we can assist you.' It's a twenty-four-hour emergency number.

I reach for my phone – just as it springs into life in my hand, displaying a long, unrecognisable number.

'Kate Palmer? This is Augusto. We spoke earlier?' He is speaking much more rapidly this time.

'I know who you are.' What a ridiculous thing to say; that's exactly the point! I clear my throat. 'Augusto, I'd like to have your badge number and—'

He interrupts me. 'Ms Palmer, your sister, you said she is a very good diver? She has had lots of training? Please now, I need you to tell me what sort.'

'Er, I don't know.' His question throws me. 'She used to teach open-water diving in Bali. Well, she said she did . . .'

'OK,' he says. 'I will tell our men here this information, which is very helpful. Thank you, Ms Palmer.'

Before I can ask anything else, he's already gone. I stare at the phone. That was my chance, and I didn't say anything. I am furious with myself. Except then, I see his number has registered. He didn't withhold it this time. We have a lifeline.

'Look!' I show Rob. 'I'm going to call him back.'

Rob opens his mouth, but a wail from Mathias upstairs momentarily silences him. I knew he wouldn't have settled. 'Just wait,' Rob begs, as he hastens to the door. 'I'm going to get Matty. Don't call anyone. Please. Not yet.'

He vanishes. I stare at the number on my mobile, swimming in front of me, and get a horrific flash of Anya first being bundled into a car, wrists bound, mouth gagged, eyes wide with fear . . . and then I see her floating in a pool, arms suspended, eyes closed, skin grey and loose hair in a cloud around her.

I hear myself make a strange hoarse noise, somewhere between a moan and a cry. Since Mathias's birth, agonising images have been randomly but regularly flaring up in my mind. I will be feeding him, holding him snugly to me, and my brain, for no reason, will suddenly show me a picture of his broken little body lying on the floor by his changing table. Or his tiny inert form, cold and still in his crib. It makes me feel so distressed when it happens I feel like I'm in physical pain, but when I tried to tell my health visitor – because what mother pictures that sort of thing? – she briskly patted my leg, told me it was perfectly normal and just meant I loved my baby and would do anything to protect him.

But now it's not only Mathias – it's Anya, too. And the torture is simply more than I can bear.

I redial the man's number, squeezing my eyes shut, forcing myself to imagine instead that I am hugging her, can feel the generous warmth of her slim body, the smell of the apple shampoo she always uses, her curls tickling and irritating the skin of my face as she clutches me back.

The call goes to a voicemail, a man rapidly speaking Spanish. But it's an emergency! He must be able to see it's my number. Who would ignore a call in a situation like this? Unless he is not genuine, and he *is* in fact in some way involved with the disappearance of my sister.

So I should be getting help. As fast as I can. I have to *do something*. I spin back to the computer and trace the emergency number across the bottom of the screen as I dial.

'Good morning, Foreign Office?'

'Hello?' I blurt. 'My name is Kate Palmer. I've just had a call from some man in Mexico, where my younger sister is, telling me that she's not been seen for two days, and that they think she's had a diving accident, but that can't be right, because she's a very good diver – and I don't know who this man is, or how he got my details.

'I have literally no idea who he is,' I'm gathering pace now, 'and I'm scared. I read some of the stuff on your website about the kidnappings, and . . . I don't want to sound neurotic, but he seemed to know a lot about Anya.' I try to take a steady breath, but my voice comes out really high all the same. 'I just don't know . . . I really need someone to help me!'

The woman on the phone calmly begins to reassure me, and starts requesting practical information: Anya's full name, confirmation of her nationality . . . I try to answer, but bizarrely am finding it hard to concentrate on what she is saying. Something has happened to Anya, maybe as much as two days ago. It can't be

47

possible. She's my little sister. I would have felt it, surely I would have felt it?

An incident. An accident. Not been seen. Rescue divers. Going into the water. I can't take your call right now. Serious sexual offences.

Exactly who is this man? And how *does* he know so much about Anya? My mind is slamming me through doorway after doorway, into rooms in which each scene is worse than the one before. 'Please,' I plead with the anonymous woman, 'you've got to help me.'

Before it's too late.

Chapter Four

'I'm so sorry that you were contacted by a regional representative, Kate.' The woman from the Foreign Office has called me back after what feels like hours, but in reality is minutes. 'The police didn't have anyone else at the scene who could speak English, and they wanted to ask you urgently about Anya's competency in the water, hence this Augusto called you – but he was merely acting as an interpreter.'

I hesitate. But their website warns of 'purported police'. How can she be sure that what she's told me is true?

'He's actually a local lawyer,' she explains, as if reading

my mind. 'We've had that verified by someone at post; that's someone based in Mexico. It's not how we like it to happen, but unfortunately sometimes people act without thinking and without going through the proper channels. It must have been very distressing for you to be told in that way, but you won't have any more phone calls now, except from me.'

'I'm really sorry, you said your name was . . . ?' I already can't remember.

'Gabrielle,' she repeats patiently. She's got a very ordinary voice, not particularly well spoken, but no obvious accent either. Indistinguishable. 'And I'm based at the Global Response Centre, which is the service you come through to out of working hours.' I imagine a slim, efficient, capable woman dressed in a neat pencil skirt, carrying files, which is oddly comforting. 'The Mexican police will now be passing information to us, and in turn I'll relay it to you.'

'And you're sure the Mexican police are . . . oh, my God!'

I've googled 'police in Mexico' while she's been speaking, and now I'm looking at some images of heavily armed men, including a balaclava-clad officer clutching a machine gun. But it is the headline searches that make my mouth fall open in horror.

```
YouTube - Mexican police soliciting a
bribe on video
FT.com - terrified Mexican police force
resigns
```

They sit above another, which simply states:

```
Telegraph - Mexico police chief's head
found in icebox
```

I'm supposed to rely on *them*? Wait for them to report on any 'developments'? Is she insane?

'I understand your concerns,' she says sincerely, when I manage to articulate exactly what I'm looking at, 'but we can't interfere with, or influence, the Mexican authorities' investigations.'

Even though I've already seen that stated on the website, my first reaction is one of incredulity. Anya is *British* – they need to help her! I want to scream down the phone that they *can't* just sit back, not when they know she's in trouble – and at the mercy of an obviously totally corrupt justice system. The police probably aren't even taking this seriously! What's one missing girl to them in the face of their evident problems? And even if they were

51

'investigating', they don't appear the kind of force to employ subtle and effective methods. They look like thugs. I attempt to convey my worries as rationally as I can, to which Gabrielle says, 'Try to stay calm, Kate,' so perhaps I'm not as succinct as all that. 'This case is now open on the system, it's "multi-view",' she continues. 'That means whatever Mexico knows, I can see on my screen in London too.'

I feel my body slump helplessly and want to weep with frustration at such small assurances. I know there probably isn't much more she *can* say, and she's trying to point out that they are not just letting the authorities there operate without being monitored. But that's no good! I want them to *do something*, not sit by and gather information that, God forbid, I will only be able to sift back through *afterwards*.

'We do recommend you report Anya missing to your local police force. They can then utilise Interpol, as a precaution, but that's all separate to the Embassy, so you'll need to do that independently.'

My head is beginning to swim.

'OK, what *do* the police there know for sure, so far?' I ask Gabrielle. I close my eyes as I prepare to concentrate fiercely, in the hope that something

52

obvious is going to leap out and it will all make sense and I'll know where Anya is.

'The daughter of the family who own the cenote – the pool – noticed the truck on Sunday, late afternoon local time. She also reported seeing a man and woman by the cenote. She spotted the same truck again on Tuesday, late afternoon,' she begins. 'Camping items and Anya's personal effects – including her mobile phone and wallet containing the card of a local hotel and three hundred dollars in cash – were found. The truck is registered to a Rafael Montoya, the dive partner she is believed to be with. At that point, the police went down to the hotel, searched her room, collected her passport and some other items and were told that your sister was seen leaving the hotel with Mr Montoya on the Sunday.'

'He'd stayed there with her?' I ask sharply.

'We don't believe so, no. Perhaps he'd come to collect her.'

But I'm now suspicious. She shouldn't have told some random man what hotel she was staying in! 'What do you know about him?' I ask, everything suddenly starting to slide horribly in the direction of items I have read in many newspapers of missing female travellers, which all seem to begin with the girl meeting a local man.

'He's a dive instructor who works for a company called Go Ghostal dives. Mr Montoya borrowed some dive equipment, which his employers have said they were unaware of, but he had secured a day's leave for Monday – Tuesday is his day off, in any case. The lawyer you spoke to, he's actually at the scene to represent the dive school in the event of any issues of liability, and he's confirmed these details are correct.

'Not all of the equipment missing from the dive school was found in the boot of the truck however, so that would suggest, in addition to the clothes left at the waterside, that at some stage – possibly as early as Sunday – your sister and Mr Montoya entered the water.'

'Abandoned clothes could also be an indicator of something else though, couldn't they?' I don't want to say it, I don't want to *think* it, but I have to. 'He was the last person with her, to see her – and now he's vanished, too?'

'If they were diving together, that would explain his whereabouts though, Kate, and the clothes,' she answers gently.

I know I've thought that myself, and that five

seconds ago I was convinced the man who rang us was in some way an accomplice, or had an ulterior motive. But why was this Rafael at her hotel on Sunday? That doesn't sit right. Surely she'd have just gone to meet him at the dive school, like you do on normal holiday excursions? And come to that, what excursion involves you needing to stay in the middle of nowhere, camping, with a man you barely know? No one in their right mind would do that. I put that to Gabrielle, who says gently: 'It does seem as if this was an "unofficial" arrangement. He'd not put it through the dive school, and Anya also had three hundred dollars in cash with her—'

'But,' I interrupt, 'if she'd suspected this man was pulling a fast one and using "borrowed" – possibly unchecked – equipment, she simply wouldn't have taken the risk. I know she wouldn't. She might not have realised it wasn't above board, which means he deliberately tricked her. It clearly wasn't for the money, if that was all still in her purse. Which means . . .'

I find I can't finish the sentence.

'I have to remind you that we can't influence, interfere with or assist the Mexican authorities' investigations,' Gabrielle says eventually – for what feels like the millionth time – although not unkindly, 'but I will relay what you've said, and my colleague at post would certainly want the local police to have evidence for them not to consider what you've suggested as a line of inquiry.'

Does she mean that, or is she fobbing me off? 'But could the local police still just dismiss my concerns as rubbish?' I ask. 'If they were that way inclined?'

'We would do all we could to address that situation, if it arose, but ultimately we can't—'

'I know,' I say quickly, because I'll scream if she says it again.

'Stay positive, Kate. Report Anya missing to your local police.'

'But you'll call me if—'

'—there are more developments? Of course I will.'

I hang up just as Rob reappears. 'Where's Mathias?' I ask immediately.

'Upstairs. He's fed, and he's asleep.'

'Is the monitor on?'

'Yes . . . just bring me up to speed.'

So, head spinning, I do, and conclude with '. . . and I'm going to file a missing persons report.'

'Kate, come here for a moment.' Rob gently moves

me over to the comfy yellow chair and, placing his hands on my shoulders, forces me to sit down. 'Tell me why you want to file a missing persons report?'

'Because they told me to!'

'You really think they don't know where Anya is?' He takes both of my hands, kneeling in front of me so he's on my eye level. 'That this man—'

I don't let him finish. 'The good thing is, Interpol are so specialist they won't even have contact with the public . . . you can trace people to within feet of their whereabouts within minutes, *seconds*, these days!'

Rob tries to stroke my hands with his thumbs as he keeps hold of them. 'That's in films, Kate. Not real life.'

'No! That's not true,' I insist, pulling away from him. I need to wipe my nose. I look around me and Rob turns uncomfortably, his pyjama-clad knee obviously digging through the rug and onto the floorboards as he reaches for a crumpled tissue that's lying on the desk. 'You said it yourself – she's tackled open-water dives in vast oceans. A pool, that man said. A pool! It doesn't make sense!'

'I know what I said, but—'

'He stole the diving equipment from the shop he

worked at,' I insist. 'He took a day off at short notice . . . Suppose it was all part of a ruse to get Anya to the middle of nowhere? You read about this sort of thing in the papers all the time.'

Rob takes a deep breath. 'Sweetheart, you're very stressed out. You've had a very difficult couple of months of it with Matty. Understandably you've been frightened of something going wrong there again, and along with other stuff,' he shifts uncomfortably, 'I think maybe it's making you—'

'Making me what?'

He is trying to pick his words very carefully. 'It's not possible to wrap people up in cotton wool, Kate.'

What's he talking about? 'I'm not trying to wrap anyone in anything! I just want to find out where my sister is. She's missing, and this man she was with was the last person to see her! He tricked her into thinking it was legitimate. Why?'

'Sweetheart, they haven't searched the pool yet. Until then, why don't you—'

'She's *not* in the water,' I say fiercely. 'She's not. They're wrong.'

'OK.' Rob quickly holds a hand up. 'OK, so suppose this bloke – I don't know – staged it all to look like a diving accident.'

When did I say that? I simply said he clearly lied to her from the word go—

'All her money was still in the car. What was in it for him?' he asks.

'Anya!' I burst with frustration. Isn't it obvious that's what I meant? 'You *have* met her, right? She's beautiful! She walks into rooms and people stop talking. They literally stop talking, Rob.' I get to my feet and step round him so I can sit back down at the computer.

'What are you doing now?' Rob asks.

I type 'Go Ghostal dive school – Mexico' into the search bar – and there it is. I go to their home page, which has a cartoon phantom peering over the top of a shipwreck and the slogan 'Come and *haunt* the most beautiful *ghost*line in the world!'

'This is where he works.'

There is a drop-down option for staff, which brings up pictures and brief biographies. The first one or two PADI instructors' pictures are framed against a bright blue sky and a very clear, almost plastic-looking sea. They look healthy and brown, like they spend a lot of time enjoying very good weather. They are wearing sunglasses and smiling comfortably at the camera.

Eduardo . . . Jorge . . . Alejandro . . . as I look down the list, a stunning picture of a girl with long dark hair, big brown eyes and caramel tanned skin appears. She's laughing, and the picture appears to have been taken on a night out. Esther Betanzo 'came to Playa to experience the good life, and since she discovered diving has never gone home!'.

'Wow.' Rob looks over my shoulder. 'Please don't take this the wrong way, but he's obviously pretty used to being around very good-looking women.'

I don't comment on that . . . Sebastian . . . has three children, is patient and friendly . . . Marta has lived in Playa del Carmen all her life and speaks Spanish, English and . . . then there is Rafael Montoya. I catch my breath.

It's hard to tell how old he is, mid– maybe late twenties? He's stripped to the waist, on a boat and has a tattoo on his left shoulder, the design of which I can't make out. His very dark hair is mussed up in the carefree way only a day at the beach can achieve, eyes attractively crinkled at the sides because he's smiling widely, revealing lots of very white, neat teeth. He is in good shape, and obviously wants people to know it – hence he's wearing no top. Rafa loves exploring, and his family joke he was born with fins! When he's not in the water Rafa can be found by it, usually on the beach. He likes cooking and culture and speaks Spanish and English.

'That's him?' Rob says. 'That's the one she went with?'

I nod, and lean in a little closer to the picture. He looks perfectly friendly, but he also looks like the kind of man not afraid to come up to you in a nightclub and tell you he thinks he can guess what kind of drink you would like . . . a smooth cocktail, right? Nothing fussy and over the top, you're too sophisticated for that. He'd be sitting down easily on the chair next to you before you could say, 'Actually, I'm fine, thanks . . .'

I would be immediately on my guard with someone like him.

Would Anya? Unlikely, but then she's a lot more comfortable in situations like that than I am. I have always hated clubs. Too self-conscious to enjoy dancing unless a drink or two up, I'd be stuck between minding that men, well, boys, were coming up to my friends, but not me – dancing closer to them, sneaking arms round their waists, ducking heads to try to chat them up over the thumping music – while also being grateful that they weren't pawing at *my* body. Either they just didn't fancy me, or I gave off some sort of 'don't even think about it' vibe.

Unlike Anya, when she came to visit me at university. The first and last visit; it was a nightmare. I can remember her dancing to Blur's 'Girls And Boys' at the union in hotpants so short I had been horrified when she appeared in our student kitchen at the start of the evening. I tried to convince her to wear something more . . . suitable, and told her she was going to end up attracting a *lot* of the wrong sort of attention, but she snorted with laughter and, sounding much older than her fifteen years, said, 'I'm pretty sure I can handle it, Kate, don't worry.' Happily it was also a traffic-light disco, and Anya had elected to pin a green 'Up For It' badge to her obscenely tight t-shirt.

I was amber, which meant 'I Might'. I didn't, though. I was too appalled at having to witness my little sister being glassily snogged by somewhere in the region of about seven couldn't-believe-their-luck boys. Eventually, worried she was getting too drunk and didn't really know what she was doing, I couldn't stand by any longer and interrupted snog number eight to insist we go home. She dismissively told me she'd get a cab later, and I could go on without her. I pointedly asked with what money would she be paying for this cab, exactly, and could she just come now, please? Her eyes narrowed, there was a moment's pause while she decided if she could be bothered to fight me or not, and then she turned to the boy, shrugged and said, 'Sorry! The fun police . . . Nothing I can do.' He nodded, picked up the remains of his pint and shot me a filthy look as he staggered back into the sweaty throng in search of his next green light.

Anya reached down unsteadily, picked up what I realised was one of *my* jackets – balled up on the sticky floor and covered in slopped Blastaway – and slurred something about feeling like Cinderella . . . Did I even know how *boring* I was?

I called Mum the next morning to tell her why I was putting Anya on the train a day earlier than planned. She laughed and said, 'Oh dear.'

'It's not funny, Mum!' I tried to shove the memory of the weaselly boys pressed up against Anya out of my head. 'It was horrible.'

'But she was so excited about coming and seeing her big sister! She so looks up to you, Kate.'

I glanced across the hall and through the door of my room at Anya, who was blearily turning over in my single bed, smearing a great streak of eye make-up over the pillow. 'I need some water,' she croaked pathetically, 'or I'm probably going to die. Get it for me, Kate. Pleeeease . . . and have you got anything to eat? Maybe a bacon sandwich?'

'She's coming back today,' I said decisively. 'I'll put her on the train in time for Dad to meet her in London once he finishes work. Could you ring and tell him?'

'Fine,' Mum sighed. 'Can Emily have a quick word with you? She's right here. She got an A-plus for her art project,' she added proudly.

'That's great,' I said absently, and then watched in dismay as Anya stuck a hand out to stretch elaborately and promptly knocked over a cup of tea abandoned the day before. She lifted her head to see what the noise was, surveyed the damage and decided to ignore it, slumping back down before turning over.

'Anya! Don't pretend you can't see it, I know you can!' I called, exasperated. 'Get up and fetch a towel! I've got to go, Mum.'

'Just a quick hello – Emily was wondering when you're going to be back for the holidays. She misses you dreadfully.'

'Really quickly, then,' I said, watching cold tea drip down onto one of my library books as Anya dabbed at it ineffectually with a discarded sock.

'Hello?' Emily's eager voice sounded in my ear.

'Hi Em.' I tried to sound upbeat. 'Well done on your art project, that's brilliant.'

'Thanks!' she said, then paused. 'You sound stressy.'

'Sorry,' I said immediately. 'Not with you, I promise. Anya,' I gritted my teeth, 'has just poured cold tea everywhere. And she won't get up to sort it out,' I added pointedly, at which Anya slung me a V-sign.

'If I was there, I'd do it for you,' Emily offered.

I softened. 'I know you would.'

'*Could* I come up and see you?' she asked. 'I wouldn't get in the way or anything.'

I felt bad. It wasn't the first time she'd suggested a visit. 'Of course you can,' I said quickly. 'Tell you what, when I'm next home we'll sort out a weekend when Mum can bring you, or something, and I'll show you where I live, and—'

'Can't I come on my own? Like Anya has?'

I smiled. 'We'll see. I'm sure we can work something out. Look, I'd better go and sort An out, OK? Before she sets fire to the room, or something.'

Em giggled, then added wistfully, 'Tell her I said hello.'

'Can't promise that, I'm afraid,' I said briskly. 'I may just go in there and kill her.'

Anya flicked a second, lazier V in my direction.

'Love you, Em, see you soon,' I said, and hung up.

We never did sort out that visit.

'He doesn't look trustworthy at all,' I say to Rob as I stare into the eyes of Rafael Montoya. Rob flicks a worried glance at me, which I choose to ignore, but he's not going to let it go.

'You cannot possibly tell any of that from a photograph.' He speaks slowly and carefully. 'I understand why you're desperate to think it, I'd be holding onto that if I were you too, because bizarrely it actually is almost preferable to the alternative, but Kate—'

I get that flash of Anya again, her legs hanging lifelessly in clear blue water, arms by her sides, eyes closed. I blink it away and stare very, very hard at Rafael Montoya's grinning picture. 'I'm going to file this missing persons report.' I look away from Rob determinedly.

'Don't you think you ought to call your parents first?'

'Because they'll know what to do?' I can't keep the tone of disbelief from my voice.

He shakes his head. 'No, because they have a right to know what's going on. She's their child.' He stops as he catches sight of my face, realises what he's said and looks crushed. 'Oh. It's because you *know* how they're going to feel that you're not phoning them . . .'

Actually it's not that, but before I can say any more I'm interrupted by the sound of crying. Mathias is, unsurprisingly, very unsettled. 'Can you get him?' I ask immediately.

'In a second, yes. This is coming out wrong. I'm sorry. I just think your parents should—'

All I can hear is Mathias. 'Please, Rob, just get him. Bring him down and then we'll . . .'

'He's OK for a bit longer, Kate. What I'm trying to say is . . .'

'Rob, *please*!' I beg, desperately. I can't bear the sound of Mathias crying needlessly, I just can't. 'He'll get really distressed otherwise, and . . .'

'He's *all right*.' Rob gives me a warning look. 'I wouldn't leave him if I thought he was in pain, or coming to any harm.'

I briefly close my eyes, swallow and then cough

to steady the wobble I can feel rising in my voice, as I fight the urge to rush upstairs to our son. 'I'll call Mum after I've filed the report, OK? She's behind us in California, so I won't be waking her up. I'm going to wait until at least seven before I phone Dad.'

'Would you like me to make you a cup of tea? Or coffee?' Rob looks at a sudden loss to know what else to say.

'Tea would be great, thank you.' I'm now just trying to placate him. 'After you've got Mathias.'

I see a muscle flex in his jaw briefly, although he says nothing, and then he's gone. I listen to him start to climb the stairs, and once the crying stops, I turn back to the computer to find the number for our local police station.

'Hello?' I clear my throat again and look at the picture of Rafael Montoya smirking back at me from his boat. 'Yes, I'd like to report my sister missing. She's in Mexico . . .' Then I hear myself add, 'I've reason to believe she's been abducted.'

They take all of the details, and say they may send an officer round, and that they will also come back to me as soon as is necessary.

But to my very deep unease, while they are kind, they seem to treat it as a routine call. Surely most of the reports they deal with from the general public are things like seeing someone hanging around a neighbour's back garden, not something like this? I don't know what I expected, but it was a lot more than I've just got. I am not even slightly reassured . . . That said, given that they – as I am now fully aware – have to concede to the Mexican authorities, what could I realistically have hoped for, from even their best efforts?

Just like that, it all overwhelms me. I simply don't know which way to turn.

And so in spite of my earlier intentions, I find myself reaching for my phone to call my mother.

Chapter Five

'Kadie, I can't understand a word you're saying, sweedie, slow down – take a breath.'

For once, I barely notice Mum's affected American accent. Normally I'd be thinking, 'OK, so she's lived in California for some ten years; there are still the forty-odd ones she spent in this country. Surely they count for something?' But not today. 'Anya is missing,' I blurt in panic, a yawning feeling of dread creeping further around the edges of my stomach and guts at hearing the words said aloud that make it real.

'Oh dear,' she sighs. 'Well, when did you last speak to her?'

I have to suppress my incredulity at that almost lazy comment. Anya's not a lost set of keys that might be in a spare handbag! How is it that I have to explain what 'missing' means? I don't know where my sister is and I'm scared! I swallow. 'Mum, this is serious, she's in Mexico and she's been kidnapped.'

There is a silence, at which I start to feel relieved.

But then she *laughs*. She laughs, and says, 'Honey, have you been at the gin?'

I'm stunned. Have I what? In the middle of the night? When I have a two-month-old baby?

I try to remind myself that of course she is going to be shocked, of course she's not going to want to believe what I'm telling her. 'Mum, I know how this sounds, but it's true. I wouldn't joke about something like this, you know I wouldn't. I had a call from a man out there, I can't remember at precisely what time, I was asleep. Since then I've spoken to the Foreign Office – their Global Response Centre – who have confirmed everything, and I've filed a missing persons report with Interpol.'

'*Kidnapped?*'

Good, it's sinking in. 'She was there on holiday,' I add.

'I know,' Mum says absently. 'I lent her the money

– well, gave it to her, you know Anya. She was thinking of calling in here before heading back home again. I told her she didn't need to ring, she could just turn up, there's plenty of space. I thought we might go for a couple of days' hiking together.'

Right. Was I the only one who didn't know Anya was going away then?

'Kidnapped?' Mum repeats. 'My God . . . I mean, do they want a ransom? Do we pay it? What's the official line?' Only when she says 'official', it sounds more like 'offishal'. My heart sinks, and I stop wondering if Anya was being deliberately secretive and why that might have been. 'Mum, have you had a drink?'

'No!' She sounds completely surprised by my question, as if it is an utterly left-field thing for me to have said.

'I can't talk to you now if you have.'

'Darling – I haven't had a drink, OK?' Her voice turns more familiar: flinty, laced with a hint of warning. 'Now, tell me exactly what this man said to you? The one who said she'd been kidnapped?'

I pause doubtfully, then say slowly, 'He didn't actually mention kidnapping. She's in Mexico, as you know. She went on a trip with a man—'

'Will,' Mum interjects confidently.

I wrinkle my nose. 'Will? Mum, that's her friend, he's not with her.'

'She definitely mentioned Will when we last spoke,' Mum says with certainty. 'They'd had an argument.'

Oh, Jesus Christ . . . I close my eyes. 'Mum, she's not with Will. She's on her own out there. She met a dive teacher, they went on a trip together and now they've both disappeared.'

'They've *both* been kidnapped?' Mum sounds confused.

It's like talking to a child. I take a deep breath. 'Mum, you *have* had a drink, haven't you? I can tell. You're trying not to slur and you're not listening to me!'

'Katherine,' she says icily, 'I have had *one* drink. It's not a terribly good line, I'm trying to absorb what you're saying to me, but you're hysterical and you're not making any sense. Perhaps you'd better give me the contact details for this official you spoke to so I can deal with them myself. I think you need to *calm down.*'

My skin prickles hotly. 'I'm not hysterical, I'm fucking terrified – and I'm trying to tell you what's happened. She was with a man, they've both disappeared; I think he might have abducted her!'

'You don't need to swear at me like that . . .' But she peters out for a moment, and I can practically hear the befuddled cogs attempting to grind into gear, trying to work out a course of action, what it is she should say next, because this is serious and yet she can't find the appropriate response in among the fug in her head. She *is* pissed. Definitely. 'So what should we do?' she asks eventually.

I feel my usual tired mixture of anger, disappointment and apathy. Aren't I supposed to ask *you* that, Mum? 'Nothing,' I answer, because now is definitely not the time to go there. 'I'm going to call you with more news as it comes in, OK? As soon as they phone me.'

'I'll fly over to Mexico,' she says decisively. 'It's no distance for me.'

'No!' I say in alarm, picturing her lurching onto the scene, demanding answers; putting backs up one minute, and then collapsing in tears the next – she'd just wind up getting into trouble herself. 'It's not safe, I don't want anything happening to you too; I'll go.' I say it without thinking, but as soon as I do, it seems so obvious. Of *course* someone has to go to Mexico. 'Just stay by the phone,' I instruct, but my mind has already begun to sift through the practicalities of getting there as soon as possible. I'm sure the Foreign Office can help me with finding somewhere to stay, getting an interpreter. And if I'm physically present, putting the pressure on, the police will *have* to take my concerns more seriously, won't they? I'll at least be able to see for myself what they are actually doing. 'Please promise me you won't go, Mum. I don't need you to do anything. I've got it under control.'

'Well, if you're sure . . .' she says. I'm feeling fairly amazed at how little fight she's putting up, when she adds: 'I'm very grateful to you, Kate. My poor little baby . . .'

The unexpectedly tender remark washes away my badly built barriers in a heartbeat. OK, she's being useless, and she's drunk, but she is *trying*, and at least she understands how I . . .

'. . . She must be so scared. My God, Kate, what must be going through her mind? Why her? Because she was a tourist, do you think?'

I close my eyes and have to take another minute before I can speak. 'I don't know, Mum. Maybe.'

'You know what I'm going to do? I'm going to ask Pastor Beck to pray for us.'

'Good idea,' I practically whisper. There's no point. No point at all.

'You know you could log onto the church website and upload a prayer online if you want to? Do something useful on that computer of yours for a change.' She is sounding brighter and more purposeful already. 'I'm going to go straight down to church now.'

'Isn't it about ten p.m. with you?' I say slowly. 'The church won't be open, will it? And I don't think you should be driving anywhere.'

There's a pause. 'I'll pretend you didn't say that.' She gives a light laugh, which makes me feel very sad. I know she will, because it's much easier that way.

'And Kate – the church is never closed to those in need. Anya is in God's loving care. We all are. Trust in that. You know I can speak to them – the authorities – if you want me to, don't you? Oh, I just feel desperate! Kidnapped . . . Oh, Anya!' She's starting to wind herself up again.

I take a deep breath. She wouldn't be like this if she wasn't pissed. 'She's going to be fine, Mum, I promise you.'

She doesn't seem to hear me. 'I can't bear it if—'

'She's going to be all right,' I say quickly, knowing where she's going and almost guiltily thinking about how I felt when Rob said the exact same thing to me earlier. 'Can you get someone to come and be with you?'

'I expect so.' She sounds distant. 'I'll call a soul buddy on the church Trouble Tree now . . .'

'Fine,' I say uncertainly. A soul buddy? A Trouble Tree? Mum emailed me a link to her church over Christmas. It was completely mad. What kind of order a) uploads sermons onto the internet anyway, b) asks God to pray for those who *don't have fully outfitted homes, because we all require a level of material comfort*? 'I'll call you when I have news,' I say finally.

'God will prevail,' she says, this time more quietly, and somehow it manages to sound ominous and chilling, rather than comforting – as I hope she meant it to be. I pretend I don't hear her, and hang up quickly before turning back to the computer and beginning to search for flights to Mexico.

As I do, I think back to being in hospital in November; shuffling about, slowly tidying up my things as best I could without lifting or bending, in my tiny, curtained-off space. There was a girl younger than me on the ward, sitting on the bed opposite mine. She too had a new baby in a plastic cot – but she also had her mother, who stood behind her, gently brushing her hair while she gratefully and peacefully closed her eyes.

Watching them together poleaxed me.

Rob comes back in holding Mathias, who is awake but clearly still very tired; he's yawning, starting to wriggle about in frustration and dragging small fists across his face as he rubs his eyes, but is also mouthing around too. 'Hold him while I get another bottle on the go,' Rob says, frustratingly, given I have to manage when I'm here on my own. And the second Mathias has been transferred to my arms – a move that doesn't result in food is all it takes to tip him over the edge – he goes ballistic. Rob looks down at his son's screwed-up, outraged little face in surprise. 'What's wrong with him?'

'He's hungry – and he's unsettled, he can sense something isn't right and it's unnerving him.' I try to soothe Mathias but he's not going to let up until he has something to eat. 'And this is pretty much what it's like – although this is a bit early, you've normally left for work before he gets going. I've usually had the cooker extractor fan *and* the hairdryer on before breakfast.' I instantly regret adding the bit about him not being around because it sounds like an accusation and I really didn't mean it like that – it's not Rob's fault any more than it is mine. It came out wrong; I meant that I'm not making it up if he asks me cheerfully how my day was and I answer, 'Pretty tough.'

'Here, pass him back,' Rob says in typically male fashion, determined to fix the problem and provide the solution. He reaches for Mathias before beginning to swoop him backwards and forwards through the air. Mathias, incredibly, quietens down and looks at Rob contemplatively, and I also gaze at him in wonder. 'That's better!' Rob says, trying not to look smug. 'What was all that fuss about, eh? I'll take him into the kitchen with me. We'll do the bottle together, won't we Matty?' And they disappear off together quite happily.

The second week after Mathias was born, a different midwife than usual came to see us and announced she was taking over the remainder of my post-natal care as the other, nice midwife was now on extended sick leave. When she arrived I was trying to make sure the room was warm enough, but not *too* hot for Mathias, and Rob was carrying him around on one arm, with a comfortable carelessness that unnerved me a bit, although I didn't say anything. He offered to make the midwife a cup of tea. Did she like chocolate or plain biscuits?

Such encouragement meant she stayed for *an hour*

and a half asking bafflingly pointless questions which included 'Have either of you ever been bullied at school?' and 'Have you been the victims of domestic abuse?' I'd actually been desperate for some help with feeding, but after ten minutes of being roughly manhandled and it *still* being agony, I just wanted her to go. My scar had started to hurt too, which I knew meant I'd overdone it and needed a lie down. We must have been her last appointment and she was spinning it out until she could push off home. Eventually, to my relief, she started to pack up, but as I began to relax, she suddenly said, 'Make sure you support each other and present a united front, won't you? Babies are very clever. They quickly work out which parent is the weakest link.'

And then she looked, pointedly, right at me.

I carried on smiling, but I was devastated.

She thought I was a weak link? And what did she mean, 'babies are clever'? I'd glanced at him: Matty was a tiny eleven days old, hardly a manipulative emotional terrorist. I said nothing, just nodded obediently as my tiny son cried – hungrily – in my husband's arms.

I wish I had told Rob how much her comment upset me. He probably would have said she didn't mean it like that, and even now, when Mathias is very happily bottle-fed, he still cries quite a lot. Some babies do, for no reason; a lot of my books say so. It's not because he's in pain, or unhappy, although I've had to work hard at not immediately panicking that he's ill or something is really wrong again. It's just one of those things that, apparently, he'll grow out of.

Instead, I told Anya what the midwife had said. 'What a complete *bollock*,' was her outraged response, which actually made me feel quite a lot better. 'I'm going to go round to her house, slam her tits in the door and see how she likes it. You're doing brilliantly, Kate.' She fixed me with a fierce look from where she was cuddling Mathias on the sofa, reached out and squeezed my hand. 'Completely brilliantly. I think you're amazing. Why don't you lie down for half an hour and try to relax? I'll watch Matty.'

'I will, in a bit . . .' I hesitated. 'Have you spoken to Mum recently? Has she said anything to you about her coming over here to meet Mathias?'

She'd shaken her head and given me a sympathetic little shrug of her shoulders.

'Oh well,' I said, and tried a smile. 'She'll brave coming back eventually, I'm sure.'

But she hasn't yet. And it can't be because of financial constraints. Not if she gave Anya the money to fly to Mexico . . . If she'd just used the cash herself, Anya wouldn't have been able to go on this trip in the first place.

Rob comes back in, Mathias lying in his arms sucking busily on a bottle. 'So did you phone your . . .' But he fades out, catching sight of the computer screen. 'Flights to Mexico?' He looks confused. 'Who's going to Mexico?'

I take a deep breath. 'I am.'

Chapter Six

'I'm stunned you're even thinking about going. What about Matty?'

I can't help but stare at him when he says that. Mathias has barely been out of my reach since they lifted him from the incubator and I was finally able to hold him. Sometimes, when he is sleeping, I am so scared that he has stopped breathing again that I have to reach out and gently poke him, just to make him move, which makes his little limbs jolt and wave around in his sleep while I exhale with relief. Rob seriously thinks it would be *easy* for me to get on a plane and fly to Mexico?

But what if something happened to Anya because no one was there for her?

'There isn't anyone else who *can* go,' I say truthfully. 'I wish I had normal parents who could step in, believe me, but I don't. I'm sorry.'

Not that I'm at all sure how I'm going to do this – the thought of leaving Mathias makes me feel physically ill.

Rob takes a deep breath. 'I know that you've always felt very responsible for your sisters, and Anya has always relied on you—'

At that, I see her; wide, panicked eyes, hands desperately stretching out to me . . . I swallow and try to keep a grip, not go to pieces. 'Could you take a few days off work?' I'm trying very hard to focus on the practicalities. 'I know it's not ideal. Your mother could help us out, maybe. She'd love to spend some time with Mathias, I'm sure.'

'But *you're* a mother now!' he exclaims. 'You have a two-month-old baby! You've only recently recovered from an extremely traumatic labour and emergency c-section! Can you even hear what you're saying?'

'I'm totally fine,' I cut across him.

'OK – maybe physically you could just about do

it, but what about the responsibility you have to us – me and Matty? We need you here. *We're* your family.'

I take a deep breath. 'You're saying I have to choose between Anya and you?'

'No!' he bursts. 'Of course not! I'm reminding you that while of course you want to rush and help her, your first consideration has to be Matty now. You can't go haring off somewhere so dangerous on the other side of the world. What if the same thing happens to you?'

'So you agree there's a possibility that she has been abducted, then?' I say quickly.

He lifts his gaze to the ceiling and doesn't answer that. 'I'm saying you can't go – no,' he corrects himself quickly and sits down, balancing Mathias carefully on his knee. 'I'm *asking* you not to go. Things have changed, Kate. You can't drop everything any time one of them calls, not any more. There are other people who could fly out there rather than you.'

'Like who?' I really am asking, because I can't think of anyone.

'Me, for one.'

'You?' I can't keep the surprise from my voice.

'Thanks for the vote of confidence.'

'I'm sorry, it's just . . .' I try to backtrack. He wouldn't know what to do! This is a man who has been known to ask me absently if I think it's cold enough outside for him to need to wear a coat or not. He's immensely capable in a lot of ways, physically strong and tall enough to be imposing when required, but he can't go to Mexico and deal with consular officials, foreign authorities, protocols and procedures – make sure things are being done right. The farthest afield Rob has ever been is Europe, and when we had that problem on holiday last May, when we arrived and the travel company tried to fob us off with a much lower-spec apartment than we had booked, he seemed so reluctant to do anything about it I felt I had no choice but to step in.

'I just didn't want to start the holiday off with a stand-up ruckus,' he said afterwards when I asked why he didn't seem happier now it was all sorted out. 'We're here to relax, aren't we? We could have just tried it for a night, and then if it was crap, moved . . .'

'What, and have to repack all over again?' I'd blinked in confusion.

'I'd have said something eventually,' Rob said tiredly. 'If I'd needed to – and given half a chance.'

And that's the crux of it – *eventually*. Not that I

don't appreciate he's just not built that way. On a day-to-day basis, Rob is the best support in the world. I had no idea how tough the first few weeks of having a new baby would be, while trying to deal with the aftermath of surgery. The house would have swallowed me up if it hadn't been for Rob uncomplainingly and quietly doing all the jobs we usually jointly undertake: the washing, hoovering, fixing the meals, making the bed . . . I simply couldn't have managed without him, and I still feel incredibly guilty that even now he has to do so much stuff I ought to be coping with – on top of a full and physical working day on site, and with broken sleep.

He is amazing, but no one can be *everything* – and he's just not a take-the-lead sort of bloke. He can't go to Mexico.

Moreover, I can't risk him going out there because I would never forgive him if something went wrong. And I can't afford to be in a position where I'm unable to forgive my husband for something. Whatever happens, I must never, ever allow my feelings about Rob to come before Mathias's right to have two parents who always do *everything* in their power to stay together. So Rob can't go. It's no good – he just can't. It's asking too much of him, of us. I won't risk it – I've seen what happens to couples when blame cannot be resolved and has nowhere to go.

'You're right.' I try to divert him. 'We need to sort something but, look, perhaps I ought to call my dad. Let me speak to him, and then we'll think about who is going out there, OK?'

He holds my gaze thoughtfully for a moment and looks as if he's going to say something, but then appears to change his mind. 'All right,' he concedes. 'Just as long as you understand that it can't be you. I mean it, Kate.' He gets to his feet. 'I know what you're thinking, I'm not stupid. I also think you should tell your father what the authorities think has happened, not just your theory.'

My mouth falls open in surprise as he carries Mathias to the door.

'I heard what you said to your mum. We have to wait for them to search this pool. It's nightmarish, Kate, but what else can we do?'

I could go there Rob! That's entirely the point.

'You understand why I can't let you go, don't you?' He looks pleadingly at me, as if I have just spoken aloud. 'You're busy trying to rescue your family, but I'm supposed to look after you, remember – and you don't make it very easy for me sometimes. You may think you're behaving rationally, Kate – but you need to trust me here. Even you have limits, and you won't be failing her if you exercise them.'

My eyes instantly flood with tears at that.

He's by my side in a flash. 'You are *not* failing her,' he says fiercely, hugging me very tightly with his free arm, even though I'm sitting and he is standing and holding Mathias, so my head is sort of resting on his waist. Through the gap at his side, just visible, are the photos of my sisters.

'All I see is that little girl,' I gulp, a mess of tears and snot. I try to wipe my eyes. 'A defenceless little girl who . . .' But I break down again, unable to say any more.

'Shhhh.' Rob holds me. 'I know, Kate, I know. You're frightened, and so very tired, still full of baby hormones . . . that and the protective, fierce love and fight you have for all of them: Matty, Anya, Emily . . . it's sort of blended them all into one, I think. It must feel overwhelming.'

I look up at him for a moment, astounded, and then just as quickly feel ashamed of my earlier, horribly condescending dismissal of my own husband. It's worryingly easy to forget, when we're staggering through the hours of each day with the single goal, or hope, of getting some sleep when we make it to bed, that we're still on the same team. He has a different way of doing things to me, but it's not necessarily wrong. 'I need to be kinder to you,' I say out loud. 'I'm sorry.'

He snorts. 'Don't be silly! You need to be kinder to yourself, more like.' He strokes a stray piece of hair from my face. 'Don't ring anyone else just yet, Kate. Especially not family. Not while you're like this, it'll only upset you more.' He moves to sit down again, and falls silent for a moment. 'I agree, though, we do need to sort who is going to go, because you're right, someone should. And I'm happy to go, I really am.'

He looks very worried though, and I wonder if he is thinking about what will happen to the jobs he has on at the moment. Yes, he may be his own boss, but equally he won't get paid if he's not there physically building all of these extensions people are having done because no one can afford to move any more. Of course, concerns about money are not something it would be even vaguely appropriate to voice, not at a time like this.

'Try . . .' He trails off for a moment, struggling to

find the words. 'Try to stay positive. We don't know anything until we know something. Do you understand what I mean?'

I nod, although that's exactly what I'm terrified of; that moment arriving. What that something is.

He leaves the room, and I stare at the grinning Rafael Montoya on my computer screen. He knows where she is, he knows where she is *right now* – and if he has hurt her, I will kill him. I imagine firing a gun at him, seeing his body jerk and fall to the ground like they do in films.

But then I also know it couldn't be enough to have him dead. All I actually want is her back, unharmed.

I close my eyes, try to shut out his face and think about my family. Even though I now have a husband and son, I still sometimes feel as if I am twenty again. I can remember exactly what it was like before it all happened, when it was just the five of us. Three happy and innocent girls drifting in and out of a warm home, with a mum and dad who were good parents, able to make us all feel safe . . .

Despite Rob's advice, I shakily pick up the phone to call my dad. I need his help – I need him.

It rings six times before a surprisingly alert and guarded voice says, 'Hello?' It is inevitably Maura who has answered.

'Maura, it's Kate. I'm sorry to wake you, but I need to speak to Dad if it's possible.'

There is a pause, presumably while Maura decides which way she is going to play this. 'Kate, dear.' She speaks slowly and patronisingly. 'He's asleep.'

'I know,' I say ingratiatingly, 'and I wouldn't ask if it weren't an emergency, but—'

'What sort of emergency?' and although she now sounds concerned, I can only picture a dog deliberately unwinding itself while not taking its eye off the intruder as it slowly gets to its feet.

'Anya is missing.'

'Oh, Kate!' She affects alarm, but then adds, 'Although I suppose this is *Anya* we're talking about. Should you really be troubling yourself with this?' She manages to sound perturbed on my behalf, yet the implied 'never mind your father and I' also hangs there, heavily unspoken.

Don't rise, I tell myself. You won't win, don't fall for it. 'Please may I speak to my dad?' I ask again. I sound like I'm thirteen; it's pathetic.

'I'm so sorry dear, no you can't,' she says almost

regretfully, as if were there anything she could do, she would, but . . . 'It's impossible.'

It's not impossible at all. He's two doors down from your room. You could carry the phone to him now.

'You wouldn't know, of course,' she continues, 'but he's had a *very* bad couple of days.'

'Oh, I'm sorry,' I find myself apologising – how does she do that?

'Thank you, dear. Although we did have to call the doctor out the night before last as he was very agitated indeed; they very nearly readmitted him, in fact. His dosage has been increased and he's *terribly* woozy. If I wanted to wake him now I couldn't.' She gives a regretful sigh. 'So you see, it really is impossible. I *am* sorry.'

As ever, I'm caught between hating the fact that this woman is allowed to play any part at all in my family dynamic, and on the other hand being forced to guiltily acknowledge that I am at least grateful Dad has someone who looks after him and does things like call the doctor to him at night. Much better that, than him being alone, or – though it's a deeply shameful admission – my responsibility. I don't think I could cope with that, too.

'In any case, Kate, he's rather off Anya at the moment.' And here comes the bite – always in there somewhere. 'She called him on New Year's Day asking to borrow several hundred pounds. He was dreadfully hurt that he hadn't heard from her for weeks, and then lo and behold, she only wanted her pocket money, aged *thirty-one*.' She laughs incredulously. 'I'm afraid they had quite an argument. Your father was most upset about it. He felt he had to refuse, because she has to learn that's not the way adults behave – take, take, take.'

I am so angry with her of all people for having the gall to say that – even if she were right about Anya, it would still be none of her business – that I'm unable to say anything. Dad doesn't *get* wound up. He only feels hurt when Maura says he ought to be, pouring poison in his ear so slyly he doesn't know his thoughts from hers any more. My dad, who delightedly used to terrify all of us, swimming around fast underwater pretending to be a shark – making his girls shriek with excitement before popping up laughing and ready with hugs. Splashing after Anya and me, with Emily on his back, her small hands clinging on round his neck, white-blonde hair plastered to her head as she giggled and tried not to slip off. My dad, who could go the *whole length* of the pool on holiday on one breath. We thought he was invincible. Last time he came to see Rob and me, he sat at the table – withered hands continually fluttering for his sticks – and said nervously, 'I need to go and sit in the car now, Maura,' over and over again, like a broken record, not even able to look at me, or aware I was there, I don't know which. Maura carried on calmly eating, bright pink lipstick having bled over the edge of her thin lips, and paused only to smooth her sleek grey bob before saying confidently, 'No you don't, David. You're perfectly all right. Eat your food up.'

A very long silence follows down the phone, but if she's expecting me to lose it with her like Anya would, she's mistaken. I bet that's what happened when Anya rang just after Christmas. She clearly wanted money for her trip, but she got Maura instead of Dad, and Maura vetoed everything – told Anya a load of rubbish that Dad probably never actually said, and Anya, hurt, told her where to shove it.

My only consolation is that if Dad really is as out of it at the moment as Maura says he is, at least he's not going to be worrying about anything.

'OK,' I say eventually, 'I understand.'

'Have you told your mother what has happened?' she asks suddenly. Maura is obsessed with Mum. She has never met her, never seen pictures of her and the only communication Mum has had with Dad since they separated has been via solicitors. She is the great unknown to Maura, which seems to have made her both the enemy and yet utterly compelling, all at once.

'Yes, she knows.'

'Well if there are any incurred costs, we shan't be paying them, if that's what she's thinking,' she says, bizarrely. 'Anya needs to learn to stand on her own two feet. It's time your mother appreciated that.'

I grit my teeth. Mum may be a nightmare, but she's still my mum, and you are still a grasping, aggressive old bag who had more than enough of your own money but still wanted more, wanted the proceeds of the sale of my parents' house, which Dad would never have parted with if you hadn't talked him into it and made him think it was all his idea. *Any incurred costs* . . . How dare she? She makes up these conflicts and positively relishes them.

'When Anya does return from her little sojourn, do be sure to let us know, won't you?'

She hangs up.

Good. That went well.

I turn to the girls' pictures. How many times do you have to stick your head above the parapet before you get the message that someone is firing at you? Dad was never going to be in a position to help. I don't know why I even hoped he would. 'Our parents are useless,' I say out loud.

Rob reappears, carrying Mathias — and another mug of tea. 'Who are you talking to?'

'I *was* talking to Maura,' I say quickly.

'Oh,' he says, and pulls a face as he sits down.

'On the upside, Dad is currently so zonked he apparently wouldn't notice if a bus hit the side of the house. She said he was nearly readmitted, night before last.'

'I'm sorry, Kate.' Rob looks straight at me sympathetically, and doesn't add, *I told you not to ring*, for which I am grateful.

I glance away — back at Anya's photo. I can't seem to take my eyes from it. Her favourite outfit, aged three, included red wellington boots — regardless of the weather — and a full-sized silver adult crash helmet; balancing on her shoulders, it was so large. She wore it not for any other reason than she just liked it, and wasn't bothered by what anyone else thought. I can see her now, peering solemnly out from under it as old ladies in shops said surprised and polite things like 'Goodness! What an unusual little girl!' Mum and I were so used to it we'd stopped noticing. I wish I had a photo of her like that, but they were in one of the albums Dad destroyed the night Mum left. I remember Anya and me walking into the sitting room at Holly Lodge to see pretty much every surface covered in a confetti made up of our family faces. Shards and scraps of me, Emily and Anya – and my parents – all over the place.

'Shit!' Anya had looked around her, laughing with shock. 'When Dad does something, he really does it . . . crazy fucker.' We stood there silently before she'd patted my stunned back. 'Come on, sis, I'll get a rubbish bag, you get the hoover. Let's get this done before anyone else sees it, OK?'

I found the two photos on my desk in one of Mum's books when I was sorting through her belongings several weeks later. I felt a bit guilty for what was effectively stealing, but then she's never asked after their whereabouts, so I don't suppose it matters that I kept them.

'In short,' I return to Rob, try to focus, 'I think we can rule out needing to keep my father in the picture until everything is . . .' and at that, I *really* struggle for words, '. . . clearer.'

Rob nods. 'So, we need to get me a flight sorted, don't we?'

But the solution has just occurred to me in a flash and I wonder how it hasn't already, it is so blindingly obvious who should go.

I snatch up the phone.

'Who are you calling this time?' Rob begins, but I hold a finger to my lips and wait while pleading silently, please, *please* . . . pick up your phone!

Pick it up now!

Chapter Seven

'Oh my God,' says Will, at which point Liesel turns over sleepily, rubs her eyes and tries to focus, staring at her boyfriend who is sitting up in bed, holding his mobile to his ear. His mouth has fallen open and in the semi-darkness – the bathroom light across the hall is feeding weakly through into their room – she can see his eyes are wide and staring straight ahead. 'Of course. Of course I will. Um, just let me—' He starts to look around him confusedly, Liesel isn't sure what for. He puts his hand up to his head and just holds it there. She can hear someone talking on the other end of the phone

– a woman – but can't make out what she is saying.

'Would they deal with me?' Will says. 'I don't know how it works . . .' He listens carefully again and then says, 'Well yes, definitely. Tell them that . . . yes, I'm absolutely sure. Well, will you ring me straight back then? OK. Bye.'

He hangs up. Liesel props herself up on her elbows and waits for him to explain – but he doesn't. He seems to have gone into shock. 'Er, Will?' She raises an eyebrow, reaching out to turn on the bedside light. 'What's happening? Who was that?'

'It was Kate – Anya's sister.' Will stares straight ahead. 'Anya is in Mexico. She went on a trip with a local man on Sunday and hasn't been seen since. They've found some of her belongings in a remote area, including her clothes.'

'Shit!' Liesel is horrified.

'The local police have started searching for her, and Kate has been in touch with the Embassy.'

'She must be terrified!'

'She is.' Will turns to look at her. 'She's asked me to fly out to Mexico.'

'What?' Liesel gives a half-laugh and sits up properly. 'You? But that's crazy!' The sound dies as she begins anxiously to search Will's face. 'Will, it's hardly gone six in the morning. You've got work today – you can't go to *Mexico*! You told her that, right?'

He looks down at the duvet.

'You said *yes*?' Liesel is dumbfounded.

Will quickly gets out of bed, reaches for his dressing gown, which is hanging on the back of the door and doesn't reply. His face is creased with sleep, his light brown hair is all over the place and he looks completely thrown.

'OK, I have two questions,' Liesel says slowly. 'One, what purpose does you flying there serve, and two, why has she asked *you*?'

Will yanks an arm into a sleeve. 'She's asked me because she's got a new baby, she can't go herself.' Then he looks down at himself, swears and starts to pull the dressing gown off again, instead grabbing for his jeans from the floor.

'She has a husband doesn't she?'

'Lee, if something like this happened to you, your parents, your brothers would be on the first plane. I'm Anya's best friend,' Will says, buttoning his fly. 'I'm the closest thing to a brother she's got.'

And at that, all the times over the years that he's managed to persuade a heavy-limbed and giggling Anya into a taxi – also having to ask the driver to stop so she can be sick – the CVs he helped her rewrite, the stern letter he sent on her behalf to the landlord who was attempting to fleece her of her deposit, the email account he set up to her delight on her laptop days before she spilled a Diet Coke over the keyboard and it died: a hundred-and-one examples he would have no trouble listing right now all appear in his mind, ready to prove what he's just said.

'A brother?' Liesel repeats softly.

Her words hang there, in the air.

Will glances at her. His girlfriend is looking away from him, knees hugged up to her chest.

'Liesel . . .' he tries to explain. 'This is serious. Kate wouldn't have asked unless—'

'Yes, I get all that, but I still don't get why *you*,' Liesel repeats determinedly. 'Real family do things like this; fathers, grandfathers . . .'

'Their father isn't well, and both their grandfathers died ages ago. Honestly Lee, there isn't anyone else, I promise you.' Will tries to stay patient, not escalate anything. 'Please. I need to get ready.' He hastens over to the wardrobe and starts to pull out more clothes. 'Do you know where my passport is?'

'Anya just has to call your name, doesn't she?'

Whoa . . . He stops dead. They woke up about

five seconds ago, and now they are into *this*? Despite knowing that every second counts – he can feel the adrenaline surging round his body in response to the fear he heard in Kate's voice – he doesn't speak for a moment. Neither does Liesel.

'Of course not! She hasn't done anything, called anyone,' he says eventually. 'No one has a clue where she is.'

'You think I don't know you,' Liesel mumbles, looking down at her long, elegant fingers which have incongruously stubby, chewed-to-the-quick nails. 'That's what I find amazing.'

'This isn't something she's done deliberately, it's not her messing around. My best friend has gone missing on the other side of the world in Mexico. It's hardly the safety capital of the—'

'So you're definitely going to her?' she challenges.

'She's a single female traveller who has disappeared. Please stop and think about the obvious possibilities that raises,' he tries. 'This isn't the time for this sort of talk, Lee. We don't have to do this now.'

He immediately realises his mistake. Liesel gives an intake of breath and looks at him sharply. 'But we *do* have to do this?'

'No!' he says quickly. 'I mean, there's no need to discuss this at all, unless you *want* to say something to me, of course.'

'You said to her sister to call you back.'

He nods. 'She wanted to know if I would go before phoning the Embassy to see what has to happen to make that possible – them meeting me at the other end, that sort of thing.'

He watches Liesel physically attempt to swallow it all down. 'OK. So how long will you be gone for?'

He shrugs helplessly. 'I don't know.' He turns away and tugs on a crumpled, long-sleeved top.

'You don't know? What about work?'

'I think you can get compassionate leave for things like this.'

'No, only if – like I said – its *actually* family,' Liesel says pointedly.

'Well, I'll sort it out somehow,' Will says. 'My passport, Lee. Have you still got it after our flight to your parents', or is it back in the drawer, do you know?'

'It's in the drawer.' He's hastening from the room when Liesel suddenly says, 'Will – do you love her?'

Oh my God, he thinks, and stops in the doorway.

'Because I probably should know.' Her voice has become a little shaky.

He glances again at Liesel, who all were in Switzerland with her folks over and ever since they got back, has been ask constantly, is he OK? Has started hinting heavi maybe this year could be the year they might think of buying somewhere of their own rather than renting, might even think about a wedding?

'I want to ask you something.' She cuts across his thoughts. 'When I flew to Mum and Dad's, and you were here for a few days on your own before you came out too, did anyone stay here with you?'

He catches his breath, torn between honesty and not wanting to do this, not now.

There is an agonising pause and then he says, 'Yes.'

He hears her give a little gasp.

'It was her, wasn't it? Anya stayed here. In our house.'

'She's my friend.' He looks at her tiredly.

'But you decided not to tell me,' she says immediately, and fixes him again with her direct stare. 'Did you sleep with her?'

'No!' he says truthfully. 'She stayed here, but in the spare room.'

She falls quiet, considering this, then nods and closes her eyes for a moment. She opens her mouth bably, Will expects – to apologise to him, which is why it makes what he says next all the more astonishing to both of them.

'We did – kiss – though.'

He's as horrified to hear himself say it as she is. He didn't want it to be like this. Had no intention of this *at all*.

Liesel's eyes widen with shock and then start to shine with unshed tears. 'Oh, I see' is all she can manage, before whispering, stunned, 'You *kissed*?'

And then she does a complete u-turn. 'But why now, why after all this time? I don't understand!' She flushes. 'Unless, has it happened before? Have you been—'

'No. I swear to you,' he insists. 'It's never happened before, and it won't again. I'm so sorry, Lee. I didn't want to hurt you.' At that, she gives a derisory snort and he can't blame her, but it *is* true.

'Well, you definitely can't leave now,' she says suddenly. 'You need to stay. We need to sort this out.'

'I can't. I have to go,' he says quietly. 'Not because it's got anything to do with . . . with what happened.'

She half laughs again, incredulously. 'Oh no, of course not, how silly of me, it's completely irrelevant!' She puts her head in her hands.

'I have—'

'No. You don't have to do anything.' She drops her hands, shakes her head defiantly, suddenly strong again. 'You have a choice, Will. Everyone always has a choice.' She looks at him, and her meaning is crystal clear. 'So what do you choose?'

His phone starts to ring. It's Kate. He hesitates under Liesel's unfaltering gaze. 'Hi Kate.' He picks up. 'They will? OK . . . well . . .' He looks down, and after a second of an agonising pause says quietly, 'Then I'll be there as soon as possible. I'll take a taxi to the airport.'

At that, Liesel pulls back the covers and swings her long legs out of the bed before standing and walking unsteadily out of the room. Will watches her disappear and closes his eyes.

'No, it's no problem at all, Kate,' he says. 'Please don't feel bad. You were right to call me. I'll do whatever I can.'

Liesel must be listening, because the second he hangs up, she reappears and says in disgust, '*Just* like a brother, eh? Well, fine,' her voice starts to shake again. 'You've made your choice, and you've had your chance.' With that, she spins on her heel and vanishes again.

He knows she means that. She won't wait for him to go after her, and he can't blame her. He can't blame her for one second, and this was exactly what he wanted to avoid, but then he didn't know Anya was going to go missing, either.

He tenses as he thinks about Anya . . . her slim wrist as her hand lifts to shade her eyes from the sun, beaming her wide, generous smile at him, curls framing her face . . . He grabs his backpack and begins to stuff items in as fast as he can.

Once the taxi is rushing him to Heathrow, while allowing for the icy road conditions, he immediately calls Kate back; it wasn't fair to discuss the arrangements further at the flat when he knew Liesel could hear every word.

'There's a flight that leaves at half ten, which providing the traffic is OK, I'll make. I've spoken to reservations and . . . What? No, it's not. I change at Dallas, which means I arrive in Cancún at seven p.m. their time this evening. That's the fastest I can get there. My work? Don't worry – I'll sort that.' He has a brief thought as to how it's going to sit with his boss when he tells her that he's not coming in today because he's on his way to Mexico. Perhaps he'll get strategic flu instead. 'Yeah – Liesel knows what's going

112

on, too,' he reassures Kate – omitting the bit where she was silently packing her clothes as he tried to say goodbye, refusing to speak or to look at him. He's finding it pretty hard to believe any of this is happening, it's so far removed from the normal morning he'd anticipated waking up to when he fell asleep next to Liesel last night.

'So they're conducting a full search at the moment? In the water . . .' He takes a deep breath. 'And what have they told you about this local she was with?' He listens intently. 'Tell me again what the company name is? Go what?' He reaches into his bag and pulls out a pen and a scrap of paper. 'Ghostal . . .' he repeats and grimaces, pressing hard as he writes. 'He's . . . Rafael Montoya. So he effectively stole the dive equipment from his employers? And do you know,' he tries to sound as casual as he can, 'if she . . . was having a thing with this man?' His pen pauses over the paper, although he hardly needs to write that bit down.

That Kate didn't even know Anya was going on this trip, let alone anything else, doesn't make Will feel any better and is far from the answer he wanted to hear. He assures her he'll call when he's boarding, and after she's repeated how grateful she is for him dropping everything, he hangs up and stares out of the window as panic gathers and churns in his gut. This is his fault, for making Anya so angry that she just upped and left. If he hadn't said anything, hadn't argued with her, she might not have gone. She would still be safe.

By the time they arrive at the terminal, he's become so desperate he practically hurls some money at the taxi driver before dashing in through the automatic doors, frantically scanning the departure boards for the American Airlines zone.

Having located it, he begins to run and weaves through the passengers who are dragging wheelie suitcases erratically behind them.

He's never bought a last-minute flight like it's a train ticket before, but it's surprisingly easy. He doesn't even wince at the walk-on price. He just wants to get there.

Given the sudden rush, then having to queue painfully slowly to go through the security scanners, makes him severely agitated. Logically he knows he still has to wait on the other side before they even open the gate, but somehow the quiet lines of resigned, dipped heads and blank faces . . . laptops being taken out of bags and shoes shuffled off . . .

make him want to yell with frustration. This is an emergency! He has to get to her!

The bucket of rocket-fuel-bitter coffee he buys on the other side in the departure lounge doesn't help either, and as the caffeine begins to hit, he starts to jiggle one leg impatiently while sitting on a rigid plastic seat, alternating between checking his watch, his mobile and the overhead screen and taking regular scalding sips of his drink. He's surrounded by a mixture of pretending-to-be-seasoned travellers making out like this is just another morning, some businessmen for whom it genuinely is, and shell-shocked holidaymakers not used to being so alert and organised at this time of day; nervous that even though they're there – have their passports and currency – they might still somehow manage to miss their flight. Will, in contrast, is beginning to feel strangely elated that he has managed to overcome the first hurdle, and is at least going to be in the same country as Anya in some sixteen hours' time and, because Mexico is behind the UK, it will still only be Wednesday evening.

It's the best he can do.

He thinks about the very first time he saw her. Plays out in his mind her walking into the bar where he was working. She strode straight up to him, smile on her sunny face and said, with no preamble whatsoever, 'I need a job, and I'd like to work here, please.'

It hadn't been up to him, of course, but his manager didn't exactly take much convincing to hire the blonde British girl with good legs and an infectious laugh.

Up until that point, Will had thought love at first sight was merely a concept peddled by desperate people keen for an explanation to the outside world for their apparent willingness to settle for someone they barely knew, because secretly they just wanted to settle full stop. Before Anya marched into it, he'd been having the time of his life on his somewhat extended gap year; long but fun hours, plenty of enjoyable banter with the other staff, an abundance of very attractive female customers to chat up, every weekend spent down at the beach. A serious relationship was the last thing he wanted. Then she arrived, and everything changed. She smiled at him and he realised whatever part she was about to play in his life, it was going to be significant.

He takes another much too large mouthful of coffee and coughs a bit, as he thinks about the night early on in their acquaintance – a good ten years ago now – when he told her he 'liked' her, while walking her home from work. She'd looked instantly uncomfortable and embarrassed, and he'd wanted to capture the childish words that were flitting about the air around them, shove them back into his mouth and swallow. Even though they'd somehow managed to laugh it off, he'd felt a little bit of him die inside when she carefully explained she wasn't sure 'they' would really work, then looped her arm through his and said while looking up at him hopefully, 'Still friends?'

'Still friends,' he'd grinned, aching at her touch, desperate to just spin her round and kiss her anyway. He should have done it – he should have risked it sooner – but he let the moment slip through his fingers because, he reasoned, at least being friends with her was better than nothing.

Except it sort of hasn't been.

The more time they spent together, the more he realised she wasn't just beautiful, intelligent and good company – she was complicated, vulnerable, bruised, too quick to anger but happy to admit when she was wrong, able to take the piss out of herself, could be ready to go out in ten minutes, didn't particularly like shopping, was fiercely loyal, brave, had a strong moral code and could make him laugh more than anyone he'd ever met. His perfect woman: the complete package.

If only she'd felt the same way about him.

Once or twice he thought he might have caught her very idly wondering – but then back at home, alone and staring up at the ceiling of his bedroom in turmoil, unable to sleep, he'd curse himself for being so indulgent and absurd. She didn't fancy him: it was as simple as that.

Instead, he concentrated on other things – moving to London, finding what his father called gainful employment, and by the time they hit their mid-twenties, he had a job he actually quite liked. It wasn't exactly going places fast, but it was gradually progressing, he was earning reasonable money and had started saving for a deposit for a flat. Anya, by contrast, was still taking different work here and there, staying with various and numerous accommodating friends – she seemed to meet people wherever she went – on sofas and in spare rooms. Often she'd disappear off out of the country. For a while she developed a thing for Italy.

In some ways Will actually found it easier when she was away; he'd get on with life, but then she always came back, and the familiar longing would return. One particular night she'd resurfaced on the radar and the two of them had gone out in Putney along with a group of other friends, some of whom he hadn't seen in ages, to get messy in a bar. He'd been mid-happy conversation when he clocked Anya sauntering back from the loos, tan accentuating her green eyes, curls falling around her bare shoulders, only to have some oily Sloane accost her from the bar.

Will narrowed his eyes as the bloke casually put his hand on her waist and whispered something in her ear, to which Anya good-naturedly listened. Instantly Will wanted to punch the fucker across the room. Anya must have said something cheeky back to him because the twat laughed, looked even more interested and gestured towards his glass. To Will's dismay, Anya unbelievably shrugged, nodded and sat down.

He went looking for her at the end of the evening when everyone was ready to leave, and it annihilated him to find her drunkenly kissing the Sloane in a dark corner. He wanted to sprint over, grab her and whisk her away from everyone, everything. How could she let someone like that touch her? Someone who wasn't even good enough to clean her shoes?

The experience made him decide that enough was

enough. He had to move on, let her live her life, or lose his sanity altogether. A week later he met Liesel, or rather, he didn't object when a work friend said one of her friends was going to join them for Friday-night drinks. And by the way, she was newly single and *very* attractive, nudge-nudge, wink-wink.

Liesel could have been the answer. Probably would have been if Anya had buggered off again and hadn't, with an uncanny sense of timing, decided it was time to stay put in the UK for a bit, meaning she was around a hell of a lot more. The harder he tried to set his feelings for her aside, the more sucked into a life with Liesel he seemed to become as a result . . . and the more guilty and unsettled he felt about *that*. He attempted to ignore his misgivings, the uncomfortably relentless pull of his own internal compass – after all, Liesel really was a good person. He genuinely liked her a lot.

It became so complicated. He squashed everything into a box, refused to give it any headspace, pretended he wasn't starting to dislike himself for determinedly staring ahead and staying blinkered. It only very nearly burst out once. At Anya's thirtieth birthday he got off his face and confessed everything to Kate. He'd met Anya's sister a handful of times over the years and liked her. She was quieter than Anya, although so were most people – more considered – and there was just something about her that made Will want to bare his soul. Maybe it was because he was desperate for someone to know, or maybe Kate was so close to Anya that it was almost like telling Anya herself, only in a much safer way. Kate promised then and there she wouldn't repeat what he'd said.

Once he'd sobered up, however, he only felt deeply ashamed of his immaturity, how disloyal he'd been to Liesel. He redoubled his efforts to keep everything in check.

Until the kiss.

That Anya flipped out seconds after it at the time barely registered with him. He'd been simply incredulous at what he'd just done. He'd known then that he had to end it with Liesel, whatever else was going to happen, which given Anya's reaction was apparently absolutely nothing. He managed to hold on until after Christmas and Liesel's birthday on 9 January – he felt he owed her that at least. He'd been going to tell her this coming weekend that it wasn't working – that he was so sorry. He'd decided not to say anything about being in love with Anya. She just didn't need to know.

But now Anya has disappeared. He closes his eyes. No one knows where she is, and she was last seen with some bloke. The noise of the airport carries on around him. He barely sees small, alert children running ahead of their bleary-eyed parents, or the couples excitedly holding hands, darting about buying last-minute holiday reads, a spare bikini just in case, toothpaste, sweets and water for the plane.

He's trying hard not to think about what lies in wait for him at the end of his journey. He *will* find Anya. And this bastard – this Rafael. His insides twist up at the thought of someone touching Anya, hurting her. Whatever it takes, he'll find her.

He can't be, without her.

Chapter Eight

'You need to stop this, Kate! Yes, it's true that she was last seen with this man and that they've found her clothes, but that's because *they think she's had a diving accident*.' Rob's voice rises in frustration.

'I said that!' I exclaim. 'You heard me say to him that they're searching in the water!'

'But you made it sound like it was no more than a precaution – as if it's a certainty she's been abducted. You don't know that the police are even considering that as a possibility!'

'Well they should be!' I burst. 'And *Will* asked *me* what else I knew about this Rafael.'

'Of course he did, after the impression you gave him – and considering you know how he feels about Anya.' Rob then adds pointedly, 'Which is the reason you asked him to go in the first place.'

'It's got nothing to do with it! I asked Will to go because they've been best friends for years.' But I suddenly start to doubt my own motives. Rob's right – I knew Will would say yes. Was it fair to play on that?

I then also remember Mum muttering something about Anya and Will having a row before she went to Mexico. I don't think Anya's ever had a serious bust-up with Will before. If they've fallen out, would Anya actually want him to be going out there?

Well – whatever they argued about, surely it pales into insignificance now, and to be honest, if the most I have to worry about is Anya being pissed off with me when she realises I've asked Will to fight our corner, I'll be a very happy woman.

'He said he was glad I'd told him, that I'd done the right thing.'

'Well, that's OK then, isn't it?' Rob looks at me unfalteringly and jiggles Mathias, who has started to whimper, up and down.

I break eye contact first, and don't answer, worriedly

thinking back to Anya's thirtieth birthday at a Russian restaurant in London. A noisy, alcohol-fuelled affair, lots of her friends, lots of laughter. And Will as I'd not seen him before, drunk as a skunk. While his very attractive girlfriend was chatting at the other end of the room to someone else, he confessed to me – completely out of the blue and in a pretty desperate, suppressed tangle of words – his feelings for my sister.

'I've tried, but I don't think I'm ever going to be able to stop loving her,' he concluded, and I felt a tug of empathy as I thought immediately of Andrew, the boy that I'd been in love with at university, who still – all these years later – had the power occasionally to pull at my heart painfully. 'It's been going on so long now I can't really remember a time before I felt like this . . . Before Anya Manning . . . BAM!'

My eyebrows flickered in surprise at this insight into my sister's private life as he laughed sadly, and I wanted to hug him – he looked so unhappy and lost, staring into space and clutching his glass. I could see he was teetering on the brink of revealing things he ought not to, things that Anya had never discussed with me, quite deliberately.

But then he seemed to realise what he was saying, and who he was saying it to.

'Please don't tell her, will you?' He looked at me pleadingly. 'It's much better left alone, she's right.'

'Perhaps we shouldn't talk about it,' I said gently, despite being curious to know more. I had wondered on the odd occasion if there had ever been anything like *that* between them, but when I'd nosily asked Anya she'd just laughed and told me not to be ridiculous, so I'd written it off and accepted they really were just best friends. Except evidently, on Will's part, it wasn't that simple. 'Let's just pretend we never had this conversation, shall we?'

He nodded gratefully, and he and I never referred to it again.

I turn back to the computer, and the face of the man who couldn't be more Will's opposite. She disappeared *two days* ago.

Two whole days. It is unbelievable.

'Here – take Matty,' Rob says, in response to the tears that are beginning to streak my face. 'I'll get you some tissues from the kitchen.'

Once in my arms, Mathias fixes me with an unblinking stare through his clear blue eyes, as if he is cutting straight to the heart of me and can see all of my deepest secrets and fears. He looks so like Emily at times that it is astonishing, but it's not just the physical likeness, it's the seeming old before their time, sitting discordantly alongside such a painfully pure, unearthly innocence. They are so very similar. The sudden, involuntary physical wrench it creates within me is enough to make me catch my breath.

I grip him more tightly. Anya has to be OK. She *has* to be. I see her getting in a car with *him*, whose face I now wish I had not seen, because it has made everything so real. My sister – utterly at the mercy, the whim of some stranger. I see the truck stopping, and then—

Then . . . I can't think about the gaps. About how my sister lost her clothes. Can't think about what happened next, and I know in my heart of hearts that every moment that passes could literally be the difference between life and death.

At that, I think about Emily again, and Mum and Dad. I hear myself having to say the words out loud: 'My sister died', and agony sears through me like a hot knife in the fresh scar on my stomach.

The phone bursts into life on the desk.

'Rob!' I shriek, and I hear him drop something with a clatter in the kitchen and rush up the hallway, before he bursts into the room and takes Mathias from me, who has started to cry.

Terrified, I've already answered and am listening intently. Rob stares at me, waits – and then I watch his eyes widen as I repeat out loud, 'So they're *not* in the pool. The divers have searched it thoroughly, and they didn't find them?'

My head starts to swim with a strange giddiness that ought to be relief but isn't – she's still missing – but I knew it! Gabrielle continues talking, and initially the words wash over me. I said so! I *said* this man was suspicious. I look straight at Rob, who whispers, 'I'm sorry.' Well, at least now the police will focus their efforts correctly, they will—

But then I realise Gabrielle has just said something completely surreal.

I am so stunned that I have to ask her to repeat it.

'The rescue team found an entrance to an underwater cave in the pool.' Her voice seems to have slowed, as if she's taking care over every word. 'It's a common feature of cenotes – submerged passages that run deep underground – and diving them is very popular in Mexico. The police have moved the search for Anya and Rafael into the cave.' She waits for my reaction.

'They think Anya swam into an underwater cave?'

I can hear the disbelief in my voice. 'That she's in there now?'

Rob's mouth falls open in shock. I can only fix on his face to anchor myself as I clutch the phone.

'The authorities think it's a possibility, yes,' Gabrielle says gently.

'But Anya hates closed-in spaces – she'd be,' I try to take a deep breath, 'terrified of going into somewhere like that.' Rob moves to me, takes my free hand and holds it very tightly. 'It'd be her worst nightmare. There's no way she'd willingly enter an underwater passage. Absolutely none at all.' I feel utterly sick at the thought of it, and I'm not even claustrophobic.

'I see, but—'

But nothing. They're wrong – Anya isn't in an underwater cave – she simply wouldn't do that. I know she wouldn't. I can't deny that, in my opinion, she does stupid things sometimes, but this would be in a different league altogether. Even she, *especially* she, wouldn't put herself in such an extreme and dangerous position.

'It would be completely out of character for her,' I insist. 'A long time ago she . . .' I begin, but then abruptly change my mind about what I was about to say. I don't want them to think Anya is some loose cannon, sparking trouble wherever she goes. She isn't, and it might prejudice efforts to find her. 'You just know some things about your family, don't you?' And I mean that; if someone told me my mother had been involved in an altercation in a shop, that she and the assistant had argued, that the assistant had asked my mother to stop raising her voice, my mother had apologised, the assistant had then . . . I would have said *stop right there*. My mother never apologises for anything. It wouldn't have sat right, and neither does this. But I have also begun to appreciate the full implications of what Gabrielle is saying.

'They must believe she's dead then,' I say stupidly, 'if they think she's in this cave. She disappeared on *Sunday*. They think she's drowned.'

There is an agonising pause.

'They're not looking for her anywhere else, are they?' I add.

Gabrielle doesn't comment on what I've just said, but continues: 'The two divers from the voluntary international cave-dive rescue organisation do need to investigate, Kate, as it seems so likely a dive trip was planned.'

International *cave* rescue? So right from the start

they must have thought this was a possibility. And what the hell does she mean, *voluntary*?

'I know "voluntary" can have amateur connotations,' Gabrielle concedes, 'but that's absolutely not the case here. These divers are experts . . . but at the moment the cenote is the focus of the operation, yes. We need to try and stay positive, Kate.'

She says something else about coming back to me when she knows more, but I am so numb, I hang up without comment and without further challenge to what she has said.

The only sound in the small room is Mathias sighing as he stretches in Rob's arms.

'She's not in there,' I manage to repeat eventually.

There is another silence before Rob ventures, 'You don't think *because* she'd be so afraid of going in an underwater cave, that's exactly why she might—'

'*No!*'

'Kate!' He motions down at Mathias, who has gone very still. 'Try to keep your tone level, sweetheart,' he implores. 'Please.'

'Men do that sort of thing – women don't need to.' I do my very best to control my voice. 'Anya doesn't have anything to prove, she knows that.'

'It's just, she's done things like this in the past; skydiving, that sort of thing. Maybe this was the ultimate. Something to really test the limits that—'

'She wouldn't have gone in there, Rob.' I am now ablaze with certainty. 'That's all there is to it.'

I watch him hesitate.

'She's my sister. I know she'd never do it.'

'I'm not saying I don't feel uneasy about them centring everything on this dive theory,' he admits. 'It's making me think about that kid who went missing in Portugal, her poor parents having to sit by while the local police seemed to mess everything up in those first, all-important hours . . .'

He looks down at Mathias, then up at the ceiling, exhaling heavily as he does, then back at me. I stay resolutely silent, and this time I hold his gaze. We stay like that for a moment, and then he gives a nod.

'OK,' he concedes simply. 'If you say she wouldn't go in the cave, I believe you.'

Relief surges through me as I hear him continue: 'But how do we make the police in Mexico listen to us, force them to widen the search? You said no one has the power to influence local investigations, didn't you? The Embassy can't do more than they

132

already are, we're on the other side of the world and by the time Will arrives in Cancún—'

'Don't say that,' I interrupt quickly, but he's right. He's absolutely right. We don't have time to wait, or to waste. We need to do something drastic, and do it *now*.

I look around wildly, as if the answer must lie somewhere in among my files, Mum's books, the papers on the desk . . . then my eyes light on a crappy magazine and the huge headline, 'Exclusive! Jordan's Marriage in Crisis'.

And I have an idea.

Chapter Nine

Earn £££s by selling your story! It's easy!
Just click below. We outsell all our rivals
and can afford to pay more!

I've come straight through to the website of a
national newspaper simply by searching for 'how to
sell a story to the papers'.

The promise of money means nothing to me,
obviously. I only care about their claim of shifting
more copies than anyone else because if that's true,
they must have some considerable power; the ability
to stir things, make people sit up and take notice . . .

And if they were to run a story on Anya's

disappearance, they'd start asking potentially embarrassing questions of the Mexican authorities . . .

What police force, keen to present themselves to the rest of the outside world as highly competent, would want a bright light shone on their search for an abducted British girl when it's going badly wrong? Their handling of this investigation could have far-reaching implications well beyond those of national pride and reputation. There's the possible effect on tourism, for a start. They might not be taking the hunt for Anya seriously, but I bet they care about *that*. And if the police think they are at risk of being exposed, with a case to answer – then won't they ensure they do everything in their power to find her?

Total anonymity is assured! the spiel continues. And we always protect our sources.

So no one even need know the information has come from me. The telephone number at the bottom of the website swims in front of my eyes, I'm staring at it so hard.

'Are you sure this is a good idea?' Rob says, worried. 'Shouldn't you discuss it with Gabrielle?'

It's too late, I've already picked up my phone, and withholding *my* number this time, I start dialling. Rob's right – normally I wouldn't make such a

136

spur-of-the-moment decision, but I'm utterly desperate to do whatever it takes to rescue Anya, or more accurately, force other people to rescue her.

My call goes to voicemail, and I'm asked to leave a brief message and contact details, so a reporter can get in touch 'immediately – if we like your story!'

That throws me: my mobile number – so much for anonymity – but I have no choice, how else will they be able to call back?

'Hello. I have a story about a British girl who has been abducted by a local man in Mexico. The police aren't looking for her properly, and unless someone does something, it's going to be too late to find her.' At that my voice cracks. 'You can reach me on . . .'

I leave our landline number, like that will make any difference in protecting our identity, and then hang up – feeling sick. Answerphones are for cheery 'call me back when you get five minutes' catch-ups, not messages the like of which I have just left. This is all so very, very wrong.

Half an hour creeps agonisingly by. Next door starts to wake up; I hear their children noisily rushing around, getting ready for school. Front doors start banging, cars blip as they are unlocked . . . our neighbours are beginning to go about another normal day.

The journalists don't call.

How long should I give them? Does this mean they're not interested? Should I contact someone else instead? Except the website specifically says, Don't tell another newspaper. In calling them, I've trapped myself in a silent no-man's-land and now I don't know what to do, or where to turn.

We haven't got this time to waste!

Rob quietly gets to his feet after another five minutes as I sit rigidly in the armchair, starts to make a few phone calls himself, cancelling jobs. I hear him apologising to a client, explaining no, it's not because of the snow, he has a personal issue that he has to attend to. He didn't have to say that, but my husband always plays things with a straight bat; probably the reason why he is a builder in demand. As I stare glassily out of the window, he makes us another tea. I haven't even finished the last one.

Mathias is adding to the sense of the surreal by staying asleep. Any other morning I'd be welcoming this miracle with open arms – perhaps taking a luxurious five-minute shower instead of it lasting long enough for me to climb in and straight back out. I'm even drinking a *hot* cup of tea – and yet it's with huge relief, for once, when I eventually hear my son mewling upstairs; it breaks the oppressive and dangerous still that has settled, now that everyone else has gone to work and is getting on with Wednesday.

Rob brings Mathias down – and when they re-appear in the room, he's pulled on some clothes; tracky bottoms and a warm jumper, and he's got Mathias dressed too – although for some reason he hasn't put any socks on him.

He feels Mathias's feet and says, 'Oh he's all right . . .' when I point it out – and God help me, I suddenly want to burst, 'Well, you've got socks on, and if your feet are cold, his will be too, won't they?' But I don't because I don't want to belittle him. Or have him say I'm being neurotic and that I have to chill out. They're just socks.

My old job was pretty average – health insurance usually is – and not exactly fulfilling, but it was busy. I saw people every day, I was responsible for training the new intake, it was a constant source of new faces, which I liked, and even having been there for nearly ten years, it had its hairy moments. But I managed. Now all it takes is a pair of socks.

I *have* to pull it together. I can't be this hermit crab now, dragging the shell of my former self around.

If I'm going to be of any use to Anya I have to step up, I have to—

Rob's phone rings, making me leap out of my skin. It's his mother – I see her name flash up on the screen.

'Can you take Matty?' He passes him over without waiting for me to say anything and, to my incredulity, picks up. 'Hi Mum.'

We're waiting for either the Embassy or a national paper to ring. It's impossible for me to process this mind-bending mix of the mundane and the grotesque. Surely he can speak to her later?

'Hello love!' I can hear her as clearly as if I was talking to her, she shouts so loudly on the phone. 'So, what's your day looking like, busy as ever?'

Rob looks carefully at me and I see him decide not to say anything, for which I am grateful.

'Yup – busy,' he says. 'You all right?'

'Yes, thanks! Me and your sister are just off for a bit of a poke around the shops with the littleys. We thought we might drop you off a pasty later for lunch, say a quick hello if you're local?'

And I can't help it, just for a moment I feel irrationally jealous of them – of my own husband – for being able to have such a lovely, normal conversation.

'I'm not around, Mum,' Rob says. 'Sorry about that.'

'OK, no bother then. Matty all right?' she asks. 'Got ever so cold again, hasn't it? I shouldn't be surprised if it snows some more. We probably won't be out for long, I wouldn't think. Keep an eye on the weather, won't you, if you're further afield.'

'Will do,' Rob says. 'I best go now.'

'Bye love,' she booms. 'Bye!'

He hangs up. 'Sorry about that,' he says.

'It's fine,' I manage.

'I didn't say anything because you don't want anyone to know yet, do you?'

Ironically, just as he says that, the home phone rings. I catch my breath. The newspaper? It has to be.

And it *is*. Very quickly I find myself talking to a woman called Claire, who is bent on aggressively checking the facts.

'So the missing girl, your "friend",' she says briskly. 'She's not been found dead yet?'

'No, they think—'

'Who's they?' she interrupts.

'The police. *They* think she's in an underwater cave.'

'I thought you said she'd been abducted by a dive instructor?'

'That's what we believe, yes, because the divers' preliminary search of the pool found nothing, and—'

'But they're still searching the cave at the moment? On the assumption she's drowned?'

'Well, yes. But—'

'So they just might not have recovered the bodies yet? Riiight.'

I begin to panic; she sounds almost bored. I'm losing her. I take a deep breath. 'Something happened to Anya a long time ago that would prove she would never do something like swim into a cave. She—'

'Look, you *have* seen the news this morning, I take it?' She cuts across me almost rudely. 'Haiti mean anything to you? There was a massive earthquake there yesterday afternoon, their time. We've got natural disasters, trapped people and emergency rescues pretty well covered today, to be honest.'

I'm stunned by how blunt she is. 'You're not interested in the abduction abroad of a British girl . . . a very beautiful one?' I hate myself for adding that cheap last comment.

'Not unless she's a celeb. And *has* been abducted

– for certain,' she says over my attempt to speak again. 'Or *is* dead. Sorry.'

'Please,' I beg. 'You've got to help me. I don't know what else to do. She's my little sister.'

There's a long pause. Then she sighs and says, 'Sorry.'

'Thank you.' My voice has fallen to a whisper.

'Look, call us back if they've searched the cave and she's definitely not in there, OK?'

No! That's not OK. 'That's entirely the point. If we wait until then, she—'

'Bye now.'

And she's gone.

I am frozen to the spot. That can't have been my last chance.

'Kate.' Rob moves towards me, but I step back as I determinedly hit the redial button. 'Hi, it's Kate Palmer. We just spoke . . . about the disappearance of Anya Manning . . . there actually *have* just been some dramatic developments.' I am trying my hardest to sound convincing. 'You're going to want to call me back.'

Rob just stands there looking at me. 'Please just stop,' he pleads. 'Please. Come and sit down for a moment. You need to – oh shit, Kate!'

I've had to dash across the study to an old Whistles

143

bag that I keep stationery in. I hang over it and retch, then again – more violently. Gasping, and eyes streaming, I stare unseeingly at the ruined cards beneath me and wait to see if my body is preparing to heave for a third time.

Rob moves silently over to me and puts a hand on my back. 'All done?' he says gently, after a moment. When I nod – a thin dribble of spit hanging from my lip, which I wipe from my mouth with the back of my hand – he quietly picks up the bag, takes it from the room, then comes back and ushers me up to the bathroom, where he wrings out a hot flannel so I can wipe my face.

'I'm sorry,' he says, 'that it didn't work, that they didn't want to know.'

I shrug and try to smile as I'm brushing my teeth, but it ends up being through yet more fresh tears. I drop the brush in the sink and cover my face with my hands as I dissolve, and he pulls me to him while I cry and cry with the sheer futility of it all.

Yet from within the deep muffle of his jumper, I hear the landline ringing downstairs. Yanking myself free, I hurtle back down the stairs and snatch up the receiver, just managing to gasp a 'Hello?'

'Kate Palmer?' It's not the woman, Claire, it's a

man, and he sounds young. Very young. 'About the answerphone message you just left . . .' he says.

'Did Claire tell you to ring me?' She's palmed me off on some junior. They're not taking this seriously, either.

'Oh – you've already spoken to my colleague, sorry, *boss*?' he corrects himself tersely.

Maybe it's because it's part of what I do for a living; train staff to listen to people on the phone so they can exploit chinks in the customer's defences and sell, sell, sell – or use the knowledge to defuse complaints – but I immediately pick up on the tone with which he says 'boss'. It's resentment. He says it like he has a massive chip on his shoulder. He doesn't like her.

'Well, I tried to,' I say immediately. 'I was going to give her some information on a story that would have exposed high-level failings in the Mexican police force that are placing a British girl in serious danger' – does that even sound vaguely convincing? – 'but she said she was too busy with Haiti.'

There's a pause – and he bites. 'Well you can talk to me,' he says casually.

And then incredibly, my mouth just comes out with something I hadn't planned to say but which seems to be there, waiting, on the tip of my tongue – as if my subconscious had it already all planned out: 'I have the phone number of a lawyer at the scene of a serious crime in Mexico . . .' I pause and wait for that first bit to sink in, let him picture it in his mind. 'The local police force is currently conducting an investigation into the disappearance of a young British female tourist. Her clothes were found by the side of a pool in a remote area, but the police are refusing to acknowledge the possibility that a local man she was last seen with could have abducted her.'

'Protecting their own?' the journalist says after a moment. 'Nice . . .'

'Exactly!' I leap on that. 'He's probably the brother of someone important, or something.'

'I didn't mean it that literally.' He sounds suddenly wary.

Oh God, I've overdone it. 'Well, true, we don't know anything for sure. That's why it needs investigating. The police just keep searching the water, even though a preliminary drag of the pool has revealed nothing. She's missing, and time is running out.' I don't need to fake the urgency in my voice when I say that. 'Someone has to do something to help her before it's too late.'

I hold my breath and wait. Have I managed to do enough? He doesn't say anything though and I'm unable to tolerate the silence. 'I came to you because it ought not to be allowed, she's a British girl – and the Mexican police force needs exposing.' Is this making him see dramatic 'paper to the rescue' headlines, Middle England standing up in outrage and refusing to abandon an innocent girl to her fate? Prizes for investigative journalism? Fat exclusives?

'What's this lawyer's number, then?' he says nonchalantly.

Oh thank God – yes, it is.

Finally, someone is going to do something.

Anya hasn't drowned in some cave.

I feel it in my bones.

Chapter Ten

I can't see anything. It is black-ink dark, and cold. I
am terrified to move my legs, am barely breathing.
The only noise is my sudden scream of 'Help!' as
fresh panic rips from me. I don't know if I'm in a
large space, or if it's touchably small. I'm unable to
reach out, completely paralysed by the fear of what
my fingers might find. Feeling a void – or tomblike
walls – would be equally horrific.

Oh God, oh God, oh God . . . The desperate chant
of my silent stream of pleading is only drowned out
by the audible chatter of my teeth. I try to clench
my jaw, stay quiet. There is literally no light, I am

unable even to see my own hand in front of my face, and it is so isolating, it's as if I'm trapped inside my own head.

'*Help me!*' I shriek again, and I'm sure I *hear* the noise. 'Is anyone there? Please! I need help.'

But the only person who might hear me would be him.

Shit, shit, shit!

'Oh please,' I begin to babble, hot tears flooding my eyes and throat, 'please, someone. Anyone!'

But there is no answer. This is not OK. This is definitely not OK. I whimper with terror, cursing my stupidity and naivety.

I can't take a breath. I can't get the air to suck cleanly into my lungs. My throat is closing in; the darkness has its hands round my windpipe – tightening, tightening. I'm shaking too, despite trying very hard to calm myself down.

I want to get *out*! I have to get out . . .

My body starts to feel hotter and hotter. 'Help me!' I rasp, but this time the sound isn't there like before. There's no raw shriek of desperation, it's an airless hiss, the kind that would barely escape from your mouth if you looked up and saw a stranger in your house looming out of the dark, beginning to walk towards you slowly with an intent and inevitability that could only mean you harm.

I attempt to swallow and start to count breaths, trying to calm myself. One, two, three, four . . . is he coming for me? . . . five, six . . . seven . . . eight . . . Are you, Rafa? . . . nine, ten-eleven-twelve! *Oh shit, shit!*

When I finally force myself to reach out, my fingers touch nothing. It would be impossible to feel my way out of here. I will certainly die if I attempt to escape. I have no choice. I am trapped.

I picture my mum and dad walking hand in hand across a field on one of our family holidays, us three girls skipping and running ahead, shrieking happily. Then I see Kate asleep, safe in her bed, Matty in his little cot within arm's reach, and then lastly, I think of Emily and me, singing happily in the car together.

And I start to cry.

Chapter Eleven

Scrunching my eyes shut, I force from my mind a picture of my family and their stricken faces silently mouthing my name, but when I open them again I still can't see anything. It's like jolting awake in the dead of night, not knowing where I am, except that instead of being able to pick out the edges of shapes as my eyes adjust, there are no shades, no tones – nothing to become visually accustomed to. It is crowding in on me. I can hardly breathe.

When I was little, if I woke up and discovered someone had absently switched off the hall or bath-room light, I'd be wide awake in seconds, frozen and staring at the end of my mattress and the door, slightly ajar. The predatory nocturnal creature under my bed was a heartbeat away from appearing, claw by claw, to grasp at the edge of my duvet. If not that, the door to the airing cupboard – just beyond in the hallway between mine and my parents' room – was silently opening, bony fingers beginning to curl around the edge; a skeletal leg was slowly emerging, climbing out *into my house*, coming to look for me . . .

Old habits die hard. The dark is so close here, I can imagine being practically nose to nose with a presence, right now. If it were holding its breath, just crouched still, staring, waiting, I would have no idea it was there, until I reached out and—

I hear the rasp of a moan and realise it has come from me, an involuntary attempt to drown out my thoughts.

How long has it been now? My senses are so deprived I'm completely confused, seconds feel like they are lasting hours. I have absolutely no idea of the length of my incarceration so far. As a rough frame of reference, all I can do – as slowly and calmly as I can – is count through what I think a minute would be.

Taking a deep breath, I count another ten.

And then ten more.

In comparison with how long I estimate I have been here in total, that felt quite short, so possibly, overall, it has been less time than I think.

Or perhaps I simply counted too fast.

Shit. This is not good. *This is not good at all.*

My pulse starts to quicken. I need to be saving this energy! Fight or flight . . . I make a conscious effort to breathe more slowly, but instead my body simply starts to judder. And I don't know if that's from fear, or the cold.

Gulping frantically, I see my mum sitting on my childhood bed in the glow of the hall light, holding my small hand and stroking my forehead, my eyes as wide as a bush baby's. 'Take a deep breath,' she says gently. 'That's it – and another one. And again. Good girl, Anya. That's better, isn't it?

'Let's think about something nice. What about you, me and Kate going to the park?' Kate is sleeping heavily on the opposite side of our shared bedroom, covers pushed back, limbs as soft and relaxed as a rag doll, snoring contentedly. 'Close your eyes,' Mum's patient voice is soothing, 'and I'll stay with you.'

So I think about the big slide at the park . . . climbing the wrought-iron steps, clutching the rails either side of me, carefully placing my feet down, each one worn and slightly slippery with use. I reach the top and look down the slide, as glossy and shiny as golden syrup. I decide not to look at the small figures of people playing on the swings and see-saw below, while a gust of wind tugs at my skirt and makes me wobble. My hands fly out to grip the rails so tightly my knuckles turn white as, sitting down with care, I shiver with anticipation – the danger of it all – take a breath and then let go . . .

The wind rushes, everything blurs: but in an instant I am safe at the bottom, grinning, my cheeks pink with the flush of relief and excitement. I clamber off, run back over the grass to the start of the steps and begin the ascent again.

I would run that sequence over and over in my mind, until when I opened my eyes, Mum had gone, the room was light and Kate was awake, propped up in bed in her pyjamas, reading *Anne of Green Gables* for the millionth time.

If only it would work out like that now, if I were to fall asleep. I wish it with all my heart.

Because I am never going to get out of here! The rapid ballooning begins again in my head. I am never going to escape . . . I will never see them all again.

Oh, God – what have I done?

Stop it! Shifting the position of my stiff muscles, I concentrate on seeing Kate in her pyjamas, reading in our childhood room.

Take a deep and steadying breath. Come on . . . calm down. Think of something safe . . .

And there I am, stood at the top of the long garden at my grandparents' house where we spent the school holidays, if they didn't come to us. The lawn was always beautifully tended by Grandpa, and in his absence nibbled neatly by the rabbits I craned to see when looking out of the small, top window of the hall first thing in the morning, before anyone else was up.

Pockets of flowerbeds with established shrubs dotted the edges of the grassy expanse that began to narrow if you were running down to the compost heap right at the bottom by the hedge, near the burned-out, blackened spot where Grandpa had his bonfires – in which sometimes we would cook jacket potatoes wrapped tightly in tinfoil. Kate could occasionally be convinced to race the length of it with me, but her legs always had that three-and-a-half-year head start on mine, and often she'd get bored with the ease of being halfway down the garden while I was still panting behind her shouting, 'Kate! Wait for *me*!' which, of course, wasn't really the point.

Sometimes when she disappeared off completely I'd eventually track her down beneath the thick, trailing branches of one of the small ornamental trees, sweeping the leaves back like a curtain to discover her reading in serene green, as if she was hiding away in her own little house. She'd sigh as soon as I appeared, like I'd ruined something for her, which I probably had, then beg me to go away. Stung, I wouldn't, – I'd deliberately do something to annoy her instead, and somehow it would end in one or other of us – usually Kate – running back up to the house in tears.

I trailed poor Kate relentlessly while it was just the two of us, before Emily arrived. If she had a friend over for tea, I'd follow them upstairs to our bedroom, and having become bored at not being fully included, would deliberately start to get in the way of whatever game Kate was trying to play until she'd get fed up. 'Just go downstairs and find Mum!' she'd plead, before shutting the door in my face. Smarting at being excluded, and from *my own room*, my favourite response was to yowl theatrically, go downstairs clutching my hand, tell Mum Kate had shut my fingers in the door (not true), and then hide behind Mum's skirt, smiling with smug satisfaction as Kate had to listen to a severe and lengthy 'we don't close doors on each other in this house, Katherine. Shutting each other out is very unkind. The more you do it, the more interesting you make everything seem to Anya. Let her come in, play for a bit, then she'll get bored and go away.'

Yeah, *right*. I'd got my own way; I wasn't going anywhere. I strutted in and casually suggested we take the duvets off Kate's bed and mine, so we could slide down the stairs on them like magic carpets. Kate gave me a 'you're such a baby' look, but her less mature friend shrugged and said, 'I don't mind, it could be fun!' Poor Kate finished up in the kitchen complaining desperately to Mum that I always ruined everything, while Mum, not really listening, laughed at Kate's friend and me gleefully whizzing down the stairs, again and again.

Thank God Emily eventually came along, otherwise it would only have become worse as we got older. 'It's not fair! How come *she* gets to stay up later?' and 'But she sat in the front *last* time', or 'She's cut its tail off on purpose' would have bled over into ruined clothes, borrowed–without–asking make-up and, God forbid, maybe even boys. I have a feeling

Kate and I would have turned out to be the kind of sisters that ended up arguing at every single family occasion, but Emily appeared just in the nick of time to dilute the concentrate, change the direction of the path and make everything OK.

I don't know where it is now, but somewhere there is a video of the three of us in our parents' room at Holly Lodge. Dad is inexplicably filming the sunset out of the window. Eventually, as if he remembers we're there, the camera pans down and Kate and I are jostling at the front for attention in our dressing gowns, dancing, jiggling around and pulling faces at the camera while Emily, not quite a toddler, sits in the background on the bed, emitting gorgeous, fat cherubic chortles of delight at the silliness of her sisters, which in turn is making my mother smile, as propped up on pillows she relaxes drinking a cup of tea, watching her girls. I predictably end up getting a bit overexcited and give Emily an enthusiastic hug – slightly too enthusiastic, because it prompts Mum to urge 'love her gently, Anya' – and cover her in kisses, which she happily puts up with, while Kate takes the opportunity to occupy the spotlight unfettered. Emily's arrival united and separated us, all at the same time. She balanced us.

Not that we didn't fight after that. Three girls?

Of course we did. In our playroom at home there was a vast, old-fashioned horsehair sofa. I think my grandparents gave it to Mum and Dad when they were first married and couldn't afford to buy anything of their own, and then we wound up with it. We used to fling ourselves on and over it, built tunnels and dens by heaving off the stupidly heavy cushions . . . it saw a lot of play action, that sofa. One of the sturdy arms was my trusty steed for quite some time, and I remember Kate objecting strenuously when I 'rode' it through her painting: while sitting on it, I deliberately flung a cushion at her art homework. I remember feeling utterly compelled to do it, and getting an actual thrill of horror and fascination as I watched the brown water jerk over the neat paints, run across the paper and drip down onto the carpet . . . I had to assure Dad innocently that it had been a complete accident. 'She did it on *purpose*!' poor Kate exploded as hot tears sprang to her eyes. 'I hate her!' She reached out and shoved me off the arm in frustration, I howled, and dramatically fell on Em, who was happily bouncing on the sofa, minding her own business. She then started crying at the surprise of being unceremoniously squished – and Kate was sent to her room. Poor old Kate. She put up with such a lot of shit.

I really loved that playroom. When Dad eventually sold Holly Lodge, we were heartbroken: I didn't think he'd actually do it, but he did. Kate was devastated. For years she'd talked about having her wedding reception in a marquee in the garden, even before she met Rob.

Kate and Rob.

They will be in their neat, semi-detached house *right now*. Their safe little nest . . .

Why didn't I just stay at theirs? I certainly should have, Kate needed me! I have no business in being here, no business at all – I didn't need to make such a stupid, dramatic gesture. I should be in my sister's house, helping to look after her.

I imagine myself walking downstairs in Kate's house to find her. They are steep steps – I've fallen *up* them when drunk once or twice – and I have certainly never counted them. But I'll try now. One, two, three, four, five, six, seven, eight, nine, ten, eleven, twelve, thirteen. Unlucky for some. When I get back to the UK, I will count them properly to see if I'm right. I bet I am – there are thirteen for sure.

I exhale raggedly. I have my hand on the end of

their banister now, can see the stripped wood floors of the hall. They were sensible to buy when they did; Kate says she couldn't afford to buy her own house now. The boards are black at the edges because Kate sanded them herself, having given up waiting for Rob to get round to it, and didn't realise that you can get an attachment that can fit into that bit. By the time she *did* find out, she didn't have the energy to go back and redo it all. Their front door has small, mixed brightly coloured stained-glass panels in the upper two portions. Kate thinks it is original glass from the 1930s. I wouldn't know 1930s glass if it bit me, but it's very nice if you like that sort of thing. Kate does, and she's proud of that door.

On the right-hand wall of the hallway, wrapped round a nail, hangs a length of candy-striped ribbon on which there are miniature pegs. This morning – or whichever morning it last was, or will be – when the post *next* comes in through the letter box, my sister will have scooped it up and sorted through it, opening hers and pinning Rob's to the mini-washing line for when he gets home from another day of building other people's houses. Kate needs order.

Into the sitting room next . . . it smells faintly of cinnamon because Kate likes to burn scented candles in the evenings while she and Rob watch TV. The walls are duck-egg blue – Kate's favourite colour. The faded yellow sofa is to the right, the cream one to the left. The vast flat-screen TV – Rob's pride and joy – sits on top of the old pine cupboard in which their DVDs live, and I know that at the back of the cupboard there is a plug-sized hole that Kate cut in the wood because it didn't occur to her to take the TV plug off, drill a *wire*-sized hole in the wood and then reattach the plug. She was really pissed off when she realised her mistake. I thought it was funny.

This is good – this is helping.

OK, so on the left of the mantelpiece is their wedding photo, both barefoot on the beach in St Lucia, brightly coloured flower in my brother-in-law's lapel, a hugely proud smile on his very brown face. Kate has a slightly sunburned flush to her pale skin. She never tans, just burns, but she too looks happy. It was absolutely the right thing for them to do, to go abroad. I told Rob if he just booked it Kate'd fall into step and stop agonising, and she did.

Next to the picture are two painted wooden turtle doves, and a small vase that sits under the mirror hanging on the chimney breast. On the right of the mantelpiece is a photo of a gowned and capped Rob next to a tiny Matty in his incubator. Kate is on the other side, looking grey and spaced out, hooked up to all manner of wires herself, still wearing a fetching hospital gown.

She told me when I saw her immediately afterwards – and she was still crawling on the ceiling with all the drugs – that I had to know two things: one, when waters break, they don't necessarily gush like you think they do. She wanted me to know that because no one told her; she wasn't even sure they *had* broken. Two – she looked at me seriously, struggling to focus with fatigue – the moment she knew she'd lost control and couldn't feel her legs because the spinal block had kicked in *wasn't* a relief because someone else was going to have to take over at last – it was bloody terrifying because she was utterly at their mercy. There was *absolutely nothing she could do* – which, she whispered, was her biggest fear.

But I don't want to think about Kate being afraid, in particular my having made her afraid. Oh God – I am so, so sorry to do this to you again, Kate! It's more than I can bear. I am so *fucking stupid*. When I am going to learn? When?

'*Help!*' I shout. It just bursts from my mouth although I don't know why I think I would get any answer this time, when I have called over and over again. One hundred and fifty-two times, at the last count. Over the noise of my rapid breathing, I listen carefully – but there is nothing.

I can't hear Rafa coming. Yet.

OK, out of Kate's sitting room. *Focus!* Turn left . . . I am in her study with its burnt-red walls. On her desk is the computer, the scarlet lamp is in the corner and then there are pictures of me and Em. I hate the one of me. I look like an asylum-seeker. It's a lovely one of Em, though.

'Emily,' I whisper in the darkness, but of course there is no answer to that, either . . . *back to the study*. Kate's work stuff is piled up under her desk, all of her insurance training files and books. Then there are the French windows out into the garden, and a small wood-burner that Kate refused to light over Christmas because she hadn't had it swept and was worried about a chimney fire.

The cream chair and the yellow-gold chair, part of the set that wouldn't fit in the other room, are rather pointlessly angled in towards the dead stove, and there are symmetrical bookcases either side of the chimney breast that are stuffed full of Mum's art books, which Kate really should finally chuck out, or have shipped to California, but she won't do either. Nonetheless, it is still a cosy, welcoming room.

In fact, the dining room is the only space in the house they've never really got to grips with. It echoes, feels merely like a walkway through to the kitchen – and the table is slightly too small for entertaining. Kate and Rob don't really do that anyway, they don't ever have loads of friends over for an evening – being more one-other-couple-at-a-time people. Mostly their friends are from school, although over Christmas, Kate enthusiastically mentioned a new name once or twice; a Tamsin, who she met at an antenatal group. She talked warmly about her, repeated something Tamsin had said that had been funny, and while I was pleased that she'd made a new friend, I also realised I was a little jealous of this interloper, which was slightly unsettling. I like being the one that makes Kate laugh, that's *my* job.

Straight through into the kitchen, wood units – everything in its place – and there's Kate. She's putting the kettle on, she's chattering away to me and carefully getting out two mugs, the teapot and the little jug. Kate is the only person I know under sixty who uses a teapot *every day*. She is opening the biscuit tin – ginger nuts and Jaffa Cakes, it won't be anything else, she and Rob recycle the same list at Sainsbury's online each week. Anyway, the biscuits are for me, because Kate will be on a diet. She doesn't need to be, she's perfect as she is. She'd say she was fat – I'd genuinely say curvy (and *not* secretly mean fat), with creamy skin. She's a modern-day milkmaid and doesn't for one minute realise how attractive she is – which is probably just as well, really.

She retrieves two teabags from the cupboard and drops them in the pot. Everything is on a tray. We are going to take it out into the garden and sit in the sun. It will be sunny because that's how I'm picturing it. In fact, it will be summer – there will be the smell of freshly cut grass in the air and a fat wood pigeon cooing in a tree somewhere.

The perfect afternoon.

I would do anything to be there with her now. *Anything*, God.

But then, why would making bargains work this time, when it didn't before?

And why should he answer my prayer anyway, when this is entirely my own fault? My own foolish, reckless – and selfish – fault?

Chapter Twelve

I think about Will telling me to grow up, as I huddle my arms about myself. He was right – and he should know, all the times he's picked me up, the times Kate has, too . . . I have had the feeling before that they have been waiting for me to realise I couldn't go on for ever as I have been. But I ignored it. Where was the harm in my travelling around, instead of struggling to buy a flat in a dreary 'up-and-coming' area when I'd never get a mortgage in any case – and didn't want one anyway?

But perhaps they didn't mean that it's a bit sad to be so unsettled when everyone else is starting to get married and have children – after all, that's just a lifestyle choice. Maybe what they meant was, it may well be my life, but that doesn't mean other people aren't part of it and bound to me, just as I am to them, and therefore we have responsibilities to each other whether or not I choose it to be that way. I am not a free wheel spinning in isolation, no matter how hard I try to be, because right now, they are all I can think about – and that will cut both ways.

What I have done is going to cause my family so much pain, again.

I have learned nothing.

Tears spring to my eyes. Somehow I always end up hurting everyone, causing damage and I am a stupid, *stupid*, selfish little bitch. I do not deserve their love, and I can't even tell them how sorry I am . . . so many things I should have said, and didn't. The shame overwhelms me, but I have nowhere to push it. There isn't the space here.

Oh, just give it all back to me!

Let me go back! Let me go back to that summer and make it all different – and I will save us all.

Our parents were off on their first proper holiday alone – without at least one of us tagging along – in what Mum said was about ten years. She had booked it, and as she rifled excitedly through a tangle of brightly coloured summer outfits and extracted a couple of rather elderly bikinis, I eyed the precarious mountain of books she'd balanced on the bed. I couldn't see how the hell she was going to get through that little lot on their five-night Italian adventure.

'You will behave for Granny and Grandpa, won't you?' she said absently for the millionth time as she stared at the piles of clothes and selected a floaty white gypsy top at random. 'I know Granny can be very . . .' she grimaced, 'annoying. But be good for them.'

I opened my mouth indignantly, but Kate got there first.

'I think Granny just likes things being in a routine, that's all,' she said from the corner of the bedroom where she was sitting on the carpet staring into a mirror and carefully plucking her eyebrows. 'I don't mind being back for dinner at six each night. It's no problem.'

I scowled at her. I loved Grandpa, but was *not* looking forward to several days of the TV at a ridiculous volume while he hogged it, watching endless athletics, cricket and other utterly pointless sports.

And as for Granny's kind but regimented 'What time will you be back, dear?' 'Where are you going, dear?' and 'I'm not sure your father and mother would like that, would they, Anya dear?' I could already feel my frustration levels rising.

When Mum had said they were going away, I'd gleefully envisaged several nights of Steve in my bed. He wasn't allowed to sleep in my room normally, as our parents said we older two had to set an example for Emily, but with them out of the country . . .

Except if my grandparents were on house alert in the next bedroom, five nights of summer sex were going to be seriously impeded. I imagined Steve, half naked on the landing, tiptoeing to the bathroom, bumping into Grandpa on one of his hundred nocturnal loo visits, and shuddered.

'I'm now old enough to have a job, get married, *drive* – yet I need my bloody grandparents to stay while you're gone?' I snapped, and began grumpily kicking Emily who was sitting on the edge of the bed carefully untangling one of Mum's necklaces for her. 'Anya! Don't!' she said patiently, and pushed my foot from her.

'Get up please, Anya darling, you're rather getting in the way lying across everything like this.' Mum nudged me gently.

'All right, all right!' I moved to the head of my parents' bed irritably, like a bad-tempered troll waiting for someone to cross the bridge, knees hugged to my chest as I glowered on the pillow. 'You don't all need to shove me.'

Wisely, no one said anything. They just quietly got on with what they were doing.

'I actually think it's insulting,' I burst eventually, and Mum sighed. 'She's' – I pointed at Kate – 'lived away from home for the last three years and got a sodding degree, for Christ's sake. We don't *need* them here!'

'Language, Anya!' Dad marched into the room clutching a neat, zippy clear folder in which I could see their passports and other important documents. 'It's not a comment on you or Kate. It's actually so that you can both do as you please, while Em still has someone to drive her around and be here in the evenings.' He ruffled Emily's hair. Em looked up and smiled at him.

I tutted in disgust. I was going to have to have a word with Emily. She didn't need someone here in the evenings. She was thirteen now, for crying out loud. It was about time she stepped up and started putting the man in Manning, because her current attitude wasn't helping – well, me, actually.

'But *Dad* . . .' I began.

He shook his head firmly. 'Nope. It's all arranged now, anyway. And Kate's in charge in their absence. Don't make this difficult, Anya.' He looked directly at me. 'Your mother is very much looking forward to this trip.'

Mum quickly glanced up at him from the bag she was cramming things into. 'We both are.'

'Absolutely.' Dad crossed to her and planted a kiss on her cheek. 'That's what I meant. So behave, you lot, all right?' He gave us one of his wry smiles. 'I don't want to hear so much as a single word of dissent among the ranks. Got it?'

We saw them off in their taxi to the airport the following morning. Dad hadn't wanted Kate negotiating a heaving M25, and then Heathrow, in his beloved Audi.

'Hear that?' I said gloomily as our happily waving and kiss-blowing parents vanished round the corner. We listened to the taxi disappear off up the lane. 'That ought to be the sound of freedom.'

Kate cleared her throat. 'It still could be,' she said, trying to sound casual. 'Why don't you leave it with me? Hey Em,' she called, as Emily, who had rushed to the end of the drive, began to mope back. 'French toast for breakfast?' I glanced at Kate with renewed interest. This was unexpected. The Reverend Sister Katherine had a plan?

Her strategy was a simple but devastating one. In fact, it was good enough to be one of my ideas; that it was conceived and executed by Kate was actually mildly disconcerting. After two days of her sneaking our cat into the forbidden zone of Granny and Grandpa's room, and practically rubbing the confused Smartie over their pillows, Grandpa was wheezing nicely. To the point where Kate was becoming worried she'd overdone it.

'I don't want to make him really ill,' she whispered anxiously to me in the hall as we listened to him coughing away in the living room. 'His allergy is really kicking in.'

'Time for them to go back to their own cat-free home then,' I murmured. 'You're nearly there now! Go and tell them we can manage for the rest of the week. Kate.' I grabbed her arm as she took a deep breath and prepared to march purposefully into the room. 'Why *are* you doing this?'

She turned slightly pink. 'No reason. You were right. We just don't need them here, that's all.' I raised an eyebrow as she disappeared. Bollocks. For once, she was up to something. I listened to her start doing the concerned granddaughter bit, and felt mildly aggrieved at how completely suckered in they were. If *I'd* said all that, they'd have smelled a rat – but because it was Kate . . .

. . . it worked. Sensible Kate convinced them we'd be fine; Mum and Dad were back on Saturday evening. That was only three more nights. She didn't think we should call them in Italy – they'd only worry about Grandpa being ill. We'd all handle it; the most important thing was that Mum and Dad had a nice break.

So the grandparents went home.

Steve stayed over that night, and the following night too. It was *brilliant*. Because we were both working at a local toiletries factory for the summer and he was on the early shift all week, he was gone before Emily got up, and Kate turned a blind eye. It was a total result.

By Friday, when I arrived home from my ten-to-five shift, I was pretty knackered but determined to make the most of the last night. I found Emily sitting at the breakfast bar in the kitchen carefully sticking a picture of a kitten she'd cut out of a magazine to the front of a bit of pink card with a Pritt stick. She was frowning with concentration and only looked up once she'd positioned the image just so, and smoothed it down so that there were no creases in it.

I had already slung my bag down tiredly and was by the kitchen sink running the cold tap, desperate for a drink. My car journey back had been fiercely uncomfortable. The bloody heater was playing up and chucking out hot air at full blast, which, given it was late August and sticky patches of tarmac were already melting in the lanes surrounding our house, wasn't exactly ideal. I'd had to drive with all the windows down as I'd rocketed home, and it was still like sitting in a furnace.

I gulped the cold water back thirstily, spilling a bit on the granite work surface before wiping my mouth with my hand and turning to face Em. 'Where's Kate?'

'She's upstairs cleaning the bathroom, again.' Emily looked at me almost admiringly. 'You stained the bath bright *yellow*, Anya.'

'I didn't have time to clean it up before I left, I was late for work.' I shrugged and dipped my fingers in my glass and flicked some water at her. She gasped and covered her picture in alarm. 'Mind my card!'

'Yeah, what *is* that you're making?' I leaned over for a better look.

'It's for Mum and Dad – like it?' She held it up and I looked at the three kittens, surrounded by stars and a cheery *Welcome Home!* across the top, the letters of which became smaller and a bit squished at the end.

'You're a bit old for all this *Blue Peter* crap, aren't you?' I said, then felt bad as she immediately looked hurt. I opened my mouth to explain that at her age, I'd been out getting my first snog, but then pictured some randy little sod getting his hands on my innocent little sister and felt sick. It was nothing short of horrific. I'd have to kill him.

And if she was a little naive, it was hardly her fault. We all cosseted her dreadfully – Mum in particular. Plus kids these days, I decided with all the experience of my eighteen years – just – had to grow up too fast anyway. There was plenty of time for her to turn into a sophisticated, know-it-all teenager.

'Ignore me. It's very nice.' I admired it and took another sip of my drink before sitting down opposite her and accidentally spilling some more. 'Which one am I?'

She spun the card round, holding it well away

from the liquid. 'This one.' She pointed to an Andy Pandy-style white cat with green eyes that looked a bit like it might be about to go off and do something naughty. I appreciated that, and winked at her.

She paused and sniffed the air. 'What's that smell?'

'Me, I expect. I've been stuck in the perfume shed all day. See?' I leaned across and she wrinkled her nose. 'Ugh! Like all Mum's sprays in one.'

'I know,' I said, remembering my earlier humiliation, breaking for lunch and saying to Steve in front of all his friends, 'Sniff my fingers and guess what I've been doing!' I flushed red with the shame at the crucifying memory of them all bursting into delighted eighteen-year-old-boy laughter.

'Anyway,' I said hastily, wanting to banish the picture from my mind *for ever*. 'I'm going to go and try to wash this perfume ponk off.'

I stood up just as Kate came marching into the room, en route to the sink. She dumped everything in the bowl and yanked the tap on so hard, the hot water thundered out. Squirting too much washing-up liquid under the stream, she thumped the bottle back down on the side. 'What's up with you?' I asked, stretching, but she didn't turn round.

Was this because of how I'd left the bathroom?

'You should have just ignored it,' I said. 'I'd have done it.'

'No you wouldn't,' she retorted.

She was right, I wouldn't. 'It was just a hair pack,' I said archly. 'And I think it's made it loads blonder, don't you?' I shook out my hair.

She didn't say anything, just pulled out a gleaming glass, rinsed off the suds and plonked it on the drainer before searching around in the water for the next.

'Are you pissed off with me?'

'Language, Anya!' she admonished me, sounding just like Dad. But before I could respond she burst, 'Look, I've got someone coming to stay tonight and I just want it to be nice everywhere, OK?' She turned and looked at me defensively.

Ah-*ha*! A slow smile spread across my face as I crossed my arms and settled back on my stool. She blushed pinkly under my gaze. 'I see,' I said. 'And who might *he* be?'

'His name is Andrew. He's at – was at – university with me.' She looked embarrassed. 'It's no big deal.'

So that explained the long game to get rid of the grandparents. The wily old fox! No big deal, my arse. I shifted through my mental Rolodex of Kate's fit male friends and acquaintances. 'Blond hair, tall, sort of rangy-looking, sporty, funny – but a bit posh?'

Kate went the colour of a radish. 'Might be,' she said in a small voice.

I looked at Em delightedly and we both went, 'Wooooo! Andrewwww!'

'Please don't do that when he's here,' she said hotly, coming over and efficiently wiping the side where I'd spilled the water next to Emily.

'As if,' I scoffed. 'So that's what all this is in aid of – Prince *Andrew*'s coming to stay for the night. He won't care if the bloody bath's clean, Kate.'

'But I do,' she pleaded. 'Please be nice, won't you?' She bit her lip anxiously. 'I just want everything to be perfect.'

'Where's he travelling from?'

'Gloucester.'

Of course he was. How *terribly* nice. 'Reasonably long way for one night. He must like you,' I said slyly. 'I suppose he's going to be gone before Mum and Dad get back tomorrow? It's almost as if you've planned it that way, Kate.'

She looked down at the floor. 'Mum would just . . . you know.'

'She'd just what?' Em looked up, interested.

'Talk a lot,' I said quickly, remembering Mum's recent mad flirting with Kate's male university friends at her graduation, all skippy and merry on one too many glasses of champagne. It *had* been a bit embarrassing. Even Dad had noticed and said gently, 'I think you might want some iced water instead, darling, it's a bit warm for anything else.' But then it was only because Mum felt self-conscious. Kate's clever friends unnerved her, made her act a bit weird. They made me feel a bit like that too, to be honest, but I could also see why Kate wasn't desperately keen for a repeat performance. 'Anyway, you don't need to worry about me showing you up, I'm going out tonight.'

'But what about Em?' Kate said quickly. 'I'm going to get Andrew from the train and then we're . . . going to go out for dinner,' she added self-consciously.

'I'm not here either, though,' Emily reminded her helpfully. 'I've got Guides, remember?'

'Yes, but you've still got to be driven there and picked up.' Kate chewed her lip worriedly and then set her face. 'You'll have to do it, Anya, I can't. I need to get ready.'

Well I had a party to go to. 'Hmmm. I suppose this is what Dad meant when he explained why they'd asked Granny and Grandpa to stay,' I said. 'In fact, have you considered what they're going to say when they get back and find you sent the grandparents packing? They're going to flip.'

'But – you didn't want them here any more than me! And for the last two nights, you know full well you've been—'

'Yes?' I innocently uncrossed my arms and let them sit loosely in my lap. 'What have I been doing that you can't actually prove, Kate?'

Kate opened her mouth in protest.

'I think we can all see you don't want anything to interrupt your big bonkathon tonight,' I said smoothly. 'And while I sympathise—'

'Anya!' Kate burst and nodded at Em. 'Shut up!'

'I know what bonking is,' Emily said. 'We've done sex education at school. In science, Mr McCreedy showed us how to put a condom on a banana and all the boys laughed. And in *junior* school, we watched that video where the mum and dad play tennis with the son and daughter, and they've all got no clothes on.'

I burst out laughing as Kate went 'Ugh!'

'We never got shown that!' I said to Em, fascinated. 'What, really? A family in the nud, playing tennis? Gross!'

She nodded. 'It was all,' she affected a deep voice, '*You will get hair in unexpected places.*'

I snorted. 'That's hilarious! Did they—'

'Does Mum know you watched that?' Kate looked appalled.

'Yup.' Emily nodded. 'We had a talk about sex and stuff afterwards.'

I was impressed. She wasn't so green after all. Which reminded me. On the subject of sex . . .

'I'd love to help you, Kate,' I picked up my bag and made my way to the door, 'but I can't.' I looked at my watch. 'Steve's expecting me at his. Big party tonight, at a friend's. You know how it is.'

'But that's not fair!' Kate exclaimed. 'I ask you to do *one* thing, and . . .'

'Only it's not one thing, is it?' I sighed. 'It's going to shag up my whole night. I'll have to take her, come back, hang around, go back and pick her up later and then babysit her all night while you're out playing Mr and Mrs.'

'I *can* hear you!' Emily interjected. 'I wish Mum and Dad would come back.' She slumped onto her hand slightly and looked at her cat card. 'I miss them. Can I phone them at their hotel?'

'No!' Kate and I said in unison, seeing both of

our illicit evenings potentially whizzing down the plughole. We glared at each other.

'You *are* going to take her,' Kate said, attempting to put her foot down. 'I've been tidying up after *you* all day, and—'

'So?' I shrugged maddeningly. 'No one asked you to. Gran would have done it if she'd been here, but you sent her home, remember? You can't have it both ways, Katherine.' I mimicked Mum. It had the desired effect.

'You are *un*believable!' She drew herself up with all the kudos of her extra five years. 'One day, Anya, you'll learn that the world doesn't revolve around you, and behaving like a baby doesn't mean you get what you want. It just makes people think you're too immature to decide anything for yourself. I'm the eldest,' she continued, 'and I was left in charge, so I say—'

'What?' I said, suddenly bored. 'What do you say? Because you can't *make* me do anything.'

Kate faltered, trying to decide where to go next, as she knew that was true.

I leaned over and picked an apple out of the fruit bowl. Emily watched us warily. 'Ask me nicely,' I said conversationally, and took a bite.

Kate's jaw flexed. 'Please Anya, will you drive Emily to Guides and babysit tonight?'

I paused and smiled sweetly. 'No. I won't.'

'*Arrggghhh!*' Kate finally lost it, flew into a rage and for reasons best known to herself, took off her shoe and flung it at me, shouting, 'I *hate* you!' making me drop my apple, which rolled under the kitchen table.

'Don't fight!' Emily was starting to look upset. 'I just won't go to Guides! Or we could ring Sophie and see if her mum might let me go and stay there tonight?' She brightened. 'Then no one has to miss anything because of me! What about that?'

I couldn't help but grin at Emily, the baby, being so mature. 'Calm down, Squeak,' I said. 'We'll sort it out now, OK?' I made a fist with my hand and looked at Kate. 'C'mon. Scissors, paper, stone – best of one. Ready?'

We hit three times before I unfurled a flat hand and she kept a fist.

'Yessss!' I breathed delightedly and then punched the air before picking up my bag. 'P.A.R.T.Y. . . .'

Kate looked crushed. At first I thought she was just going to accept it – but as I went to go upstairs, she put her hand out on my arm and said desperately,

'Please, Anya. *Please* will you do it?' It was then that I noticed her carefully painted nails – and she'd done her toes, too. Most unlike Kate. I hesitated and she looked at me hopefully, sensing a chink in the armour.

'Kate, I won fair and square!'

She kept looking at me firmly. Normally she'd have accepted it by now, but I could see just how determined she was.

'Fine,' I sighed, and gave in. 'Pick up Prince Andrew and go out for your meal. I'll take Em.' Steve would just have to come over instead. It would still give us an empty house for at least an hour or so.

She looked at me sceptically, like she was waiting for me to say, *Ha ha – not really*. 'You mean it?' she breathed. 'You're not messing around?'

I sighed again. It was probably going to be a shit party anyway, to be fair, but she didn't need to know that. And I *was* pretty wrecked after the last two nights of not much sleep. 'Yes, I mean it. Can you leave Mum's car keys out for me?' I attempted yet again to go upstairs.

She paused, then said in a small voice, 'Can't I take Mum and Dad's car?'

I came back and looked at her incredulously. 'Are you for real? You're going to make Em and me drive the junky old oven while you two ponce about in comfort? Anything else? Want us to find a choir of angels to sing a chorus when his train arrives at the station?'

'It's just, Andrew's parents bought him his own brand-new car on his twenty-first,' Kate mumbled.

'And a gold-hoofed chocolate pony called Mr Trippy Trap, no doubt,' I said. 'What a lucky boy.'

'I don't mind the red car, Anya.' Emily got to her feet. 'I'll go and get my stuff.'

'Fine! I give up,' I retorted crossly. 'We'll take that one then, you take Mum and Dad's. Jesus, I hope this bloke is worth it, Kate.'

'He is,' she said softly. 'I mean, it's only been four months, but I really think . . .'

'Yeah, sorry,' I cut her off shortly. 'I haven't got time. I'd better go and ring Steve, tell him we've had a slight change of plan.'

'Thanks,' she said sincerely, and I left the room loftily, feeling secretly rather pleased with myself. This was going to result in a useful bargaining chip with Kate – always helpful to have in the back pocket.

Once Emily was ready, we both walked out into the heady summer evening. The sweet scent of honeysuckle was heavy in the air as she happily chattered away about the cat card. I wasn't really listening, thinking instead about Steve. We climbed into the stuffy car and both quickly wound down the windows.

'Woof! It's boiling in here!' said Em, flapping her pink T-shirt. I glanced at her denim shorts and slightly gangly, foal-like legs.

'Where's your Guides outfit?'

'In my bag,' Em said. 'I'll change when we get there. It's too hot.'

'You wait . . .' I turned the engine on.

A blast of searing dry air whacked us both in the face.

'Ugh!' Poor Em began to wilt almost immediately, a rose flush creeping across her pale cheeks. 'That's horrible! And it's making your perfume smell even worse.'

'Don't worry – we'll get a through-draught going,' I assured her confidently. 'Got your seat belt on?'

She nodded, but I double-checked it was clicked in anyway – it was fine once you'd done it, but there was a knack to it. 'Right.' I revved the engine. 'And they're off!'

I floored the accelerator, sending a cloud of dust up in the air as gravel spat out behind us and we bombed off the drive, to Emily's shriek of delight, which the show-off in me found very pleasing.

Hurtling up the lane, which was perfectly safe because there was hardly ever anyone on it anyway, we whizzed past the fat hedgerows – shedding cow parsley petals onto the road behind us – and then screeched to a stop at the top.

'Quick!' Emily said. 'It's so hot! Go, go, go!'

I didn't need any encouragement, and crunched the small car into first. We took off again. Em leaned forward and put the tinny car radio on. The theme to *Men in Black* filled the car. 'Oh, I love this one!' she exclaimed ecstatically.

I pushed away a bit of hair that had swept across my face and shouted over the noise of the wind, 'I love Will Smith more!' We flew down the road happily singing in unison, Emily bouncing up and down in her seat, on cue with the lyrics, making me laugh out loud. She grinned back at me.

I was suddenly filled with complete random happiness, and just for a second wished I *was* going out later – it was a perfect evening – but hey, whatever, the boy I loved was still coming over to see me. I slowed down as I began to approach a crossroads. Emily was still singing, a single lone car smoothly passed in front of us and as it disappeared to our left, we were off again.

But barely twenty feet up the road, I heard a sudden pop – even over the music – and instantly turned off the radio. I put my foot on the brake and pushed my hazards on. As we came to a stop, I listened carefully. The hot air was still rushing as the engine hummed. 'Did you hear that?' I said to Em, who shook her head.

'No, what?'

I sniffed, and even over the hot air blasting in our faces, and my cloying perfume, we both smelled it. Smoke.

'Shit!' I said in alarm, and fumbled to switch the engine off. We both looked through the windscreen in front of us. Unmistakable wisps were beginning to rise from under the edge of the bonnet. My heart pumped fatly. 'We've got to get out of the car, Em,' I said, trying not to panic her with the sudden shaki-ness in my voice.

'OK.' She reached quickly down to her feet for her small bag.

'Just leave it,' I instructed, unclipping my seat belt. 'Come on!'

'I can't get my belt undone.' I couldn't see her

face, her long hair had fallen across it as her little fingers pushed down redundantly on the red Press button, the catch refusing to release the metal clasp.

'Let me.' I shoved her hands out of the way, noticing the smoke, darker now, beginning to rise more determinedly. I pulled at the belt but it wouldn't budge. I clicked the Press button furiously. It did nothing. The mechanism had completely jammed. She was trapped. I heard her yelp, and looked up to see a tiny lick of flame at the front of the bonnet before it disappeared again. 'Right, you'll have to slip out under it.' I turned back urgently, and with strength I didn't know I had, I fiercely wrenched the belt, but it was one of the old-style ones in which there was no give, because otherwise it wouldn't actually function as a seat belt in the first place. There was just a tightened loop of belt, which I was going to have to force back through the buckle to create any slack at all. My fingers fumbled and struggled.

Emily was starting to become frightened. 'Anya, I want to get out.'

'I know Em, I'm trying. Don't!' I said as her hands tried to clasp over mine and pull frantically at the buckle.

'Why won't it open?' Her voice was rising. 'I'm scared!'

Instead, I turned to try feeding the belt back through the loop; make it loose enough so that she could slip out from under it, but that was no better, it was gummily bonded stuck with infrequent use. I quickly gave up. 'Can you get this over your head,' I said, 'and then maybe I can pull you out from the bit over your lap?'

She tried, but it was absolutely taut across her rapidly rising and falling chest. I needed something to cut the belt with, and foolishly looked around our feet or on the back seat for something sharp as Emily waited for me, her big sister, to fix it, to make it all OK. Of course, there was nothing, and the smoke was continuing to thicken, although thankfully there were no more flames. I glanced up, which was when I spied a nearby farm. And made a split-second decision.

'OK, Emily, listen to me,' I said urgently, but as calmly as I could manage. 'I can't get the belt off. You see that house just there?' I made her look – her eyes were wide and frightened, but she nodded as I pointed it out, fewer than a hundred yards up the road. 'I'm going to go there and get help, and I'm going to be so fast that by the time you count to two hundred, I'll be back.' I threw my door open and scrambled out. 'Keep trying the belt while I'm gone. Now start counting.'

'One, two, three . . .' Her voice was surprisingly clear and steady.

'Good girl.' I smiled shakily at her. 'Keep going!' And then, as her face was obscured again, her fair hair falling across it as she turned back to the catch, I began to run. I kicked off my flip-flops and sprinted faster than I had ever moved in my life, lungs pulling for extra air, in which I could already taste the tang of acrid smoke. I ran as fast as I could, barely feeling the sharp bits of grit cutting into the soles of my bare feet, and I did not look back.

Chapter Thirteen

I hurtled into the concrete yard, at which a panting collie lying in the shade jerked its head up and scrambled to its feet, barking with outrage.

I hated the local farm dogs. They would lie in wait for you, lurking around gates or at the end of the long drives ready to pop out of hedges and snap at the wheels of your bike, barking crazily – or at your ankles if you were jogging past on a run. They weren't family pets; they were bored, feral and I was usually more than happy to give them a very wide berth.

It raced over to me and began to leap about as I tried to pass it; I felt the sharp scratch of a rough paw down my bare thigh and the whistle of teeth nipping the frayed edge of my cut-offs. 'Get away!' I roared down at it, in spite of my heart being up in my throat and my mouth dry with the exertion of running – both to my surprise and the dog's. It dropped back uncertainly and encouraged, I rushed up to the front door and began to hammer on it with my fists. 'Hello?' I shouted. 'Hello! Can you hear me? I need help!' The dog began to bark frenziedly again, dropping back on its haunches and unleashing a volley of noise that drowned me out completely – yet it was also now blocking my exit, and no longer looking so unsure of itself.

Mercifully the door juddered open and a confused man who looked about the same age as my dad appeared, chewing away on a mouthful. I very vaguely recognised him, but then all the farmers round us looked the same. They all had the identical uniform of filthy trousers and old shirts, as well as thinning hair and rough, red skin. His eyebrows flickered at the sight of my bare feet.

'My sister.' I took a gulp of breath, suddenly conscious of how mad I must look. 'She's stuck in our car and I can smell smoke. I can't get her out, the seat belt is jammed and I need to cut it—'

He pushed past me before I could finish, ran to the edge of the yard and looked down the road. The dog and I watched him turn on his heels, hurry back and vanish past us into the dark hall of the house. I heard him shouting something to someone out of sight about calling the fire brigade. Then he re-appeared holding a bloody great kitchen knife, and as if I wasn't there, broke into a run without a word. The dog instantly scrabbled after him, and I followed. They were much faster than me though and by the time I had reached the road again, I could see they were already halfway down it.

But further down it still, the whole of our car was now completely engulfed in angry, orange flames.

I could only just see the outline of the roof and the front edge of the bonnet. A huge cloud of toxic black smoke was billowing up into the silent sky that was just starting to streak with the first rosy colours of early evening. I stopped in my tracks, stunned, then took a hopeless step forward and then back again. And then I think I screamed – and shrieked *no!* because I couldn't believe what I was seeing. Only then did my legs start up again as I hurtled towards the car – and Emily.

I'm not sure how close I got to it before he stopped

me and held me back as, kicking frantically, I tried to pull free, shouting at him to let me go, arms flailing, fingernails scratching his face as I stared wildly at the burning car. I could feel the heat on my skin even from where we were.

Lying motionless in the dark, I reach up and wipe the hot tear that is sliding down my face. I remember very clearly running towards the car, how still everything felt, the smell in the air, flecks of floating ash, collapsing into the farmer's arms, the sound of my weeping, the distant and then louder sirens – I have replayed it through with total clarity a thousand times. And when I do it's with the same questions every time. Did she call for me? Did she know what was happening? Did she suffer or, please God, did she pass out from the smoke so that it was painless?

I saw a film about the First World War some years later, and when a young soldier came to have to go over the top, just before he was forced up the ladder he cried for his mother. The knowledge that Emily too was alone, because I left her, aged only thirteen . . . I don't think it will ever stay shut in the room in my head. It bursts through, smashes windows when

I least expect it and the rest of the time sits there waiting for me to come and find it.

Initially I refused to believe that she was in the car.

I remember fiercely insisting to one of the fire brigade who quickly led me away that they must look *around* it. Emily was a slim girl, she would have wriggled out while I was getting help . . .

I don't recall what they said to me. By then things were becoming confused. I have no idea who strapped up my bleeding feet, or wrapped me in a blanket. I answered questions automatically. I stopped repeatedly asking if they'd found her outside the car and fell quiet altogether. When I was told gently that someone was going to take me home, I didn't even put up a fight. I just did as I was told.

I can see Kate's face now as she opened the front door, ready to go and collect Andrew. She was wearing a pretty, floaty grey summer dress I'd not seen before, had clean hair, a happily expectant smile – which fell away when she saw me numbly flanked by two policemen. They told her there had been an accident, and our neighbour – who had appeared nosily at the sight of the police car on the drive – rushed over, hugged her and furiously told her not to panic, that everything would be OK.

Our kitchen started to fill with people. Poor Andrew arrived in a taxi and hovered awkwardly in the background, not knowing what to do or say, as unsuccessful attempts were made to trace our parents, who couldn't be found at their hotel.

Then the confirmation came through, the police sat us down in our living room and told us together. They were so sorry. Kate immediately started to cry. I don't remember what I did. Just sat there mute, I think.

Our ashen grandparents returned, both appearing to have aged a hundred years. It was the first time I had seen my grandmother in tears as she hugged first my rigid body to her and then Kate's. Another taxi arrived to take Andrew back to the station. The phone began to ring as the news spread locally, we missed a call from our frantic father because a rubbernecker had got in there first, clogging the line up, wanting to be among the first to contact us with condolences. Instead, Dad left a message saying they'd been told to ring us urgently, what the hell had happened? My grandmother was unable to call him back, was too upset and my grandfather was talking to the police, so Kate had to do it. She was sobbing as she said, 'There's been an accident, Daddy. You need to come home – right now. She's dead!' I remember it specifically because she hadn't called him Daddy for years.

I found her curled up on the bathroom floor afterwards, clutching the card that Emily had made only hours before, weeping, her face puffed up as if a snake had bitten her. When she saw me, she blurted: 'I was supposed to take her. It should have been me – I would still have insisted on using Mum and Dad's car. That way she'd never have got stuck. You won the toss – it was all my fault, and I didn't even let you take the safer car when you asked me! If I had . . . if I had . . . Ohhhh!' She moaned with pain and I automatically went over to her and half sat, half collapsed down and put my arm out to her.

I wanted to say that it *wasn't* her fault – I'd been there, I got out of the car. I made the decision to leave Emily while I went for help. I abandoned our sister. How could Kate blame herself? But I was simply paralysed. I kept seeing myself in slow motion; that tiny, deadly space – getting out, backing away from Emily, turning and running . . .

And then, I imagined what had happened next, what I *hadn't* seen.

I should have stayed with her. I should have kept

trying to get the belt undone. I shouldn't have got out of the car.

I was unable to say it to Kate, though; I didn't know how. All I managed was to reach out silently, placing my hand on her arm – and she was in too much pain to do anything but clasp it tightly as she cried.

Then our parents arrived back.

I don't suppose there is a blueprint for how people will behave in a situation like that, but I didn't expect my mother to fly at my grandparents the way she did – she was hysterical, screaming, 'My baby girl. My daughter!'

They should never have just left us, she shrieked, so what that Kate had said we could cope? *She* had asked *them* to stay, the decision was nothing to do with Kate!

He could see that, my grandfather started, through a coughing fit, but—

But what? They didn't even think to ring, to say they weren't there?

'But Kate said—' began Grandpa.

What? What did Kate say? Were they saying it was Kate's fault? Mum demanded.

Kate's eyes widened with fear where she was

standing, waxen, in the corner of the kitchen. 'Of course not!' Grandpa stammered, as Granny burst into tears again and my grandfather placed a protective hand on her arm. They were, he began brokenly, so very sorry that—

'Get out!' Mum shouted at them, adding that she would never forgive them, would never speak to them again. Dad tried to calm her, holding her back as she clawed like some deranged animal, shrieking at her parents-in-law to *just get out!* when they didn't move, rooted to the spot in shock.

Kate and I watched as finally they stumbled from the room, horrified by what we'd just witnessed. For a moment no one spoke, but then our father turned to Mum and said desperately, 'It's not their fault.'

'They said they'd be here. I trusted them, and look at what they've done!' She was shaking violently. It was as if they'd forgotten Kate and I were there. I glanced at Kate, but she was looking down at the floor.

'But we weren't here either! No one—'

'You don't have to tell me you didn't want to go, David!' she burst. 'I know!'

'Alison please, I have to go and deal with the procedural requirements, for . . . for Emily's identification.' Dad's voice broke as he interrupted her. 'How am I supposed to do *that*?' His voice cracked, and he sounded like he was really asking her, but Mum rushed out of the room and he followed. We heard a door slam, and sobbing. I wasn't sure which one of them it was.

The only ones left, neither Kate nor I moved until finally Kate looked furiously up at the ceiling. I realised she was crying and took a step towards her, but she turned and made for the door too, before vanishing upstairs. I stood alone in the kitchen, horrified by what I'd done.

Surreally, Princess Diana also died that Sunday, and images of smashed-up cars were everywhere, although they had already been burned onto my brain for ever. We were in raw shreds, locked inside our own family tragedy, isolated within our grief.

Mum barely left Emily's room in those first few days. To have crossed the boundary and joined her would have felt like an intrusion. When I did find it briefly empty, I tiptoed in and sat on Em's bed. Mum must have heard me, though, because suddenly she was there too, sobbing, wrapping me in a tight hug and saying, 'You must have been so frightened. My poor, poor baby.' Kate appeared silently in the doorway and looked on, pale as a ghost herself, before melting back and quietly closing the door to her bedroom.

I started trying to tell Mum that I was sorry, that Emily must have been so scared too, and— But she shushed me, wouldn't let me speak, seemed only to want to hold me, so I obliged. I didn't want to upset her further. Once she let go of me, she simply withdrew again.

In fact, up until the funeral, I think all four of us were suspended in disbelief. It was only on the day itself – which we were allowed to go ahead with only once the cause of the fire had been finally established, as an electrical fault – that it all hit us and felt real. Which is the point of a funeral, of course.

It was an overwhelmingly packed church, people I didn't even recognise were crying for *my* sister, which was weird. The farmer was there, smart and scrubbed in a suit he looked uncomfortable in. I didn't make eye contact with him, I couldn't – and he stared straight ahead, although I spied his wife take his hand when the vicar said the laughter of children taken before their time can be heard in the purest of sounds, like the everlasting babble and flow of water over stones.

I really hated the priest saying that; it felt like nothing more than a cheap soundbite that he'd sombrely practised in front of the mirror, so the congregation would look at him admiringly. I wanted him to talk about Emily, and wished that my grandparents were there, familiar faces rather than the sea of mourners I didn't know dabbing at their eyes, but Mum had refused to let them attend.

It was during my father's faltering reading that the really hideous thing happened. The small coffin sat at the front of the church, and finally I made myself give it a first proper look. Initially as I stared at the box I saw Em's tiny hands fumbling with the seat-belt buckle, but then to my horror I found myself wondering what was actually in the coffin. Was it just – remains? Was it her whole body? Was there anything in there at all? I'd seen the car burning fiercely there in front of me . . . I didn't see how . . . Stricken, I tore my eyes away and focused on my father, standing in the pulpit. He had identified her. He knew.

I couldn't look at it, or him, again after that, and it was as much as I could do to stay on my feet for the rest of the service. When we all filed slowly into the churchyard afterwards, I giddily stared at the ground, only saw the coffin lower out of the corner of my eye. I wished I had Steve standing next to me – I needed him, physically wanted to lean on him – but he was standing towards the back at a respectful distance.

Instead, I became aware of Kate's hand in mine. I knew that she was crying, could hear the sniffing and feel the judder of her sobs moving up my arm, but I was statue-still, my mind full of macabre thoughts that I didn't know how to give voice to, even much later when the house finally emptied of the last guests and Kate appeared in my room, clutching her pillow.

'Can I sleep in here with you?' Her eyes were red-raw and her voice exhausted. I nodded and folded back the duvet so she could get in. We huddled together like we had when we were little. 'Are you OK?' she asked, and I nodded again, because I didn't have the right words to say. Everything was tangled in my head.

'I feel so sad,' she whispered, and her eyes flooded again. 'I want her to be here, with us.'

She fell asleep eventually. And I suppose I must have done too because I remember dreaming I was in an unfamiliar house, going from room to room, but every one I entered had a dead body in it, wide eyes staring straight up. They weren't Emily, but random corpses. When I woke up the following morning Kate had gone, back to her own bed.

With the funeral over, everyone else's lives returned to normal while the course of ours was changed for ever; *we* were changed for ever. The four of us were without Emily, and yet she was there in everything we said, felt or did. People told us that time would heal. I think they meant we had to learn to live alongside it as best we could.

We really tried.

At first, Kate and I were tragic curiosities, a delicious drama in a village where everyone knew everyone else and nothing much ever happened. Because Kate had only just returned from university, she would have been a novelty anyway down at the pubs where bored blokes she'd once been at school with now hung out. Tired of seeing the same old faces and the same old outfits on girls they'd already tried it on with every Saturday night, Kate was a breath of fresh air.

Had Emily not died, they wouldn't have got a look-in, those blokes. I'm sure Kate would have stuck to her existing plans for that September – a place in a flatshare with some of her university friends in Camden, a trainee role in a marketing company, living near and still seeing Andrew – but none of that happened. She decided she wasn't going to go to London. She didn't feel she could leave our parents. Especially Mum.

'I can't,' she said to me. 'You've seen her, she's just – there's nothing there. Dad can't deal with her on his own. I owe it to them to stay and help.'

'But I'm here,' I pointed out.

She shook her head fiercely. 'No. You *have* to go to uni. I can't leave you, have you miss your chance. I've already got my degree.'

I opened my mouth to say it was OK, I didn't really want to go to university anyway. I wanted to stay at home with Steve.

'It means the world to me to know that I can do this for you,' she insisted. 'It's the least I can do. I owe it to you too, Anya.'

She didn't, she didn't at all.

'But what about Andrew?' I said a moment later.

She shrugged and tried a smile. 'Oh – I don't think that's going to work out anyway. He's going to move to London and . . . we've tried, but he doesn't really know what to say to me any more. It's all different now, not like it was. You know what I mean.'

I did. I had found myself becoming very angry with Steve for whingeing over tiny, insignificant things that really *weren't* problems in the grand scheme of things, and similarly he was becoming frustrated with my lack of interest in him, specifically rushing round to have sex with him as soon as both of his parents were out. It *was* different, but at least I still had him.

'I'm sorry,' I said automatically. 'You really liked Andrew, didn't you?'

She nodded. 'I think he really liked me too – but, well, there you go. Things change.' She looked round the room. 'You haven't done any packing at all. I could help you.'

'OK,' I said. It seemed to be very important to her, this university thing.

We were all trying to do the best by each other.

I managed a year. I hated it. I'd only got the place because Dad had applied for me, but the flaw with that plan was, I couldn't apply myself. I sat in lectures thinking, what was the point? Who cared about Descartes' dream theory? That was all it was – a theory peddled by some ancient guy – and all of the other people on my course were weird too. As for the people on my corridor . . . the girls seemed completely immature, getting pissed, shagging random blokes then crying everywhere because said bloke gave them the shocking news they weren't really up for 'anything serious'. The boys were exactly that – boys trying to pretend they were far cooler than they actually were, that they could handle ten pints every night, and regularly did. Except they'd end up violently ill, then get up and do it all over again the next day.

I didn't make friends. Their 'problems' irritated me, were nauseatingly trivial. So what if they hadn't finished an essay on time? None of it mattered. Couldn't they see that? They were wasting their lives sat in some stuffy room listening to a corduroy-suit-wearing, stale-sweat-stained and sour-breathed beady weasel of a tutor, self-importantly regurgitating other people's ideas like they were his own. Most of the time I felt angry with everyone, I felt like an outsider. I wanted to go home.

And then I received a letter from Steve saying he loved me, but that a long-distance relationship . . . and other things . . . were proving tough. He thought we ought to split up. I rang him instantly, panicked and in floods of tears, but he was resolute. Desperate at the thought of losing him, I dropped out and rushed back to Holly Lodge.

I tried my hardest to convince him everything would be OK now I was home, that I loved him and I knew he loved me, but he just kept shaking his head and saying, 'It's too late.'

I wanted to hit him and have him hug me all at the same time.

He didn't need to tell *me* that.

Chapter Fourteen

In my absence, day-to-day life at home had settled into a new routine, one I barely recognised. Kate had taken a receptionist's job at a local doctor's surgery. Naturally, they loved her. By all accounts it seemed she had revolutionised the place. She was running the house, too – and had what was fast becoming a serious boyfriend, a very good-looking bloke called Rob.

'You wouldn't remember him, he was there before your time,' she explained to me while making tea for us, 'but I met him down at the pub with a couple of the old girls from school, about six months ago now.'

I listened from my vantage point, perched on a kitchen stool. He'd seemed nice when I'd been introduced to him the previous night. Not exactly a boat-rocker, but that was probably a good thing for Kate. I could see he'd been a valuable distraction. But a long-term option?

'Do you still think about living in London, like you were going to?' I asked.

She shook her head. 'I'm not going to leave,' she reassured me kindly, which wasn't what I'd meant. I reached for my drink and was about to explain that I thought maybe she *should* go, when she said, 'I've got a confession. I saw Steve in town this afternoon.'

I looked up quickly.

'I wasn't going to tell you, what with my despising him and everything.' Her face flushed with anger. 'He asked me to say hello to you.'

My heart thumped hopefully, although I also blurted, 'Was he with her?' I hated myself for asking.

Kate nodded, and my insides cramped up painfully.

She hesitated, then said, 'He's not worth it, Anya. Writing you a *letter* of all things. OK, so you were away, but—'

I looked down at my mug of tea. There was a long pause.

'Shall I make shepherd's pie rather than lasagne for tea tonight?' she offered gently, knowing it was my favourite. 'You'd like that, wouldn't you?'

The truth was, I still had no appetite. I hadn't tried to lose weight, but since I'd had the letter it had melted magically from my bones with sheer stress. I felt like I was going to cry again and tried not to – it was wrong to be able to cry so much for Steve when I hadn't been able to about Emily.

'You will get over him, An.' Kate was looking at me steadily. 'I promise you. Trust me on this one.' She gave me a sympathetic little smile. 'So, shepherd's pie, then?'

I nodded emptily, but, pleased, she reached for the potatoes.

'Do you still hear anything from Andrew?'

She hesitated, and pretended to busy herself with getting a plastic bag out of the cupboard for the peelings. 'I think he's gone to Singapore now.' She shrugged, as if it were no big deal. 'Nice, eh? He's got a flat out there, a girlfriend . . . He's done well for himself.'

Both of us fell quiet for a moment while we

215

wondered if Kate had been meant to be that girl-friend, living in Singapore, being carefree.

'Things just move on,' she said, breaking the silence. 'I did think for a bit that maybe I'd try London, but everyone's settled in their house-shares – I haven't even spoken to most of them in ages . . . And now there's Rob. I couldn't very well . . .' She trailed off, and seconds later, the kitchen door opened and the man himself walked in holding his car keys, giving us both a huge smile. 'Hello Anya!' he said easily, then walked straight to Kate and gave her an unselfconscious kiss. 'Hello, beautiful.'

She blushed and smiled back at him. I concluded that perhaps I was wrong. He was at least very easy to be around. There was a lot to be said for that.

And secretly *I* began to enjoy being around them. It was as if they had somehow morphed into the parents while I'd been away – apparently in the absence of our own, who seemed to be struggling in that, and pretty much every, department.

I'd never witnessed first-hand the balance of a marriage tip, realised how fragile it could be in the face of outside influences. It would be sad to see it happen to anyone. I found it frightening to watch it happen to my parents. I know I was eighteen

– technically an adult, old enough to be married myself – but I don't think being older lessens the effect if your parents' marriage hits trouble; it's just different. Everyone expects their parents will be together for ever, don't they?

Before Em's death, ours hadn't really had any disasters hit them – maybe that was part of the problem. OK, Mum's parents had both died when she was young, but that had never seemed to be something she visibly struggled with. She was happy, they were happy . . . so we were happy. But when we lost Em, the strands of 'them' didn't knit closer together. They pulled apart.

The first round of Christmas and birthdays, which of course were never going to be anything but dreadful, were actually not the worst because they passed in a blur, but by the second Christmas, Mum in particular had hit a new low. We probably should have all gone away, tried to make it feel different, not just our usual traditions – only minus Em – but by eight p.m. on Christmas Eve she'd already drunk a bottle and a half of wine. When Dad eventually took the glass from her as she sat curled up in a chair in the sitting room, she barely seemed to notice, just flicked a glance at his retreating back as he disappeared off to the kitchen, then returned to staring at the fire in silence. I'd tried to jolly her into watching a film with me, requested a game of Scrabble, even asked her if she knew where the wrapping paper was – knowing perfectly well it was upstairs in Kate's room – just for something to say. She was barely monosyllabic. It was like *she'd* died.

Rob came into the room. 'Dinner's ready – Kate's made roast pork,' he added proudly. 'It looks great.'

I got up, but Mum didn't move.

'You coming, Alison?' Rob said.

'I'm not hungry.'

'Well, why don't you sit with us anyway,' Rob suggested equably, and to my huge surprise, she wordlessly did as she was told. Got up and sat at the table, albeit in silence. For a while, the only noise in the kitchen was the scraping of plates and my overly hearty, 'Kate, this is delicious!' Dad smiled at her briefly. 'Yes, it is. Thank you, Kate. Thank you for trying.'

Mum's head jerked up sharply. 'What do you mean by that?'

Dad paused, his eyes darting round the table. 'Exactly what I said. Thank you for going to so much trouble and trying to make it as happy . . . as it can be.' Then he did something very unexpected, for him. He picked up his glass and said, 'To Emily.'

We all froze, but then Rob picked up his glass gamely. 'Emily.'

'Emily,' I whispered, and Kate was a fraction of a second behind me.

My mum looked up at the mantelpiece, where the welcome-home card was framed and hanging in pride of place, Em's picture below it. For a wild moment I thought she was going to raise her glass too, but instead she said, voice trembling, 'How many times? I know if we'd been here . . .'

Dad put his glass down, put his head in his hands with exhaustion and said, 'I didn't mean that, at all—'

'Yes, you did! Just say it, *say* it, David!'

'But it doesn't matter what I say, does it!' he challenged back. 'Because you don't believe me. You're never going to believe me! I don't know what more I *can* say. Keep blaming yourself if you want—'

I stiffened.

'It won't bring her back!'

Mum shuddered, as if someone had both electrocuted her and thrown iced water over her all at the same time. Kate reached out and quickly placed a hand on Mum's arm, but she didn't seem to notice, she just got to her feet and stumbled away from the table in her haste to leave the room.

I saw Rob firmly take Kate's hand in his. I looked at Dad. 'Aren't you going to go after her?'

He shook his head and cut a piece of meat furiously. 'No, I'm not. And no one else is to, either,' he said as I went to stand. 'It's Christmas Eve, for Christ's sake.'

We could all hear noisy sobbing upstairs. I couldn't bear it, and tentatively got to my feet. 'Please, Dad. Let me go to her.'

He clenched his jaw, let his knife and fork clatter down and just for a moment I thought I saw his eyes shining with unshed tears. But before I could be sure, he'd swung his legs round and banged from the room as well. Shortly afterwards, we heard the front door slam and a car leave the drive.

'I'll just go and make sure she's OK,' I said eventually.

Kate nodded, and quietly began to gather up the abandoned plates.

I found Mum crying incoherently on their bed. 'I can't do this any more,' she said when I came in. 'It's too much. It's all too much.' For a minute I was terrified she was talking about doing something stupid, but I stayed with her until she fell asleep, or passed out – I wasn't sure which – and the following morning she was up for breakfast. Completely silent again, but up nonetheless.

Hell, it was a fun Christmas.

They limped on until Kate moved in with Rob about seven months later. I was in France, nannying for a local family over the summer holidays. It was the first time they'd been properly on their own since it happened, and Kate's phone call came after only a week.

'Mum's left Dad.' She sounded stunned. 'She's just gone, I don't know where. She left him a note saying she can't do it any more. He's beside himself. I'm so sorry to ask, but can you come home?'

'Beside himself' was pretty far from it; he'd had a complete meltdown. When we got back from the airport we discovered him weeping in the kitchen having ripped up every single family photo he could find. It profoundly upset me to see my big strong dad like that because – very unfairly perhaps – it was so disappointing. I didn't want to see him so stripped back. It wasn't right. He was supposed to look after us, wasn't he? But then what had started it all wasn't his fault, either. We had to get the doctor

221

out to give him a sedative in the end, which is when all *that* began.

He had checked into a considerably less glitzy version of the Priory when Mum finally rang to say she had settled on America – but we weren't to worry, she assured us, her voice bourbon-warm – she'd found God there, and *everything was going to be OK*. It was going to be *just fine*. No, she wasn't going to be able to come home, it was too painful. But we could go and see her (and God presumably) whenever we wanted. We could go and live with her too, if we liked. Although we had our own lives now, she could see that . . .

It was all too surreal. I had to laugh.

I really did.

But Kate was devastated. She even flew out on her own to see Mum – I think to try and talk her into coming back.

'She's not going to though, is she?' I asked on Kate's return.

All she could do was shake her head. 'No, she's not.' She didn't seem to want to discuss it any more than that.

I'm not sure what else we could have said in any

case. If we had talked more . . . Would it have made it easier? I don't know. We did what we thought was right at the time. I assumed she had Rob to confide in – and I was beginning to sympathise with Mum's approach. I wanted to get away, didn't really want to be at home any more either. I didn't recognise it. There were ghosts everywhere I turned, some in physical ex-boyfriend form. Everything had changed so profoundly, so quickly, I felt lost. In the absence of closeness, distance was the next best thing. It was one or the other – we were dealing in extremes.

Predictably I chose the place that, short of outer space, was about the farthest away I could get from everything: Australia.

'I needed a change of scene,' I explained to the nice bloke Will at the bar where I'd found a job. He was a Brit too, and we were cleaning up after a long shift. He'd asked me a little bit about myself and, to my immense surprise, I'd actually told him.

'I expect,' he said carefully, 'you just need some space to work out how you feel about everything.'

I refolded my cloth so it exposed a clean section and wiped another one of the tables. Why I was unburdening myself to this tall, boyish English bloke of all people, I didn't know.

'Whereas your sister, Kate, she's chosen to stay put. It's just an alternative way of handling things,' he suggested thoughtfully. 'It doesn't make either of you right or wrong. Different personalities deal with things in different ways. You just have to do what you can to get through it, somehow . . . I imagine,' he added cautiously, and I was grateful to him for not saying anything shit like, 'I understand how you must be feeling.'

'I'm not just going to leave Kate and Rob to deal with my dad, though,' I added quickly. 'I haven't just done a bunk.'

'I believe you,' Will said, and I relaxed a bit. I could see he meant it, and wasn't thinking the worst of me.

Not that I needed to worry about Dad, as it turned out, because *luckily* he met Maura at one of his self-help groups, not long after my arrival in Australia.

'The only thing she's helped herself to is our dad, the old bitch,' I said, again to Will, while we were buying some food because he'd offered to cook for me. He laughed, and somehow that reaction made everything feel not quite so bad. He was very easy to talk to, probably – I'd come to the conclusion – because I didn't fancy him. He wasn't my type. Rangier and leaner where, say, Steve was shorter, stockier. I tried valiantly to push Steve from my mind. 'Kate's told me all about Maura, and I don't like what I hear.'

'I'm sure it won't last long,' he said. 'It's classic rebound stuff, isn't it?' And then winked at me.

He never was a good judge of that sort of thing.

When I slapped Will, two weeks ago, for what he said to me, I confess I wasn't initially sorry. It felt good. Just for once, I'd made my point. He could be in no doubt I was *really* angry with him. I was angry, full stop.

But seconds after a surprising surge of triumph – and release – coursed through me came dismay and regret. I'd hit him. *Never* OK, whatever the circumstances. I waited for him to shout or push me away. But to my confusion, he did neither. He just stood there and took it.

I never even told him I was sorry. Or that he was right. And here I am, pushing the limits again. Only this time, I haven't got away with it.

And Kate? She's probably going to think my not telling her about this trip was in some way about needing to get away from her. It wasn't. More mistakes, more confusion. More stuff left unfinished.

Exhausted, I close my eyes for a moment. I thought we had been there for each other, Kate and I, but I suppose in lots of ways we haven't been.

For the millionth time, I feel myself running away from that car. I should never have left her. How frightened must she have been?

'Stay with me Em now, please,' I beg. 'I'm so sorry I wasn't with you.'

Of course, I have asked her many, many times over the years to forgive me, but saying it here, in this dark space, completely alone and trapped, she suddenly feels very near. Unless now I really am starting to lose it completely.

More waves of fear and fatigue engulf me. Where is he? Is he close, will he find me? Oh, I am so, so tired . . .

'Em?'

Holding my breath, I wait. But she doesn't answer, of course. Lucky really, because that *would* freak me out.

Might even finish me off completely.

Chapter Fifteen

The six-year-old **girl who went missing** from her parents' house is found dead at home.

The local teen **girl went missing** in Aruba, **Mexico** while on holiday with her parents.

The **girl** was reported talking to three men outside a bar in **Mexico** City, before **going missing.**

Rob is safely in the kitchen, and so I'm doing an online search for 'girl goes missing in Mexico'.

Logically, of course, I know I shouldn't be doing this – and I'm reminded of the time I was pregnant and, panicked, had to ring my midwife while Rob was at work. 'Hello, my name is Kate Palmer.' I'd tried to stay calm. 'You did my booking recently – I don't know if you remember me, but I had to go into the Early Pregnancy Assessment Clinic because I had a bit of a bleed? They said as far as they can see everything is all right, but it really freaked me out – and since I've been back at home, I've been looking online and now I'm even more frightened.'

'This is one of those occasions when it's best to not look on the internet,' she'd said kindly, 'because there are lots of sources that aren't reliable, and you'll frighten yourself to death – it'll give you more stress than reassurance.'

I'm sure this is no different, and I don't even know what I'm hoping to find: suggestions? Clues? But at least it is something to do. I've heard nothing back from the journalist, and there's been no call from the Embassy either.

A **girl is missing** in Mexico: She would have called me, she would have known we would worry, I read on.

So if your loved one **goes missing in Mexico** scream as loud as you can and don't stop.

This item immediately grabs my attention. That actually does sound helpful – advice from someone who has been through this.

But it turns out to be a blog forum about a girl who vanished after a night out while on holiday, last seen getting into a car with two men outside a well-known tourist bar. Lots of people have added comments speculating as to her whereabouts, and wondering if she is still alive. The general consensus is that she is not. 'Man!' someone writes. 'How dumb would you have to be to get talking to strangers like that? Why do people act like the rules don't apply just because they're on vacation?'

'She'd have been dead before they even started looking for her,' writes someone else. 'I think it's something like 95% of all people who go missing are killed within the hour?'

I freeze at that.

I should narrow my search. I quickly leave the

blog and tap in 'girl goes missing in Cancún', fingers trembling.

Several items appear relating to a teenage girl who nearly drowned when the snorkelling-trip tour boat she was on began to sink. She was flown home to America in a coma and later died of heart failure. How awful. I clench my jaw – but Anya has *not* drowned . . . she hasn't.

I begin instead to read a newspaper report from 2008 about a local girl who went to a nightclub when her parents thought she was at a sleepover. She vanished after being seen with a young man in the club, who the police were unable to identify. A pile of her clothes and an item of jewellery were recovered at a local hotel, but the girl herself was never found.

I stop dead, reread the last bit and hear Gabrielle's voice saying, 'A pile of clothes was found on the bank.'

We gave that ring to our daughter for her sixteenth birthday and she never took it off. I scan the father's interview. She would have been forced to remove it. And it was valuable. Whoever attacked my daughter was not a thief interested in financial gain.

Again, alarm bells ring in my mind. All that money found in Anya's bag . . .

I quickly open another tab and Rafael Montoya stares insouciantly back at me. 2008 – he would be the right age to be out clubbing then. I hesitate, and then quickly type: 'How can I find out if someone has a criminal record in Mexico?'

```
How to find out if someone has a criminal
record. One of the fastest ways to see
if someone has a criminal background.
```

I listen carefully for Rob, and hearing nothing, enter the website. It asks for the person's first and last name, and the state they live in. I enter the details, hit 'search now' and seven Rafael Montoyas come up, all of whom presumably have criminal records. It also lists their ages . . . and there is a Rafael who fits!

Shit! I start to scrabble around for my purse because I can't view the records without paying $25 for a month's trial membership, but my phone begins to ring, making me jump guiltily.

It's Gabrielle. It turns out that the journalist made almost instant use of the phone number I supplied him with.

'My colleague felt the mood of the authorities had been tense but cooperative,' Gabrielle says. 'But after the reporter called . . .' she pauses, 'it seems the atmosphere has become increasingly bad-tempered.' She waits for me to say something.

I stay silent.

'Kate, when an incident like this happens abroad there are lots of challenges to face,' Gabrielle says. 'Relations can be very delicate – the balance easily upset. Sudden interference can prove extremely counterproductive.'

I swallow. She suspects it was me who gave the reporter the phone number.

'If people begin to feel defensive, it can shift the focus from the common goal – in this case, finding Anya. The journalist first questioned the involvement of the lawyer's clients – the dive school – then suggested the police couldn't be following procedure, as they were clearly no closer to finding Anya. He finally implied the search was deliberately being obstructed to protect the Mexican local Anya was last seen with. As you can imagine, Augusto, the lawyer was only too happy to repeat all of that to the Mexican police. At best, it's been unhelpful. At worst—'

I cast my mind back to the images of the armed

232

men in balaclavas I found on the computer earlier. Was it crazy to think they could be manipulated or pressured – and that I could be the person to do it?

I didn't think. I grabbed at the only chance I had.

'It's reckless journalism. He should be aware of the responsibility of reporting on a current investigation. He's managed to enrage a lot of people very quickly.'

And I still want to ask her about what I've just found. This girl went missing in circumstances uncannily similar to Anya's, and I'm pretty sure I now know for certain that Rafael Montoya has a criminal background. 'So what's happening now?'

'Well, the water search has been halted.'

It's *what*? I sit up.

'The police don't want to leave themselves open to further accusations of incompetence, so they've sent for a professional police dive team rather than allow the voluntary divers to continue. That's confused and frightened Rafael Montoya's family, who are at the scene and obviously want the cave search to continue in the interim. They're also very unhappy at the insinuation that Mr Montoya might have some sinister connection to Anya's disappearance.'

'But the rescue divers hadn't actually found anything in the cave?' I ask quickly.

'No,' she admits, 'they hadn't. Except for a guideline – but it's too old to belong to Anya and Rafa; it would have been left by previous visitors. Even so, the rescue team followed it until its conclusion; not that there was anything. They were going to go back in and check the offshoot passages, but that's now been suspended.

'So it seems that the journalist's interference does appear to have prompted the police to initiate a land-based search, albeit an ill-humoured one,' she continues. 'My colleague has reported that it will begin once more officers arrive, and the police have also confirmed that they are now considering all lines of inquiry.'

I hardly dare speak for the stab of fierce triumph and relief. So it *did* work! Whatever she says, it forced them to act. I am so grateful to that journalist.

I did the right thing.

'I'll be in touch as things progress,' Gabrielle says. 'Please come back to me if you have any other questions though, won't you, Kate? Try not to contact anyone else. It may seem like a good idea, but it's better that we handle this, really it is.'

So she knows. I don't confess, though – I just assure her I won't do anything I shouldn't, which is true; I don't need to now.

'Gabrielle,' I begin uncertainly, as Rob comes back in. 'I found something I think I ought to mention . . .'

And I tell her about the other missing girl and the police record, not quite meeting Rob's eye as he sits down and watches me, listening carefully.

'If it is the same Rafael Montoya, the authorities will be aware of his background, and *if* it has any relevance to this case.' Gabrielle is patient, but firm. 'Stay positive, Kate. I'll come back to you.'

'You found all that while I was in the other room?' Rob says eventually, once I've hung up. 'For God's sake, Kate. You have to let them do their work. Please, no more online searches. You need to—'

'They've suspended the water recovery,' I interrupt. I probably should qualify why they've changed their minds – that it's because of the journalist – but it doesn't matter really. The fact is, they have at last started looking for her. 'They're going to start a land-based investigation now. They don't think this is an accident any more, either.' Again, that's not entirely true, but . . .

Rob pales and, chastened, falls silent.

'We need to call Will.' Suddenly I feel dazed, and am now thinking back to the blog forum, to the post which said they're usually dead within the hour of

235

going missing. 'We need to tell him that we were right, Anya *has* been abducted.'

Will's delayed flight gate number finally flashes up on the screen as he's thinking about Liesel – wondering if perhaps he should call her to apologise again, tell her that he wishes it hadn't happened like this more than anything, when his mobile lights up. He inspects the number, and answers quickly.

'Hi Kate.' But it's not Kate. It's her husband, Rob.

As Will listens to Rob's faltering words, everything seems to scrunch up from within him and pulse out in shattering waves of shock across the airport. He is vaguely aware of people walking past him; a girl across the way is reading a newspaper with a headline that more snow is on the way – 'The Coldest Winter Freeze for 30 Years Continues'. There is a last call for a couple flying to Berlin, but Will just stares ahead, mouth slightly open.

The girl with the newspaper, sensing Will staring, thinks he's looking at her, but when she frowns up at him, he's somehow looking *through* her, gripping his phone. She sneaks another glance, curious now. He's fit. She instinctively glances at his left hand. No ring. *In*teresting . . . but then to her surprise, she sees his eyes have filled with tears. He closes them slowly, and his forehead creases like he's in extreme pain and trying to contain himself. He shakily hangs up and then his hand reaches out and fumbles for the small bag that he has on the seat next to him. Grabbing it, he gets uncertainly to his feet and she watches him stumble across the airport, bumping into someone as he goes, before he eventually disappears out of sight. She wonders briefly what the hell that was all about, before losing interest and turning back to the shock news on page two that Simon Cowell will be leaving *American Idol* and this will be his last series of the smash show *for ever*.

Chapter Sixteen

Shivering, I listen carefully for him. I think of his telling me he was going to look after me, watching him playing casually with a knife as, giggling, he asked me to tell him a secret that no one else knew.

Rafa was alarmingly on edge by the time we arrived back at the cenote this afternoon – although it might not be Tuesday afternoon any more, I have no idea.

But then, now that I think back to it, he wasn't exactly relaxed when we first arrived at the water on Sunday night just a little bit too late. The light was fading, and he had gone from being chatty and

239

enthusiastic in the truck to comparatively subdued and reflective. 'We can't dive now,' he said dismissively when I eagerly asked him what the plan was. 'I don't want to have to set up camp in the dark.'

I was disappointed at that – I'd been psyching myself up on the drive over – but in fairness, he did insist on getting us organised while I looked around.

It was honestly one of the most beautifully serene places I have ever seen in my life. The edges of the pool were lined with lush grasses, and I was transfixed by the floating lily pads, some of which were flowering; delicate white cups of petals on very clear and in places very blue water. I was only too happy to sit dreamily in the last rays of the afternoon sun while Rafa methodically and silently set about arranging everything.

I woke to find him standing over me saying softly, 'Anya? Everything is ready.'

'Oh, wow! Thank you!' I smiled lazily, and stretched like a cat. *This* was service. 'I should pay you now,' I said, and sat up blinking, looking around for my bag. Apart from anything else, it would be just my luck to lose the bundle of notes we'd agreed on.

He waved a hand. 'No. Let's make sure you are totally satisfied first. And you always pay afterwards.

For everything in life,' he admonished, before grinning and turning to get the food pack out of the truck.

Well, it was his call. 'This is an incredible place,' I remarked, looking out over the water.

'It is an uncommon cenote, which is why I thought you would like it.'

'I love it,' I assured him. 'I think it's perfect! You were right, it was worth the effort.'

'You haven't even been in it yet!' he teased.

I spied some worn stone steps leading into the water. 'Isn't it a bit weird for someone to have gone to the trouble of putting in access somewhere so remote?'

'They are very old, Mayan,' he explained, and I felt a bit foolish. Of course they were. In an attempt to try and save face, show him I wasn't a complete philistine, I turned back to the water and said enigmatically, 'The Maya believed in an underworld, didn't they, that you could reach via the caves? Isn't it presided over by the god of death?'

Rafa didn't say anything at first, just nodded. 'Some think so. They believe he comes looking for his victims.' He watched me for my reaction, and I realised what he was doing, deliberately giving me the heebie-jeebies – all part of the service – cute!

'Almost like,' I lowered my voice to a dramatic whisper, playing along, 'he's hunting – or stalking them.'

I looked back towards the steps, which was when I noticed the bone of some small animal nestled next to some grasses, probably a bird or something. 'Oh, look!' I pointed it out to Rafa. 'You think he's already been?'

He snorted, but quickly kicked it into the water. We watched as the circles began to spread over the surface – then everything went still again.

In spite of myself, I did actually feel the hairs on the back of my neck stand up, so when I glanced across the pool and saw a figure standing motionless on the other side, just watching us, I leaped out of my skin and swore aloud.

I made Rafa jump too. 'What?' he said, shaken, but didn't share my relieved laughter as I pointed across the water to what I realised was just a little girl of about twelve and *not* in fact the god of death. 'She must live round here. How amazing to have this as a back garden,' I remarked, but Rafa said nothing, just stared at the girl as I smiled and waved at her. She regarded us warily for a moment while twisting a piece of her long hair round her finger, then spun on her heels and ran off, disappearing in between the trees.

I turned my attention back to Rafa and the steps. 'Isn't it the Maya who say that the world is going to end on 21.12.2012? Bit melodramatic, aren't they?'

'Some people think it means a big disaster will come, yes.' He was still looking at the point where the little girl had vanished. 'Others perhaps just a change, maybe spiritually. We don't really know.'

OK . . . Either he was stretching the joke a little bit *too* far, or I'd offended him. I felt a bit bad then, for taking the piss out of something he was, after all, entitled to have respect for, and a bit ashamed of myself. 'Sorry,' I said immediately. 'That was rude of me. I take it back.'

'Hey, it's no problem.' He seemed to snap out of his study. 'You know what?' He rubbed his face thoughtfully. 'I think we should maybe not dive here after all. I know a better place. Let's leave now.'

I stared at him in confusion. 'But we've just arrived! And you've set everything up. Can't we just go and see in the morning if . . .'

His smile vanished. 'I thought you said you'd been an instructor. So you know that you have to trust the local expert and do as he says, yes?'

I hesitated. I wanted to dive, but he had a point. If something wasn't sitting right with him, we had to move on, however frustrating it was for me. 'Don't you think it's safe here, then?'

'Oh, it's safe,' he said. 'But thinking about it, maybe it's too big a cave for your first go, you know? I can see you're nervous – you screaming at a little girl is telling me this,' he grinned. 'It's too much, this one. I know a better place, a "baby" cave. And then maybe we come back here after.' He looked at his watch. 'Come on. You'll have to help me.'

'But isn't it a bit late to be heading off again now?' I said in dismay, not liking the thought of all the repacking and *un*packing at the other end. 'We'll be arriving in the dark. You said that wasn't a good idea.'

'You're scared?' he deadpanned.

'No, I'm not *scared*,' I retorted.

'We leave now, and that way we get maximum dive time. I don't want to waste it travelling.'

'I really don't think the cave will be an issue,' I tried, shielding my eyes. 'And anyway, I'd rather one that's big, on my first go, than one that's really,' I paused, 'small and tight.'

He looked at me with interest. 'You're afraid, aren't you? I don't mean nervous. I mean actually scared.'

'I'm fine,' I lied. 'I really want to dive it.' I kicked off my flip-flops determinedly. 'Let's stay. Honestly, I'm too tired to get going again now, anyway.'

His face darkened momentarily. 'Whatever,' he said. 'Your choice. But don't say I didn't warn you.'

I looked at him, worried, less sure of myself.

'Just don't freak out when we go past the skull and crossbones sign tomorrow, will you?'

I blanched. 'What's that there for?'

'To make sure you don't carry on any farther without someone who knows what they are doing,' he said simply. 'Because it's so dangerous. Anyway, you should get some sleep. Big day tomorrow.' He gestured at the tent. 'Sweet dreams.'

'You made the right choice,' he assured me as we bounced along the uneven road in bright sunshine the following morning. 'You really did. It's always best to embrace your limitations in life.'

I looked at him. 'I'm not scared as in too frightened to do it at all,' I corrected quickly. 'I just . . . gave what you said some thought last night, and maybe it *is* better.' I shrugged non-committally. 'To start small and work up.'

'Absolutely,' he smirked. 'You're so right.'

I narrowed my eyes, but didn't say anything. Perhaps I deserved that dig. If I had listened to him, we'd be in the water by now. I'd probably have already done it.

'Are we nearly there yet?' I asked coolly instead, but there isn't a way to say that on a car journey without sounding like a five-year-old. He knew it, and looked amused. 'I'll tell you when we're ten minutes away,' he said. 'How about that?'

I had, it turned out, quite a while to wait. Despite his confidence, Rafa seemed to be a little lost, taking us up a couple of tracks and then muttering, 'This isn't right . . .' at the first, and absently, 'This is no good either,' to himself before we appeared to stumble on the one he was after.

Once we'd parked up I got out of the truck, walked a little way to a small clearing, looked at it, and then turned back to Rafa in dismay. 'That's it?'

The small pool looked not unlike a puddle of water that had drained from a silage pit; brown and murky with disgusting bits floating on the surface. A forlorn tree had its roots in the water, and I couldn't help thinking it was one desperate plant that would attempt to get any kind of nourishment from *that*. The cenotes in the area were meant to be spectacular. This was a crappy, muddy puddle.

He barely looked up at me, so busy was he getting the bags out. I supposed he felt bad for it taking a lot longer to get here than he'd realised, but he was being a bit premature, unpacking. I really couldn't see that there would be anything in there that could justify half an hour's exploring, let alone a day and a night's camp.

'I appreciate you bringing me somewhere really authentic and off the beaten track,' I said slowly, looking at the sludge and thinking of the roll of dollars that I was also very pleased was still sitting in my bag. 'But this is ridiculous.'

Rafa stopped what he was doing, looked down at the floor, sighed heavily, straightened up and walked over to me. He had his dive knife in his hand, and reached out languorously to cut away a couple of long pieces of twine that were hanging inches from my face. 'So, you don't want to do this one either?' he said pleasantly. 'You know, looks really aren't everything, Anya.'

I raised my eyebrows in surprise. Was I starting to piss him off? 'What time is it, please?'

Rafa inspected his watch. 'Quarter past two.' He turned and walked back to the truck.

My heart sank. Even if we left again immediately, by the time we got back to the original site it'd be dark again. A three-day extravaganza, he'd promised me. Day two, and I hadn't so much as got a toe in the water. But in fairness, that *was* partly my fault as well. I sighed and looked down at the unflushed loo. He seriously thought that under that surface there was something worth exploring?

'Fine,' I said. 'Let's just do it.'

But instead, he patted a blanket he'd laid down on the ground. 'Let's take five a moment. I want you to be happy and enjoy this. Why don't you come and sit down, and let, me explain to you *why* I thought that this cenote would be perfect, and then—'

But out of nowhere, he was interrupted by another truck roaring up and a pretty angry-looking, sweaty fat bloke leaping out, gesticulating wildly and gabbling away in Spanish.

To my huge surprise, Rafa sprang up from where he was sitting, rushed up to the man and began shouting violently in his face, while repeatedly jabbing a finger into the man's chest, forcing him to step back. The driver was quelled for a moment – Rafa had gone puce with rage and was shaking his head insistently – but bravely dodged round him, reached into the truck, pulled out one of our dive masks and held it up in the air triumphantly.

Rafa turned to me furiously and said, 'This is the landowner, he wants payment for us diving here.'

'Well, that's OK, isn't it?' I said slowly. 'It's his property.' I walked over to my bag, got some of the cash and held it out. 'Is this enough?'

The landowner immediately snatched the notes from my hand, shoved them into his pocket and smiled ingratiatingly at me. 'Thank you,' he said in English. 'I hope you like the dive. I will come back in an hour with some refreshments for you. My wife is an excellent cook.'

'Oh, that would be lovely, thank you,' I said happily. Rafa threw me an incredulous stare, shook his head and stalked angrily back to the truck, to my embarrassment, but his rudeness didn't seem to bother the landowner in the slightest, who waved cheerfully as he hopped back into *his* truck and drove off.

'Well, don't just stand there,' Rafa snapped. 'We've got a dive to do.'

'So now you're angry with me too?' I said. I would never have spoken to a client like that.

He ignored me, coolly replying, 'By the way, did you ask him how much your "refreshments" will cost?'

Oh, shit. I tutted inwardly at myself. He was right.

I'd been distracted by their row, and the landowner had pulled one of the oldest tricks in the book. I was uncomfortably reminded of a trip I'd done years ago in Turkey where, similarly, I'd been encouraged to choose my fresh fish while it was still swimming in the tank. I'd forgotten to ask the cost upfront, in my excitement had eaten it and was then told it was £50 – which of course I didn't have.

At least I had cash this time.

'Well, I won't take it out of *your* money,' I said tersely.

There was a long pause.

'Hey – look . . . I'm sorry, Anya,' Rafa said smoothly, after a moment more. 'That guy just really pissed me off.' I watched him clench his fist. 'I don't appreciate being told what I can and can't do like that – but you're right. We can just go somewhere better.' He smiled at me disarmingly, and I was again struck by how good-looking he was. 'You deserve somewhere pretty.'

But strangely, all of the delay and procrastination had removed some of the mounting fear that had been eating away at my gut in the middle of the night. 'No, you're right – I just need to get it over with.' I took a deep breath. 'And we've paid now.'

'Oh . . . ok,' he said, and his smile faded, before seeming to recharge quickly. 'Well, let's cave-dive, then!'

'Honest to God!' was the first thing he said to me when we surfaced half an hour later. 'I was sure it was this one, but it can't have been. I don't know what to say.'

There had been no cave in the cenote. It was a total dud. Nothing of interest at all, which the land-owner would have known, the thieving git.

Rafa swam to the edge and clambered out. I gave him a long, hard stare. Was he, quite literally, taking me for a ride too? All he'd done so far was drag us all over the place. I was beginning to doubt he was an expert in anything but bullshit.

'Rafa, tomorrow, can we go back to the place we were at yesterday?' I said carefully. 'I think I *could* dive it. I'm not afraid any more.'

He gave me a huge smile. 'Tomorrow, you can do whatever you like. I think that's a very good idea to go back. Shall we leave now, and we can stop some-where to camp on the way?'

I was about to say yes – I'd sleep up a tree if it finally enabled me to get a decent dive in – when the landowner pulled up again with the food he'd promised, and which I'd forgotten about. It actually did look delicious, and to my huge surprise he didn't ask for payment. Perhaps I'd misjudged him. 'Let's just stay put,' I whispered to Rafa. 'I think he's trying to make it up to us.'

Rafa looked at the landowner sceptically, but after we'd eaten, when I offered to help him put the tent up and suggested an early night, as we would probably be needing to leave *before* it got light the following morning, he seemed to recover some of his good humour, even producing a bottle of rum while I sorted through my bag. I declined, but he knocked back a good couple of measures anyway, to my surprise, given I never drank the night before a dive and I was still a paying customer. Doubt began to niggle at me.

'So tell me, Rafa, what's the best cenote you've dived?' I asked.

He glanced at me. 'I like the Birdcage,' he said. 'And Luke's Hope.'

Hmmm. I knew they both actually existed. But obviously, as I had never been in them, I couldn't ask much more to test him.

'Where did you do your training?'

'Here, in Playa. What frightened little questions.'
He smiled shrewdly at me. 'Tell me, Anya,' he had
started absently playing with his knife again, 'why do
you want to do this dive so badly when it scares you
so much? What demons are driving you, eh?'

His directness drew me up short. I shook my head
as if I hadn't a clue what he was talking about. 'I
don't have "demons",' I laughed.

'Oh, really?' he said softly. 'I don't believe you. Girl
here on her own, determined to do something so
dangerous. You're very interesting to me, Anya. Come
on,' he leaned forward eagerly, 'tell me! After tomorrow
you'll never see me again.' He giggled. 'Tell me a
secret no one else knows . . .'

I hesitated. 'I don't have any secrets.'

He instantly looked bored. 'Fine, don't play then.'
God, he was unpredictable. One minute he was
perfectly charming, the next, it was like being with
a sulky child. He'd be bloody hard work as a boyfriend.

He began to dig the point of the knife into the
ground irritably.

'Well, you tell me a secret,' I said bluntly. 'And *then*
I might tell you one.'

He looked up at me, interested again, and said,
'I'm not cave-dive qualified and I'm ripping you off.'

My mouth must have fallen open because he roared with laughter. 'I'm messing with you!' he said, and then pointed the knife at me. 'Although that's what you think, isn't it?' He had one eye closed and his tone was playful.

'Of course not!' I lied, thrown.

He started dig-digging with the knife again, then paused and looked at the blade in fascination. 'Are you never struck by how something like this could just – so simply – slice your skin?' he said. 'What I mean is,' he said, at the expression on my face, 'it's an everyday item you use to cut food, or rope – but just like that . . .' I jumped as he slammed the blade into the ground. He was gripping the handle so hard I could see a vein bulging on the back of his hand. Then he reached for the rum again.

I kind of did know what he meant, yes, but, unsettled, I decided I wanted to go to bed. 'I need to get some sleep.'

'Don't be like that,' he wheedled. 'Stay up for a bit, let's talk a while . . .'

'I really do need to get some sleep, Rafa,' I wrapped my top more tightly around me against the gathering chill and got to my feet. 'I'll see you in a bit.'

254

I was zipping up my sleeping bag very tight when the tent front opened and he appeared. 'Anya?' he said. 'I'm sorry. I didn't mean to frighten you.'

He climbed in and I shrank imperceptibly away from him, an automatic reaction.

'Don't be mad at me,' he begged. 'You're so nice – and fun – and you're brave, not like other girls. I can see you are really not OK with this dive, but you're doing it, I like that . . . I like you.' He tentatively reached out and touched my hand. 'You're also beautiful,' he whispered.

There was a pause before he said quickly, 'I feel embarrassed now.' He covered his face for a moment and then peered at me through his fingers. 'It's the rum talking – ignore me.'

He looked very cute – and I couldn't help it, I was flattered to be spoken to like that. In spite of myself I smiled – and at what he thought was his cue, he quickly leaned towards me.

It was a perfectly good kiss on a technical basis, I even automatically responded for a heartbeat, but it was utterly devoid of any feeling, and I really hadn't wanted the trip to be about this. I hadn't come halfway round the world for a no-strings fling. After a second or two longer I knew I certainly didn't want anything *more* than just a kiss – and Rafa was starting to become a bit . . . enthusiastic.

'Rafa.' I pulled back. 'This isn't such a good idea.'

'What isn't?'

'This. I'm sorry. I think we should stop.'

Rafa's face was impassive in the dim light of the tent, barely illuminated by the moon outside.

'Well I don't,' he said.

Chapter Seventeen

I felt my heart jolt and a cold wash of doubt flood over me. 'To be fair to you,' I tried lightly, 'I *am* very attractive.' I edged back slightly, and suddenly the instant rapport I felt we'd had when I'd first got talking to him at the dive centre, and the decisions I'd made based on it, seemed ludicrous, as I saw the situation through the eyes of an outsider.

He continued to stare at me, for longer than was comfortable. But finally he turned away and looked at the ceiling of the tent. 'Oh *Gooodddd*!' he moaned softly. 'What am I *doing*?'

I exhaled slowly. 'Are you all right?' I asked. He

didn't answer me, just carried on staring up guiltily. 'You're thinking about your girlfriend, aren't you?' I hazarded, but he flushed, so it seemed I'd hit home.

He'd been arguing with her when I'd first walked into the dive shop. Drop-dead beautiful, she had long, glossy, almost black hair, effortlessly long legs and healthily tanned skin. She was also clearly feisty, violently trying to pull her arm from his grasp. They both jumped at the sight of me, and she took the opportunity to yank herself free, running out from behind the counter. She hurried past me as if I wasn't there, snatching up her handbag en route. I saw a compact mirror fall from it and roll towards the feet of her boyfriend, but didn't say anything.

'Esther!' he called after her, but she ignored him, allowing the door to slam behind her.

He and I had stood there for a moment in embarrassed silence.

'Please excuse us,' he said eventually. 'We were—'

'Having a domestic?' I offered. He looked confused, not understanding my turn of phrase.

'Your girlfriend dropped this, I think,' I said, bending to pick up the mirror. I passed it over to him. He opened his mouth as if he was about to say something, but appeared to change his mind and slipped it into his pocket instead. 'Thank you.' He held out his hand. 'I'm Rafa.'

'Anya.' We shook, and I sat down on a plastic chair angled close to a desk. He took a seat opposite me, turning the computer screen towards him, ready to help me with my enquiry.

'So have you been together long?' I asked him cheekily.

He hadn't been expecting that, and looked slightly taken aback at my directness, but then laughed with good humour. 'No. Not really . . . you want to know what the argument was about too, I suppose?'

I shrugged and smiled at him disarmingly. He didn't know it, but he was about to give me a fat discount on his usual rates . . .

Sitting back in his chair, he looked at me with interest. 'OK. So suppose I told you she was my boss's wife – we all work together – and I keep asking her to leave him and be with me, but she won't?'

My eyebrows flickered.

'And *you* weren't expecting me to say that, were you?' He looked at me mischievously. 'So, you want to find out about diving in the area, I take it?' He turned to the computer.

'Yes please. It's cenote diving I'm interested in. So why won't she leave him?'

He shrugged. 'He's a lawyer, I'm a shop boy. As they say, you do the math. You're dive-qualified, I take it?'

'Yes, I am. I used to be a dive instructor in Bali.'

'Oh, cool.' He glanced up briefly in acknowledgement of the common bond. 'So, you want a day trip, or something longer?'

'Something longer.'

'Just for you? Or you and – your boyfriend? Or friend?'

'Just me,' I said cheerfully.

'You're here in Playa on your own?' he asked conversationally.

'Yes, I am. I should warn you, though – I've only got a budget of $300, and I want to dive a cave.'

'Ohhhh. You want to *cave*-dive . . .' He whistled and sat back in his chair again. 'Hmmm. Well, overnight-assisted camping dives are pretty pricey. We could hook you up with another group, maybe. Unless . . .' He hesitated. 'I'll take you if you like? It wouldn't be through the school, but I could do you three days all in for $300 cash. I can't do it for less than that if I'm going to have to take

Monday as unpaid leave. I've already got Tuesday off.'

Three days all in? That was pretty tempting.

'You'd be helping me out too,' he confessed. 'Esther isn't going to like it at all . . .'

I realised then what he was up to; trying to make his lover jealous. I studied him carefully. He wasn't quite old enough to know tactics like that never worked out long term. But hey, who was I to argue if I was going to get a cheap dive trip out of it? I shrugged, smiled sweetly and held out my hand. 'Deal.'

Only we'd ended up playing our parts a little *too* well . . . 'You're right, I *really* shouldn't be doing this,' he repeated in a low voice.

'Oh, come on, Rafa,' I tried to reassure him. He was overreacting a bit now. It was just a kiss. Perhaps he was more drunk than I'd realised. 'Don't worry about it. Let's just pretend it never happened, shall we?'

He swung back violently to face me, but before he could say anything else, the zip on the tent flap suddenly flew up and a bright light shone right into our shocked faces. I screamed and Rafa yelled something in Spanish as the dumpling-like, greasy head of the landowner loomed in through the gap in the canvas.

It turned out he very much did want paying for the food – and it seemed he'd deliberately left us to relax under the impression he was being generous, because now, he also wanted payment for camping privileges, too. I couldn't believe it. We argued the toss with him, but he was having none of it, and eventually left with yet more of my dollars in his fat little fist.

'I thought we were alone.' Rafa seemed dazed. 'I'm sorry. I really thought that he had gone and wouldn't be coming back.'

'Forget it.' I turned over, away from him. I'd had enough – of both of them – and just wanted to sleep.

'I'll make it all better for you, Anya,' Rafa said softly as I closed my eyes crossly. 'I promise. It will be a good day tomorrow. You're going to remember it for the rest of your life.'

He actually did give me food for thought, not that I'm sure he intended to. I spent a lot of the night awake, thinking about my reasons for doing the dive. By the time the morning came round, I felt thoroughly confused.

'I have a fear of tight spaces,' I said aloud to him over the truck engine the following morning. 'Last night, you asked me what was driving me to do this. I just want to see if I *can* do it.'

He shot me a look of bemusement, then laughed. 'You crazy girl! If people are afraid of snakes, you hold one little grass snake, you don't get in a whole box of them. That's fucking funny, though.' He shook his head.

'The thing is,' I said, not seeing how it was funny in the slightest, 'I'm really not sure it's such a good idea after all.'

'Oh my *God*!' he said, and laughed again. 'You're unbelievable! Anya – look at me.'

I glanced over at him.

'Do you believe in fate?'

I saw Emily's small fingers pulling at her jammed seat belt. 'Um, I struggle with it,' I said slowly. 'It would seem to make for a pretty pointless and cruel world.'

He pulled a face. 'Whoa, I just meant don't panic, because no matter what you do, if your number is up, it's up.' He looked at me curiously. 'Don't you think that's a comfort?'

'So, in a way, you can never be held responsible

for anything, because your actions can't alter destiny, you mean?' I looked out of the window.

'Exactly!' he laughed. 'So relax, OK? You can decide when we get there, but it won't make any difference if you do it or not. You have to understand: what will be will be.'

I fell quiet, and we continued the rest of the journey in silence.

It was still beautiful when we arrived back, and peaceful, even for a Tuesday afternoon. In fact, it was completely deserted.

Rafa seemed positively elated. 'No one here today!' he shouted cheerily. 'Mind you,' he looked at his watch, 'that nosy little girl probably doesn't go back off to school for a little bit. So – we have some time to kill . . . Are we diving, or are we not diving? Shall we lie down under that tree and finish what we started last night instead?'

It was a comment so out of keeping with the tranquil surroundings, I actually jolted. I shot him a look of surprise. He was smirking back at me. I laughed awkwardly and said, 'Um, on balance, diving, I think. But as far as the cave goes, can I decide when we're in the water? Is that OK?'

'Whatever you want is OK, baby.'

Baby? I frowned and turned away. Quickly slipping out of my clothes, under which I was already wearing my bikini, I glanced up again. He was unashamedly watching me undress.

And slowly, the peace began to distort into an isolating stillness. In broad, crude daylight rather than the darkness of the tent, Rafa's interest was sleazy, not flattering.

'We really *don't* have to dive, you know.' He was completely fixed on me – and I was almost certain I could hear him beginning to breathe excitedly.

'Let's dive first,' I said lightly, stepping back.

He looked at his watch again. 'OK,' he shrugged. 'Just a quick one then!' He giggled helplessly at his own joke. 'So we're not sure about the cave until we're there, yeah? Although – you know what? I'm going to *help* you. I'm going to *help* you overcome your fear, I promise.'

He raced off to the truck to get the dive kit. He seemed manic, like he was on something. I stared at his retreating back. He was starting to scare me.

He hadn't been serious about what he'd said the night before, about not being cave-dive trained, had he? And why did he keep looking at his watch? What was he waiting for?

Then I remembered him saying about the little girl going back to school in a bit . . . he appeared to be waiting for us to be completely alone.

And all that asking me about fate, in the truck. Saying you couldn't ever be held responsible for anything, that it was all preordained: that I didn't need to worry, doing a dive wasn't going to make any difference . . .

Any difference to what?

My heart began to speed up, but I tried to keep cool as he passed me my kit.

I was starting to pull on my suit when it occurred to me that he'd been steadily moving us on since Sunday, each time we'd been disturbed.

Was he trying to bluff his way out of having to dive? The cenote he'd taken me to the day before had been a complete sham, after all—

'Ready, then?' He looked at me.

But then if that was the case, why was he so happy to dive now?

I wavered. I didn't want to do it. I didn't want to place my life in his potentially untrained hands. But neither did I particularly want to stay out of the water with him.

He shielded his eyes from the sun. 'What's wrong, Anya?'

I tried to keep my face impassive. Could *all* of this just be my imagination? It could, couldn't it? I attempted to breathe normally, while darting a look around me. There was no obvious escape route.

'Come on then,' he said, looking at me curiously.

I had no choice but to do as I was told.

'Trust me.'

It was the last thing I heard him say.

Chapter Eighteen

Having found he has a criminal record, I cannot stop trawling the internet for something, anything more it can tell me about Rafael Montoya.

There isn't much; several Facebook and LinkedIn profiles that aren't his, and a Facebook profile that *is*, but is also locked apart from his pictures. There are, however, plenty of shots of him grinning away on nights out – most of them with his arm slung round various girls. I clench my jaw and decide to try another line of attack and type in 'Cave divers, Cancún'.

It brings up numerous options, and I'm just

deciding which one to visit when I notice the top-ranked one, which says 'cave-cenote diving – the ultimate experience in Cancún', is displaying in purple, not blue – which means someone has already viewed it on this computer.

And then I notice another link further down that has also been looked at. 'Cave diving in Cancún. Here you will find information about cave diving in Mexico.'

Despite the adrenaline that is still somehow pushing me on, my underlying exhaustion is such that I have to stare stupidly at the screen for a moment before I realise the significance of what I'm looking at.

Anya. She used this computer while she was here over Christmas to plan a trip.

A cave-diving trip.

My heart stops.

I slowly reach out, access the full history, find the dates that she was here and with one tremulous click, there it all is – searches for flights, hotels, several dive schools. She even looked at videos on YouTube.

My mouth falls open as I start to watch one of them. I barely hear the commentary telling me that *some cenotes, incredibly, have layers of water that just don't mix* because I am transfixed, horrified at the sight of

270

two divers drifting in dark water, slow torch beams sweeping around to the sound of their regulated bubbles of breath. That's eerie enough, without the ominous choral soundtrack that suggests they are about to be struck by a vengeful God at any moment.

They look vulnerable and tiny under the clearly visible solid-rock ceiling. I imagine one of them to be Anya, just as the camera leaps to an overhead view, taken from a helicopter, of what appear to be numerous lakes dotted in among dense green trees. 'There are *thousands* of cenotes left to investigate . . .' the deep male voiceover declares. 'Our divers will return . . .' Then it cuts to an end shot of the divers squeezing through an unfeasibly tight, underwater cavity, having to wriggle onto their sides before they disappear into the black.

I simply stare at the screen.

All this time I've been insisting she's claustrophobic, that there is no way she'd be in there . . .

. . . when she fully intended to do a cave dive from the outset.

I've made them abandon the water search.

Oh my God . . . *oh my God*.

I scrabble for my phone as fast as I can, and Rob comes back into the room to hear me frantically

271

trying to convince Gabrielle that I know what I said earlier, but I've just found proof – actual proof – that she's in the cave.

'You have to tell them to go back in!' I am sobbing with fear. 'They can't wait for this other team to get there – it'll be too late. Tell the police I'm sorry – it was me, *I* phoned the newspapers here, and I won't be looking to expose them as incompetent, of course I won't! I was just desperate, that was all. Please – please make them let the divers go back in.'

I am aware I must sound hysterical. Gabrielle doesn't dismiss what I say, but with maddening calm tells me she will have to 'relay the information'.

'What the hell has happened?' Rob says, the second I've hung up. He takes my arms and forces me to face him. 'Kate – look at me. What have they found? Tell me!'

'She was planning the trip while she was here at Christmas. I found her searches! You were right.' I nod at the computer.

He releases me and starts to scan the page rapidly. 'Shit,' he says. 'Oh, Anya . . .'

'I swore blind it was out of character.' My voice begins to rise. 'How, *how* could she have watched this,' I push round him to show him the video, 'and

272

wanted to do it herself? She couldn't have found something more dangerous if she'd tried! How could she be so *stupid*?' I shout.

'What did Gabrielle say?' Rob says quietly. 'Can the divers go back in?'

'I don't know!' I rake my hands through my hair. 'I don't know because I told that journalist she'd been abducted, and once he phoned the police there . . . Oh God, Rob, what have I done?' I start to rock on the spot. 'It all seemed clear! That man looks so suspicious – he's got a criminal record.'

'I imagine a lot of people out there have,' Rob says. 'And it could just be – I don't know – for nicking a car, or something.'

I stare out into the garden. 'I've got to phone Will, tell him I've made a mistake – tell him that he's got to *force* them to let the divers back in.'

'Kate,' Rob says quietly. 'If she really is in there—'

'No!' I shake my head determinedly, eyes shining with fresh unshed tears. 'She's going to be OK.'

I cannot have just cost my sister her life. Again.

'You were the one.' My voice is trembling. 'You were the one last time who told me I had to be strong. I just need to phone Will.' I start to tremble uncontrollably.

273

'I might just give Mum a call.' Rob is watching me carefully. 'Ask her to come over and—'

'No!' It rushes from my mouth. I cannot cope with her now. I may have known my mother-in-law for some twelve years, but we still don't have *that* kind of relationship. I don't relax when she's in my house. She bustles, notices what food is in the fridge – or not, as is usually the case – when she gets the milk out to make a cup of tea. She sees the mountain of ironing, and refolds the item on the top of the pile while saying brightly, 'I used to do a little bit every evening when the kiddies were in bed, which meant it always got done.'

She doesn't mean it as criticism, but on the average day I can find it hard. Right now, her presence – however well meaning – would be unbearable. All I have room in my head for right now is *my* family; Anya. I don't want anyone else.

'Please don't ring her,' I plead.

'OK, OK,' Rob assures me, 'I promise.'

We both hear crying upstairs.

Rob grabs for my phone. 'I'm going to hold onto this while I go and get Matty, then I'm going to come straight back down and *I'm* going to phone Will. Stay off the computer – no more searches, no nothing, OK?'

274

Harassed, he makes for the door and I hear him go upstairs two at a time.

I turn back to the computer – how can I not? – and on the site of a cave-diving rescue organisation I start to scan the fatality reports; incidents its volunteers have been called to. They are numerous, heartbreaking and harrowing. One report laments inexperienced divers going on dangerous dives that they are not equipped, literally and mentally, to deal with, documenting a trip on which the victims went too deep, after apparently wanting to 'just look around one more corner'. They were on their way out of the cave when they simply ran out of air – and were found drowned, holding hands. Other incidents include people becoming entangled in guidelines, or simply not using lines at all, a commonly made mistake, apparently. It seems any kind of significant problem occurring in an underwater cave is, in all likelihood, fatal.

'Kate!' Rob is standing in the doorway holding Matty, staring at me in despair. 'We agreed! No more searches!'

I don't even push my chair back from the desk. I just start to cry.

Rob sets a snugly wrapped Matty carefully down

on the rug and comes over to me, forcing me to look him in the eye. I can see the pity and deep sadness there, the pain at having to watch me go through this. 'Kate, please stop. I'm begging you.'

'I can't believe she would do this,' I whisper. 'It's so dangerous. Wouldn't she know what it would do to me if something went wrong? How could she take such a risk, just for kicks?' I cannot stop thinking of that dark, enclosed water.

We both fall silent.

'Come on,' Rob says eventually, and squeezes my hand. 'You're right. We're not going to give up, Kate. Let's phone Will.'

Chapter Nineteen

Will looks out of the window at the dense white clouds surrounding the plane. The sun is shining so piercingly up here it would be too bright to look at directly – painful even. Other people on board are palpably excited to have escaped from beneath dull British skies laden with more snow, yet all Will can think is how cold it would be out there, brittle. He focuses on the ice crystals in the panels of the window. He is trying to concentrate hard on these small details, because he's finding it almost impossible to hold it together.

He kept his headphones on right through boarding,

to prevent any conversation from any quarter, because he was frightened that if anyone spoke to him – not necessarily a word of kindness, just any interaction at all – he might lose it. Having to remove them for take-off was almost unbearable. 'Could you also please turn off your phone?' the air hostess said, seeing it resting on his lap. 'You can have it on flight mode once we're airborne.' She smiled warmly. All he was able to do was nod dumbly and let his gaze drop. He felt as if everybody must be seeing straight through him, as if his devastation was horribly evident to all and sundry.

He simply can't process this in his mind. He has longed for Anya for so many years now that the feeling of *not* having her, to some degree, is second nature to him, but he knows he has never stopped hoping that some day she'll be his.

How could any man deliberately want to cause her physical harm?

He closes his eyes slowly, seeing her as he last saw her; curled up on his sofa, sleeping peacefully next to him. Her face was, for once, completely relaxed, her expression soft with a faint flush of warmth on her cheeks from the fire. She looked so beautiful. He'd watched her breathing peacefully for at least a minute or two before he'd made himself stop, in case she woke up and caught him staring like a teenage boy.

Thank God he told her he loved her before she left. Having already taken the chance to hold her and kiss her, saying it seconds later wasn't even meant as a last-minute plea – it was a simple statement of fact. He never meant it to be under circumstances no decent bloke could ever be proud of, but he also knows he will never regret it.

That she pulled away and got so angry, shouted about friendship to him, walked out into the snow so stubbornly – he followed her at a distance to make sure she got to the tube station OK, and only trudged home once he was sure she'd actually caught a train – none of that matters any more. How that evening ended isn't enough to detract from what he *knows* was real. He didn't imagine it; she kissed him back. For a split second the girl he loves more than anything was in his arms and kissing him.

He squints furiously at the clouds and focuses hard on them, because he is trying desperately to push the picture of Anya screaming – someone advancing towards her – from his mind. He stares out as if he is transfixed by the view, even though he is aware he is being asked if he would like a drink. He ignores the question knowing that the hostesses are busy, will assume because his earphones are now back in he can't hear them, and quickly move on to the next passenger.

Which is exactly what happens.

He is terrified that he is already too late, and wonders what she would think about him now, dashing out to her rescue, waving a hero's banner. He has a sneaking suspicion she would find it funny. He smiles at the thought and then, just as quickly, it bleakly fades. No, she wouldn't be laughing. She wasn't heartless – she was never heartless. In fact, her big problem was she felt things too deeply, had been so scarred by her experiences that she barely trusted herself to feel anything at all.

It didn't take an expert to see it: she was obviously happier when things were at arm's length. She was so vibrant, so happy; the life and soul of any social occasion and he's sure any of her friends would say she was great fun, a wonderful girl, no party complete without her – but did they actually *know* her?

Very few people did, he's almost certain of that.

He challenged her on it several times, not just the last time at his place . . . but you can't force someone to admit otherwise when they adamantly insist you've got it wrong, that they are *not* scared of intimacy — they are just private, there's a difference — and they *like* constantly being on the move, thanks very much, seeing new places, making new friends; who doesn't?

There are only so many times you can risk saying it for fear that you'll end up driving them away from you completely. And has he just managed to convince himself she had a problem letting people in because that was what he wanted to believe; because it conveniently explained why she wouldn't let *him* in?

Except that nothing was convenient about Anya, nothing at all. She messed up his life. It would undoubtedly have been simpler if she had walked just one door on to the next bar in Sydney and not come into the one he was working in. He might even be married by now. He tries to imagine being married to someone and can't, not even to her — because the idea is too ridiculous. For one, she would never marry, full stop; didn't believe in it, which given her parents' history was completely understandable. But now he wonders how much of that too might just have been something she said because she had never been tested by the opportunity actually presenting itself.

Of course, there is nothing to suggest anything would have worked out between them anyway. Despite what he is utterly certain they both felt during that kiss, he is wary now of freezing time and permanently making it into *everything*, just because he will probably never be proven wrong. Will never have to feel the pain of watching her walk down an aisle into someone else's arms, or see her proudly holding some other man's baby.

But he would do both of those things and a hundred more if it meant she were still here. He would let her just *be*, do whatever she wanted him to do – go away, be her chaste best friend again . . . whatever it took.

Because that's what you do when you love someone, he thinks. You want what is best for them, even if it's at a cost to yourself. That's why he is here now, why he got on the plane despite dreading what is waiting for him at the other end, because it's the very least he can do to help her family and that, he knows for sure, is what she would want.

She was everything to him.

He hopes she knew that.

Chapter Twenty

I think my only hope now is his girlfriend. She knows I came here with him. If he returns without me, she'll be suspicious, won't she? My muscles convulse uncontrollably – so cold, cold, *cold* . . .

Focus, and think straight. Only, might he just tell her my holiday has ended and I've gone home? Would she care? She probably hates me, and I can't blame her. So that means potentially no one is actually going to miss me until Friday, when I'm supposed to check out of my room.

Three whole days.

Jesus . . . what if he just leaves me here?

'Stop it!' I say hoarsely, aloud. 'Get a grip!'

It's not as if I don't have plenty of water – even if I don't have food. It would take a lot longer than three days to starve. And it might not be three days now, anyway. I might have been here at least a third of that already. So stay calm.

Huddling on my rock, I realise it's true what they say, silence *is* deafening . . .

I fix on the rhythm of my breathing instead . . . but it sounds fast, almost like I am panting—

Because I am very, very afraid. What is worse, him coming for me, or abandoning me here? I really don't know.

The trouble is, no matter how much I talk to myself, count minutes through, mentally try to stay positive, I can feel the fight and energy beginning to drain from my fingers and toes.

It's becoming a battle with my body. Trying to stop my head from lolling forward is an effort; it suddenly jerks upward and my eyes widen with surprise in the darkness. I find myself blinking several times in confusion at the sound of the cold water sloshing around my lower body, which I can't actually feel.

I can't stay awake for three days.

I think I'm running out of time.

Having already had several moments of sheer panic, I'm starting to become aware of my tired body slowly weakening further, which is frightening me in a different way. I need to stay with it.

Come on, Emily! Help me play a game, to stay focused. What about . . . things I like and that make me happy:

1. Hammocks on beaches at sunset.

2. Holding Matty.

3. Getting so lost in a good movie I feel like I've lived another life for an hour or two by the end of it.

4. Birthday teas – proper old-fashioned ones with sandwiches (several types), crisps, party rings, a big trifle, brandy snaps – and the all-important cake: sponge with jam and butter-icing filling.

5. Spontaneous hugs.

6. Lucozade. Granny used to buy it for us if we were ill and off school. It reminds me of being tucked up in bed and being looked after.

7. Laughing so hard your tummy hurts.

Hmmm. It turns out I am not as original as I would like to be, eh, Em? Next I'll be adding the smell of cut grass in summer or storms when you're inside and cosy. Yawning, I decide to try something else.

Things I will do when I get out of here:

1. Say sorry to my family for putting them through this.

2. Say sorry to Will for slapping him and storming off.

3. Try and let people in a little bit more.

Yeah, I don't want to play this one any more. I slam my eyes shut as they start to well up, and attempt to stay still.

After a moment or two, I feel my hand fall slightly to one side and let my fingers dangle numbly in the water before bringing them back up to my mouth to gently suck the bitter-tasting moisture. I have to stay hydrated . . . but suddenly the water is closing in over my head to the muffled sound of bubbles of my own breath. My arms flail around in panic before I instinctively push myself back up and gasp with the shock as I break the surface, the mineral-heavy water on my lips as I reach out for my rock again.

The effort it takes to drag as much of my lower body back out of the water as I can is huge – not a smooth or elegant manoeuvre. I'm worried about cutting myself, but eventually I'm back to where I was, just now incredibly frightened of moving at all. I don't understand what just happened. Did I slip?

Did I fall *asleep*?

I could have drowned!

I start to shudder uncontrollably. I need to get out of here, Emily.

I need to get out of here fast.

Chapter Twenty-One

Will's phone is going straight to voicemail. He can't have landed in Dallas yet, must still be airborne. Every second that slips away knots my stomach a little tighter, makes my heart thud a little faster. Waiting to speak to him is unbearable – and I hardly notice the doorbell go at about eleven, until Rob comes back into the study moments later and says, 'Your friend Tamsin is here. Shall I let her in?'

Dumbfounded, I stare at him as he confesses, 'It's just – well, I asked her to come over.'

My eyes widen in disbelief. He must have phoned her when he took my mobile upstairs with him. But

I particularly told him I don't want anyone to know. And while we've seen a lot of each other recently, and I've spoken glowingly about Tamsin to Rob on more than one occasion – I like her a lot – surely, if he was going to tell anyone what has happened, I would at least have expected it to be one of our older friends, whom we've known for years.

Then it clicks. He's remembered my telling him she's a psychologist . . . but it's not one of the 'could you come and see if my wife is having a breakdown' variety, she's an occupational psychologist. That's how we got talking at the antenatal group. She knew a bit about my company, having done some freelance profiling for them. Oh, how could he do this to me?

'I don't want to see her.'

He opens his mouth, but obviously thinks better of whatever he was going to say – and disappears. I hear the murmur of low, embarrassed voices, then the door closes again before he comes back in.

'You called someone to assess me?'

He flushes guiltily.

'You think I'm going mad?' My voice starts to tremble with energy.

'No!' he says immediately. 'I think you're in shock – and after everything you went through with Matty

290

so recently . . . you can't stop crying, you look really pale and you're breathing so fast . . .' He bites his lip. 'I thought someone you knew rather than a stranger, just to look at you, see if maybe we need a doctor to come out and give you something. I don't know . . .'

Dad appears in my mind the second he says that – Maura handing him one of his numerous, unidentifiable pills; popping it in his mouth like a baby.

'Kate, I'm sorry. It's just you seemed so . . .'

'So what?'

'I can see this is opening up everything else too.' He is trying desperately hard to pick his words carefully. 'From the past, I mean, and I'm frightened that—'

I reach over, grab the photo of Emily and thrust it in my poor husband's face.

'That little girl was the best of everything. She'd be twenty-six now, Rob, and not a single day goes by when I don't wonder where she would be living, what she'd be doing, who she would be friends with. I think about the man that she was meant to marry and have her children with – and I wonder what he's doing now instead. I go over and over the things she never got to experience, all of the things I would have loved to have done with her; the weddings, watching our children playing together, family days at the beach, Christmases, birthdays. So no, this hasn't "opened anything up" because it's never closed. Every time I look at Mathias, I see her in him, and while yes, it's a comfort of sorts, it also kills me a little bit more each time too, because,' I pause, my voice now thick with tears, 'because I will always, always want more. I can't help it. And now, *now*, Anya too?' I gesture back wildly at the second picture frame. And as I say it, in my mind I see myself blithely opening the front door at Holly Lodge to reveal a trembling, teenage Anya, flanked by a policeman on either side: *that* was post-traumatic shock, Rob. Poor, poor Anya.

Why didn't I ever talk to her about what she saw? She was so brave, and I never told her. I just packed her off to university and messed up everything between her and Steve. What if he was 'the one'? She might be happily married to him now, settled – safe.

'You know what I remember hearing someone say to my parents after Emily died?' I challenge Rob. '"God never sends you more than you can bear". Well, *bullshit*!' I rake my sleeve roughly across my face to wipe my hot eyes. 'I am *not* going mad, I just can't

bear this – I can't. I want Anya! I want them both
. . .' I dissolve completely at that, and Rob moves to
hug me, but the pain is so great that this time it's no
comfort. I want it to be, but it simply isn't, so my
phone starting to ring – my mother is calling – is a
relief, and I quickly untangle myself from his arms.

As I pull away from Rob completely, I remember
watching her do the same thing to my dad. It always
seemed to me to be such a cruel thing to do, to push
away someone trying to help you (although at the
same time I can remember wanting to shout with
frustration at Dad when he didn't go after her), but
perhaps she, too, was simply in too much pain to be
held.

'Kate? I've been thinking.' Unlike earlier, Mum's
voice sounds tight, high – and frightened. 'I should
go to Mexico. I'm so close. It's wrong not to, isn't
it? It would be wrong not to go.'

The sentiment may be there, but so is the plea in
her voice. She still wants me to lie to her – tell her
again that no, she mustn't fly out there. It's too
dangerous, and it won't help. That she must stay where
she is. She is begging to be absolved of responsibility,
even though she knows that she ought to be dropping everything because it's her child.

But I also know that's exactly why she is unable to go.

I take a deep breath. 'I want you to stay where you are, Mum.'

She says nothing, just stays silent.

I can pinpoint almost exactly when I realised that my relationship with Mum had somehow flipped and I felt more like the parent, and she the child. It was when I flew out to America to ask her to come home, shortly after she walked out on Dad. She refused point-blank, and said she couldn't stay in 'that house' while everything pulled away from her. She couldn't explain it, she insisted, she just knew she was unable to come back. When I had my own children I'd understand how what had happened to Emily had left her feeling utterly empty. I wanted to say that I was still there, and so was Anya . . . I don't know why I didn't. 'You don't have to come back if you don't want to. It's OK,' I'd said slowly, although it didn't feel OK at all, it felt very frightening to watch my mum sat huddled in front of me, staring into a place I didn't know how to rescue her from. I wondered if she was thinking about her own parents, but didn't want to ask in case she wasn't, and I made things even worse. Everything had become so unrecognisable so quickly.

'I should go to Mexico,' Mum repeats.

Perhaps I ought to let her. After all, she should be there already. So should Dad.

But then she does a strange sort of gulp and says, 'I just can't . . . I can't see the body of another of my children, Kate. I cannot do it.' Her voice cracks and then I know I am listening to the sound of her crying, alone in the small tiled-floor condo that overlooks the pristine gardens and shared pool. It's not hysterical, drunken sobs. Just bleak, frightened, quiet weeping. It's one of the saddest sounds I have ever heard, and it breaks my heart for the millionth time.

'Mum, please can you get someone to come and be with you?' I am gripping the phone so tightly my knuckles have gone white. 'I don't think you should be alone right now.'

I hear her exhale, as if she's trying to get herself under control. 'I'm all right,' she says after a moment.

'Well, will you at least promise me you'll stay put?'

'I promise.' A note of relief is creeping into her voice. 'Are you going to call me, as soon as . . .' she pauses, 'as soon as there is news?'

'Of course. Try to be brave, Mum. You're doing well.'

I see Rob's eyebrows flicker at that comment. 'She's

not in a good way then,' he says, once I've hung up. 'You shouldn't be telling *her* to be brave.'

'She just said she thinks she should fly out there, but she can't bear to see another of her children's bodies.'

Rob winces visibly.

'It's very hard sometimes, that she's all the way out there,' I manage, before tailing off. I'm not sure I will ever understand how she could just up and leave like that, but she genuinely felt she had nothing left – and perhaps she was right. After all, An and I were twenty-somethings, adults. Perhaps she did have a right to salvage her life . . . although I still can't ever imagine not being there for Mathias if he needed me, however old he was.

Rob squeezes my hands. 'It's not . . . straight-forward, is it?'

I manage to shake my head and we sit in silence for a moment, but are interrupted, to my surprise, by Mum calling me back. This time she doesn't even bother with hello, and with no preamble says, 'Kate, does your father know what has happened?'

I'm stunned. In about ten years she has not made direct reference to Dad. I've mentioned him, of course, but not once has she asked so much as how he is.

'I phoned him, yes, but Maura wouldn't let me speak to him.'

'Wouldn't *let* you? What do you mean?'

'Mum, do you think *you* could just call him?' I say exhaustedly. 'That would really help me right now.' Rob might have a point – in trying too hard to protect people, maybe you really can do more harm than good. I don't for one minute expect her to agree, but after a moment's pause, and to my astonishment, she says, 'Fine. Give me his number then.'

I do. 'I'll speak to you shortly,' she says, and rings off.

I tell Rob what's just happened and he looks surprised but says, 'Well, let's not hope for miracles,' then looks appalled as he realises what he's just said. 'Shit, what I meant was—'

'I know what you meant,' I say quickly – and look at my watch. Will *has* to have landed in Dallas by now. Surely?

And he has. This time it barely rings before he answers with a quick 'Hello? Kate? I've just picked up your messages to call. I was just about to – what's happened?'

I take a deep breath and tell him that I have made

a dreadful, dreadful mistake. Anya *is* in the cave, but I deliberately obstructed the search, and now the divers aren't allowed back in.

'Please, do whatever you can to make them look for her, Will.' I am horribly aware of the burden of responsibility I am putting on him, but I have no choice. 'How soon can you be there?'

Chapter Twenty-Two

I always thought I was good at being in my own company. I've never felt I had a problem being alone.

In fact, I've always insisted alone is better – 'you shouldn't need another person to complete you' is one of my favourite phrases. But perhaps I might have just been hiding behind that.

I do need other people. Not just literally: of course I need someone to come for me. Right now I am as helpless as a baby, lying here totally reliant on others . . . but I also need, and want, the people I love – who it looks like I am going to lose. It's not dying that is frightening me, it's leaving behind the others: Kate, Matty, Mum and Dad, Rob – and Will.

I particularly regret that Will and I parted on such sad terms. I assumed we'd have plenty of time to set things right. I was wrong. And when we have been friends for all these years, for it to end like this, with so much left unsaid, is tragic.

We have been best friends for the length of time that when nosy people nudge one of us and say, 'So have you two ever . . .' we both laugh easily and insist, 'Absolutely not!'

Should they persist, adding slyly, 'Do you think you ever might . . .' I'll smile and say, 'If we were going to, we would have done it by now.' To which Will nods emphatically and says, 'Trouble is, I just don't fancy her. It's taken a long time for her to accept it, but you can't make someone feel something they don't.'

Of course I've considered it. You always do at some point with a friend of the opposite sex, and anyone who says otherwise is a liar. Will propositioned me, in the nicest sense, when we'd not known each other long and were about to go travelling together. But I didn't want complications. I actually did think he was attractive, I always have – he has a nice kind face.

But I just wasn't in *that* place, and I stand by that; I made the decision that was right at the time. There is, I am now sure, only the moment you are in; that's all. Nothing else is real. I'm not even sure *this* is real any more.

There was only really one other time when it might have spilled over – my slightly uncontrollable thirtieth birthday meal out in Waterloo. We ended up as a party of twenty-seven, which, while fun, really stressed the waiters; I'd told them we'd be no more than sixteen. People just kept turning up, some of whom I hadn't seen in an age and had forgotten I'd asked. Anyway, there was a lot of happy hugging, laughter and catching up going on when Kate came up to me and quietly said, 'I think Will's a bit drunk.'

I'd looked down the very long table. He'd looked up, met my eyes solemnly, raised a shot of vodka and downed it in one. I laughed and turned back to Kate. 'Yeah – he is. He can't handle shots. Pints, yes, shots, no.'

Kate sat down on the edge of the seat, made me budge up and said in a low voice, 'He just told me that he's asked his girlfriend,' she nodded down the table at Liesel, 'to move in with him, but he thinks it might have been a mistake. He likes her very much, but – she's not you.' She paused excitedly. 'Only, he can't tell you because he thinks you're worried it would mess up your friendship. He asked me not to say anything. But I think you should know.' She looked at me breathlessly. 'So, what are you going to do?'

The hand holding my own shot had frozen en route to my mouth. 'Nothing,' I said lightly, and managed to knock it back. 'He's right. You shouldn't have said anything.'

'But you're so right for each other!' she exclaimed. 'You and he could . . .'

'Could what?' My voice began to take on a warning tone. 'Have a lukewarm fuck-up that turns out to be a huge mistake and wrecks everything?'

'If he stays with her,' she said urgently, 'you'll lose him eventually anyway, An. That's just the way things work. Married men don't stay friends with their female friends.'

My insides shrank with dread at the thought of not having Will in my life. It must have shown on my face, because Kate added quickly, 'I'm just saying . . .'

'Well don't,' I said shortly. 'It's none of your business.' I could tell that hurt her, but I didn't apologise.

302

It was making me very uncomfortable, discussing Will in *that* way. To my relief, a waiter appeared bearing a blazing cake and everyone began a bright chorus of merry singing. We said no more about it.

I blinked, another year passed and on 17 December – about three weeks ago – I went round to his for a Christmas meal. Liesel had already flown out to her parents, and he was due to join her two days later for two weeks. His first Christmas with her folks.

'Are you looking forward to it? Xmas with the in-laws?' I teased, clutching my empty wineglass as I huddled by the dying fire.

'I suppose so, and they're *not* my in-laws.' Will nodded at the log basket. 'Put another on, if you like.'

I shook my head. 'Not unless you're staying up – I should make a move soon.' I yawned. 'Before the tubes stop.'

'You know you can stay here tonight if you want,' he offered.

'I haven't got any stuff with me.'

He rolled his eyes. 'Yeah, because Liesel hasn't in fact got drawers full of stuff you can nick. It's up to you: you can go back, or just stay and come into work with me in the morning.'

I hesitated. It *was* late, and bloody cold outside. 'Oh, go on then.'

Oddly, I felt a bit funny, curling up in bed knowing that Will was just through the wall – but it had been a full-on red wine, and I was asleep before I knew it.

I woke to see him standing over me, smiling. 'There's been a slight change of plan,' he said, and drew back the curtain. I gasped. The sky was a thick grey-white, and falling snow was tumbling past the window. 'How heavy is it?' I blinked and sat up.

'Heavy.' He grinned gleefully. 'No work for us today! I've made some coffee, and bacon sandwiches. Come on! Get up!'

We had a really lovely day. One I'd hoped to remember a lot longer. We made a snowman, we went sledging in the park, did an emergency food run in case it got any worse, and then we lit the fire, opened a fresh bottle of wine and put a movie on.

'The snow's getting heavier,' I exclaimed happily, tucking up on the sofa in one of Will's jumpers and a pair of Liesel's leggings, which, given the length of her legs compared to mine looked ridiculous – not that it really mattered, of course. 'How great to get this before I ship off!'

Will paused in between putting another log on the fire. 'You're going away again? Where?'

'I haven't decided the exact location yet,' I said truthfully. 'Maybe Mexico?'

'How long for this time?'

I shrugged. 'Don't know that, either. It's just a thought at the moment. I'll wait and see what happens. This is fun, isn't it?' I patted his leg happily as he sat down next to me and turned back to the TV, taking a sip of wine.

He didn't answer, just crossed his arms and said, 'Wake me up when the movie's done,' before closing his eyes. I assumed he was just tired from all the fresh air. With the warmth of the surprisingly efficient stove filling the small room, it wasn't long before I had set my glass down with a yawn myself.

When I woke the room was dark, lit only by the flickering of the TV. The remains of the fire were glowing in the grate and the curtains were still open. Big fat snowflakes were falling again and, transfixed, I let my head just rest on the sofa as I watched them float past.

'Beautiful, isn't it?'

I looked over and realised Will had woken up. He was staring out of the window. 'God knows how I'm going to get to the airport tomorrow, if it's even open.'

'Maybe we'll be stuck here for ever.' I smiled.

'Maybe,' he agreed – and fell silent.

I sighed, and he glanced at me. 'Why the sigh?'

'Not being able to go anywhere, or having to do anything. It's nice. Peaceful.'

'You run around too much.'

I rolled my eyes and playfully turned my head to him. 'No I don't.'

'You do. You never stop. You need looking after.' He glanced down and then, out of nowhere, blurted, 'I wish you'd let me do it.' And then, to my stunned surprise, before I could say anything, he leaned over and kissed me.

Everything was quiet. I could hear only the fire and, behind it, the stillness of the room. For the briefest of moments I closed my eyes . . . but then I realised what was happening. It was *Will* – I pulled back sharply. 'What are you doing?' I whispered, horrified. I was shocked to realise tears had sprung to my eyes.

'Anya?' He looked at me in disbelief. 'Don't cry. I didn't mean to upset you. I'm so sorry. I would never want to hurt you, never – I love you too much.'

I leaped up at that, appalled, and put my hands over my ears, beginning to feel unaccountably angry. 'Shut up! Liesel isn't here, and this is wrong.' I pushed my feet into my shoes. Suddenly the small warm room, the snow outside – it all felt stifling. I had to leave.

'What are you doing?' he said. 'You can't seriously be considering going out in weather like this?'

I didn't answer him.

'Anya,' he said carefully, 'please don't. It doesn't have to be like this.'

'It does now!' I shouted. 'Because you've fucked it all up!'

'Well, then, perhaps you might as well just give it a go,' he challenged, and tried a brave smile. 'It's never too late! And you've nothing left to lose now, have you?'

Why was he acting like it was all a game? 'You did this on purpose?'

He looked at me like I was mad. 'Of course I did! I'm not in the habit of accidentally kissing people!'

'You didn't stop to think I might be perfectly happy as we were?'

'Nothing stays the same for ever, Anya,' he said quietly.

That made me *really* mad. 'You think I don't know that?' I choked on my words, properly upset now, hot tears rushing to my eyes.

He exhaled slowly. 'I think you can't keep running away from everything under the pretence that you're too busy having fun; responsibility, jobs, feelings, being a grown-up.'

My hand shot out and I slapped him round the face. He didn't even flinch.

'You don't think I've had my fair share of shit?' I could hardly get the words out, I was trembling so much.

'You've had at least five people's share, maybe more. But bad stuff happens to lots of good people, Anya. You can't stop living, refuse to get involved.'

'How dare you!' I shivered with anger. 'I've travelled, I have friends all over the world, I've had lots of interesting jobs. All this, because I don't fancy you?'

'That's not why I'm saying all this.'

'It's exactly why you're saying it. And it's an unbelievably cheap way to behave.' Marching across the room, I began to look for my bag.

'Anya, you really can't leave, not when it's like this outside,' he insisted. 'I get it, you're angry.'

'Yes, I am. And this is me leaving.'

'Please,' he hastened after me, 'just stay, and we'll discuss things properly.' He put a hand on my arm.

I shook it off and yanked my coat on. 'I don't want to talk to you for – for a really long while.' Tears flooded my eyes again, and I pulled the front door open.

'I'm sorry,' he said desperately. 'Please don't leave.'

I did, though, and determinedly trudged all the way to the tube station, glad that the streets were practically empty so that no one could see me crying. I decided I bloody well *was* going to go to Mexico, and the sooner the better. How could he have done it, ruined everything?

He phoned me the next day, but I ignored the call, and the dozen that followed, one of which came through while I was actually at the airport, waiting to board. He must have finally got the message, because he didn't leave one for me.

I clench my eyes tightly shut. I'm so sorry, Will. Ignoring you must have seemed such a childish way to behave, even if I *was* hurt – and frightened. It's just, I wasn't able to go there. I couldn't unpack it, there's too much. Shutting it off, boxing it all up was the only way I could cope; it would have swallowed me up whole otherwise.

But now, when there is nowhere to hide and it's all confronting me, I can't say it is a strategy that has necessarily worked, or made me any the happier. I just don't know. I don't think I know myself at all.

Had I known that less than a month later it would all be ending like this, would I still have walked out on Will that night?

Might I have even . . .

The sound of a splash makes me jump and catch my breath. Is it *him*?

But no, it must be me . . . this water feels higher somehow . . . how is that possible? Now it seems to be round my waist . . . the tide must be coming in. Mystified, I reach up to see if I can feel a ceiling above me, but I can't – there is still space, the *same amount* of space, I think . . . But this is a freshwater system. Isn't it? Yes, I'm sure it is. There *are* no tides. But when I bring my hand back down, I inexplicably find my shoulders are *in the water*.

It must be rising . . .

Or am I sinking?

I close my eyes to prepare myself for the effort of hauling myself back out again. But the directions are somehow all wrong. I go to place my hands on the rock, only feel nothing . . . and somehow plunge myself *under* the surface, before coming up coughing and spluttering and spitting water.

'Emily!' I shout. 'Help! I'm getting a bit tired, going a bit mental . . .' And then I hear laughter . . . probably also me. What am I talking about – of *course* it's me!

I blink. Quick! More distractions! More things to focus on – the capital city of Malawi is . . . Lilongwe. Capital city of Peru is . . . Lima. Capital city of Slovenia is . . . I don't know . . . But then I've never known that one, so that's OK.

I hear laughter again. Who *is* that? Is it him? But then I guess, as he said, if this is to be my fate, it won't make any difference to the outcome if Rafa comes for me or not. The die will have been cast a long time ago.

Teeth starting to chatter, I decide that if I get out of here, maybe I will go to Slovenia – find out first-hand what their poxy capital city is.

Or perhaps Emily and I will just go home instead.

Chapter Twenty-Three

'I've got two hours until my connecting flight, then it's another two hours in the air and however long it takes to drive from the airport. Is the Embassy representative still going to meet me?'

Will is so physically and emotionally exhausted that he can barely make sense of what Kate has just confessed to him. All the fury he has been focusing on this unknown man – the supposed enemy – suddenly has nowhere to go, and his panic comes full circle. It is his fault after all. She meant to do the dive. He should never have said all of those things to her about needing to grow up.

He chews it all over again and again as he sits there alone in the busy airport waiting for his connecting flight, confused and frightened, drinks yet more bitter black coffee and mechanically eats a plastic-tasting pastry while picturing Anya ducking under the water, staring defiantly back at him. His stomach is twisting and churning by the time he boards his last plane. Leaning his head back on the hard headrest, he tries to close his eyes. But he can't sleep. Of course he can't sleep.

As soon as the seat-belt sign is switched off, he gets up sharply and asks the couple next to him if he can please make his way by? Rather than standing up, the woman half moves to the side and Will has to edge past in an ungainly way so he doesn't end up sitting on her knee. Thankfully the man who is with her isn't so lazy, and nods in response to Will's quiet 'Thank you.'

He starts to walk up the back of the plane towards the loos. There is a queue; several people in front of him, arms crossed, staring blankly out of the small windows. He joins the back and waits, eyes downcast, focusing on the strip of carpet lined with emergency lights. Someone shuffles past him back to their seat and they all move up one. He looks up and briefly around, envious of the other passengers whose biggest problem right now is feeling a bit creased and tired. Unlike them, he had no plans to be travelling today. He should be at work. Anya should be safe.

He senses someone staring and instinctively looks up. A woman in her twenties is looking brazenly back at him and flashes him a confident smile as their eyes meet, smoothing down glossy dark hair tied back in a pony tail. 'Don't you just love the "plane-fresh" feeling?' she says drily. 'I swear I get on looking normal, but by the end of it . . .'

Will manages a flicker of a polite smile, thinking: *I don't want to talk to you – I'm really sorry, but I just don't.*

'So are you visiting someone in Cancún, or are you on vacation?' she asks casually.

'Visiting.' He hopes that will be enough . . .

'Awesome!' she enthuses.

It isn't.

'I have family out there.' She smiles another dazzling, perfect smile. 'Whereabouts are you headed?'

Oh God . . . He hesitates. 'I'm going to meet my girlfriend.' He feels bad for saying it, she's just being friendly, but he really doesn't want to get into this conversation. Not at all.

Her smile doesn't falter, but she says a little more coolly, 'That sounds fun. She must be excited to see you.'

'She doesn't know I'm coming.' He says it without thinking.

The girl's eyes widen and she clutches her hand to her chest. 'That's so sweet!' And then she gives him an actual genuine smile, a friendly one. 'You're from England, aren't you? That's a long way to fly for a surprise. Is it her birthday or something – ohmi*god*! Are you going to *propose*? I know it's none of my business, but are you?' An older woman in front of both of them half turns curiously too, having been listening in.

Will feels something catch inside him.

'You've got to tell me now!' the girl laughs. 'I can't not know.'

'Yes,' he finds himself saying, 'I am.'

'Ahhhh!' both women say instinctively.

'She's going to be psyched! Have you got the ring and everything?' They move up one again, and the older woman looks very disappointed to have to go into the cubicle and miss Will's answer.

'No,' Will confesses.

'Thought it better to let her pick it our herself? Smart move.' The girl nods approvingly.

'She's not really the flashy jewellery type,' Will says, thinking about Anya's beautiful bare hands and elegant long fingers. Artistic hands, his father remarked when Will had first introduced Anya to his parents. Anya had laughed and said she couldn't draw so much as a stick person. She could reach an octave on a piano, but that was also her musical limit. She'd refused to go to piano lessons when she was younger, and now very much regretted it. His mum had smiled at that. They'd liked her.

'Honey,' drawls the girl. 'Trust me, she's the flashy jewellery type. We say we're not, but secretly, we *all* are.'

Will tries to smile courteously, but says nothing. *She's not, actually,* he thinks. *You know nothing about how special she is.*

The door opens, the older woman comes out and beams indulgently at him as she makes her way back to her seat.

'Well, good luck!' the girl says, stepping into the cubicle. 'I hope it all works out for you – and that she says yes!'

317

'Thank you,' Will manages, and she closes the door.

The occupant of the second loo finally vacates, and as he shuts himself in the cramped, unpleasant-smelling space, damp, used tissues spilling out of the bin, he stares at himself in the small, harshly lit mirror. Why did he feel the need to say all that to a complete stranger? It was an out-and-out lie, not real. She's not even his girlfriend.

He closes his eyes briefly and sways on the spot, not just from the movement of the plane.

None of this feels real.

He opens his eyes again.

Except it really *is* happening.

And he has to start preparing himself for what lies ahead.

At seven p.m. local time, he is hurrying off the plane onto the springy runway feeling crumpled and greasy, although the comparative warmth of the Mexican evening begins to rejuvenate him. Lifting his head, he quickens his pace.

As he has no luggage to collect, it is no time at all before he is in the back of a car, pulling through busy evening traffic, trying to absorb what an earnest stranger – the Embassy representative – is saying to

318

him. He clutches his bag to his lap tightly, dazed by the neon lights of the city streets flashing past. They are going straight out to the site.

He opens his dry, tired eyes what feels like moments later, to find the car is bouncing and lurching all over uneven ground. Suddenly wide awake, he sits forward a little on his seat as the headlights catch the surface of an expanse of dark water. There is a small crowd of people milling around on the bank. He swallows and starts to feel sick.

Climbing out of the car, he is immediately struck by the palpable air of tension. Some men appear to be arguing with two policemen, but Will can't understand what is being said.

Before he can ask who they are, a Chevy roars up and as the engine cuts, a very attractive woman jumps out. She even earns a few admiring glances as she hurries over to a man standing back from the edge, and straight into his arms.

'That's the lawyer, the man that first called Kate,' the Embassy representative murmurs. 'And I guess that's his wife. Word is spreading . . . I think most of Mr Montoya's family are here now.'

It turns out to be two of the male members of Rafa's family who are arguing with the police, trying to persuade them to let the voluntary divers back into the cave given the police team *still* hasn't arrived. The police are shaking their heads determinedly and are trying to coordinate the newly arrived reinforcements ready to conduct the land search.

'That's Mr Montoya senior.' The Embassy representative points to one of the gesticulating men. 'He's insisting that he doesn't see what "evidence" could be compromised that hasn't already *been* compromised by the divers going back in — and the officers are telling him it's not his concern.'

They pause and listen some more. 'Now the father is saying that of course it's his concern, Rafa is his son.'

Will watches the older man lunge forward at one of the officers, only to be held back by the other younger one. He shouts something, eyes shining brightly.

'He's just said that his son is no criminal, he's a good boy. A good son,' the representative says uncomfortably.

Will continues to watch in silence. He doesn't need any translation to see that the father's increasingly desperate protestations are not making the slightest difference to the police. But then everyone stops what they are doing as an official-looking car pulls up and several men climb out. 'The Chief of Police,' the Embassy representative says. 'Excuse me, I have to go and talk with—'

'May *I* speak with him?' Will asks.

The representative shakes his head. 'I'm not sure that's such a good idea.'

'I just want to tell him I think he's doing an excellent job, coordinating all of this,' Will says. 'Please.'

The representative looks at him extremely sceptically, but disappears. A few moments later an unsmiling, surprisingly tall man in his late forties with thinning grey-flecked hair and pockmarked skin is standing in front of Will, face inscrutable.

Will clears his throat and turns to the representative. 'Please could you tell him that—'

'I speak English,' the man says.

Embarrassed by his first gaffe, Will nods and says, more bravely than he feels, 'I'm sorry. Could we perhaps speak alone for a moment?'

The representative immediately opens his mouth, but the Chief of Police holds up a silencing hand and steps towards Will. They both move until they are out of earshot. He folds his arms behind him, looks at Will and waits.

'I hear your team of divers is still delayed,' Will stammers. 'As the other divers are still here, would it be possible for them to—'

'I can't discuss the operation with you,' the Chief of Police says smoothly, and Will realises he has only granted this audience to make the point that he actually doesn't have to do anything anyone says, because he is in charge – no one else.

Will feels a wave of panic well up within him. The divers *have* to be allowed back in. 'The woman who called the newspapers in England, I know her. She's very, very sorry,' he says.

The Chief of Police doesn't react, just dismissively begins to walk away, confirming the interview is now over.

'I have some money,' Will calls out desperately to his retreating back, thinking of the flat deposit he's been saving for the last few years.

The Chief of Police pauses, and slowly begins to turn. Will's heart is thumping. This is farcical. He has just offered a bribe to a very senior police officer. Who does he think he is? Suppose it offends him? Makes matters worse?

The Chief of Police is staring at him in apparent outrage, but as Will wracks his brain to think what on earth to say to haul this back on track, he chuckles and begins to walk back towards Will. 'I don't want your money, little man,' he says softly. Will flushes. He is horribly out of his depth. The representative was right – he shouldn't have tried to sort this. What he's doing is no better, or more helpful, than Kate's well-meant interventions.

'Although *if* we did allow them back in,' says the Chief of Police casually, 'you would of course want to tell people, I think.' He takes a step even closer to Will and says deliberately, 'I think you would want to tell very many people what a great man I am. How I overlooked rudeness and inter-ference, the assumption that we will do as we are told, the implication that we could not possibly rescue this girl and boy, because here in Mexico we are just criminals and lazy incompetents.' He smiles charmingly. 'Because that's what you think, isn't it?'

'Not at all,' Will stammers.

The Chief of Police laughs lightly. 'Oh, I think you do. Just as we think you tourists always need us to look after you. You come out here, you drink, you get in trouble, you think it is acceptable to behave like you would not behave at home. Because this is *my* home, you see, Mr . . .' He looks at Will enquiringly.

'My name is Will.'

'Will,' he repeats pleasantly. 'Well, Will, *I* know how it works here. And it's not how you see in the films.' He leans in closer and whispers, 'It's much worse.' He guffaws. 'So you can contact these journalists too, can you?'

Will stares at him and says quickly, 'I'll make sure everyone knows that you changed your mind and let the divers go back in because you are a generous and compassionate man. Nothing more or less than that.'

The Chief of Police appears to consider that, and nods meditatively. 'But you must actually do it, or I might have to come and find you afterwards, eh?' He leans towards Will, eyes twinkling. Will has no idea if he's joking or not. He feels like he's in an episode of *The Sopranos*. It would be funny if not for the fact that this is about Anya's life.

'I give you my word,' Will says sincerely.

The Chief of Police laughs properly at that. 'Good for you. Well, we will have to see, won't we?' He pats Will idly on the shoulder. 'We will just have to see what we will see. My name is Ramiro Garza. That's spelled G.A.R.Z.A.'

And then he turns and walks away, leaving Will just standing there, not sure if that actually just happened, and if it will make the slightest bit of difference anyway.

Chapter Twenty-Four

My eyes flutter open. Just black. I am still here . . .
I *think* I know where here is.

I try to move, but can't. My legs seem to have
frozen. With a huge effort I reach down. I feel no
temperature difference in my fingers, but when I
bring them up to my mouth they are wet. I must
still be in the water.

OK. This is getting serious now.

Another list, Emily . . .

My least favourite things:

1. Caves.

2. Wasps.

3. People who talk about themselves in the third person. Anya doesn't like that.

Emily giggles. I definitely hear it.

'Em?' I say, confused.

She is not *actually* here. Is she? I force myself to think carefully. 'Em?' I try again tentatively. She does not answer, of course she doesn't. She died thirteen years ago. Thirteen . . . Unlucky for some . . . unlucky for us. I shudder again.

I could use a hug . . . Em with her arms around my shoulders. Small hands linking together, the brush of her long hair as she kisses my cheek lightly and holds me to her, the warmth of her small body. For ever fixed in my mind, always wearing . . . I pause. Always wearing what? I can't remember what she was wearing the day she got in the car. A pink t-shirt and what? What else? Oh, come on!

I try hard. Very hard – but I can't. This is ridiculous! I won't dwell on it though because she's still here, holding me. I reach up to my shoulders in wonder: will I *actually feel* her warm skin? But the movement kills the moment. My hands clutch at nothing.

I squeeze my eyes tightly shut, deeply distressed. I am losing them all. They are all slipping from my grasp even though I'm trying, trying so hard. I know it, I can feel it. And I'm afraid.

I am going to be alone too. Like Em was.

I will have to try and be brave as well.

Chapter Twenty-Five

'Did you speak to Dad?'

'No, he wouldn't talk to me – or at least that's what Maura said. I tried, Kate. I promise you.'

And for a brief moment I feel horribly cheated. I so wanted there to have been some miracle moment when they spoke, mended everything, and then Dad would call me, tell me he was going to sort everything out. But I am not a child any more, and it doesn't work like that. Sometimes I suppose the resolution is that there *is* no resolution.

'Well, thank you for trying.'

'How strong you are,' Mum says, after a moment

more. 'I don't know how your father and I managed it. Or maybe we didn't. Maybe it was despite us. I *am* praying for her, Kate,' she says earnestly. 'For all of us.'

This time it doesn't annoy me when she says it. 'Keep going, Mum. I'll call when Will has rung me with an update.' As I hang up, it occurs to me for the first time that Mum was only five years older than I am now when Em died.

When I consider everything Rob and I have been through already in the short time since having Mathias, and how tough we – or I – have found it, I feel suddenly incredibly sad for my parents. I can't claim I now want to absolve them of their actions – I don't. But perhaps I appreciate them a little better. We are all making choices and trying our best, hoping it will be good enough.

Glancing over at Rob – who has a sleeping Mathias lying on his chest, his own eyes closed – I think about Andrew hovering in the background at Holly Lodge as we waited for news of Emily, and remember Anya saying, 'I hope he's worth it.'

If I met Andrew in the street now I might not even recognise him. He, like Emily, stays fixed in my mind as he was then, not as he would be now.

I didn't even move away. Have *I* changed? I suppose

I must have, although I still drive past Holly Lodge from time to time, turn down the lane, see other people's cars on the drive, lights on in the rooms that I can picture so very clearly full of our things. Full of our family.

I talked to Rob about relocating once, about seven years ago.

'But to where?' He seemed genuinely confused by my suggestion.

'I thought maybe London?' I suggested hopefully.

He'd blinked, like I'd said Mars. 'But what would I do for work? My business is here.'

And that was the end of that.

If Emily had lived, would I have carried on seeing Andrew? Moved away? Married him, maybe? For a long time I confess I wondered.

Anya and I had a holiday together in between one of her many trips, when I was particularly restless both with work and living with Rob. We recklessly – well, for me – used some of the money our grandparents had left us, and went to Barbados together, for two weeks. We hired a little house in a private complex on a golf course; Anya sorted it. I didn't even know you *could* hire places like that. We rented a car too, which I drove of course, and spent our time mostly heading to Sandy Lane to lie on the beach next to the rich people.

We had a lot of fun. Enough to make me properly question if Rob was, really, the one. Anya inadvertently started it.

'You know, I never saw you as still living in the same place, with the same school friends and a local job . . . If you get married and have kids,' she lay back on her towel and closed her eyes contentedly under the hot sun, 'the picture will be complete. I thought it would be you doing things, going places – and me staying at home. Funny, eh?'

I said nothing.

'But I mean, whatever makes you happy,' she added. 'Are you?'

I wasn't sure how to answer that honestly. I thought fleetingly of Andrew, and then of Rob. Sufficiently happy to think it was madness to imagine saying to Rob, 'We need to talk.' Occasionally itchy enough to wonder, 'Is this all there is, for ever?' But then, given everything that had happened, I was surely always going to have an emptiness that Rob – no one – could never be expected to fill.

I didn't say that to Anya, though. Why didn't I? It seems crazy now that I didn't.

'Sometimes I'm happy. I am right now.' I smiled. 'Shall we stop at the supermarket on the way home and get some more rum – and ice cream?'

'Yes!' Anya said decisively. 'Let's.' She sat up and reached for her hat. 'Oh – and I got chatting to the bloke two doors up. They're having a barbecue tonight, he and his wife, they've got lots of friends coming over and he asked us to join them. That's nice, isn't it? I think we should go. It'd be fun. They've got a cute dog, too.'

That reminded me of something I knew she'd like. 'You know Rob's mum and dad's dog? Dudley?'

Her eyes gleamed. 'I *love* Dudley. He's so naughty! I'm going to get a Westie just like him.'

'We went round the other day and Dudley was in disgrace because he'd eaten the remote control. Rob's dad said, "It's a bugger having to change channels with the dog, but there you go."'

Anya laughed and lay back down as I smiled.

'We'd better leave soon, I suppose.' I looked at my watch after a moment more. 'Seeing as,' I added wryly, 'we're going to end up going *into* Bridgetown at least twice on our way back, and wind up at the

Garfield Sobers roundabout God knows how many times . . .'

Anya lifted the hat she had balanced over her face and gave me a look from under it. 'It's hard,' she said defensively, 'when you don't know a place.'

'An, there are only two main roads on the whole island. One that hugs the coast, and the other that's, like, five miles further inland but still goes in a massive circle. It couldn't be easier. And yet we keep on coming back to Garfield . . .'

She laughed, and flicked me a v sign – even though earlier in the day we'd been so lost we'd been yelling furiously at each other in the car. My 'I can't drive *and* map-read!' was drowned out by her shrieking, '*I can't concentrate when you're all up in my face like this!*' before flinging the map in a temper over onto the back seat. When we finally arrived at the beach, I broke her sulky silence by saying, 'If you're going to be in a mood you can stay in the car, or we might as well just go home.'

She got out, banged the door shut and marched off ahead of me down the track to the sea. I sighed, collected our stuff and followed after her. She walked fast – deliberately – and as we reached the beach, I watched her turn right and begin to stride across the soft sand, long hair swinging. Her pretty chiffon trousers over her bikini swished crossly . . . and then a socking great wave came in from nowhere and completely drenched her.

I bit my lip as I looked at her standing there, gasping and soaked, trousers forlornly clinging to her, hair plastered to her face like a little drowned rat – and then burst out laughing. She turned slowly, gave me a murderous look and there was a split second when she had the choice either to laugh with me, or plunge even further into a mood.

Her face split into a huge grin.

I smile briefly at the memory.

Anya – the eternal optimist . . .

And what of our mum and dad? Would they have stayed together if things had been different? Maybe. I might have had parents who came together to see me in hospital when their grandson was born. Mum hasn't even met Mathias – well, not yet.

I glance at Rob and Mathias. Rob is such a good dad. We have made good partners, he and I. Wherever Andrew is, whatever he wound up doing, I hope he has a good life. But I no longer wish I was sharing it. Things *have* changed.

I imagine Anya smiling at that.

She is so much to me, not just my sister. She drives me crazy, can be selfish, moody, opinionated and strident. But she also has such a good, good heart. She makes me laugh; we share the same sense of humour without trying. I love her, and I'm so proud of her. Proud of the way she keeps on going and tries hard to stay true to herself. I've watched her struggle with so much and come through it: Steve; the one-night stands and flings that followed him – they were never her, I know they weren't. The thing about An is that she is so independent, so strong – and even over Christmas, when I sensed she was unhappy about something, she didn't discuss it. I let it go because I was knackered, put off the chat for another day . . .

Tears rise and thicken at the back of my throat. It's almost a relief to hear the front door bell and have an excuse to leap up.

'I'll go,' I insist. Rob can't stop me because he has Mathias on him. It's only as I'm walking down the hall and see the outline of a tall figure waiting on the doorstep that I falter and feel my blood go still. They probably would, wouldn't they? Send someone to tell me in person. They wouldn't say something bad over the phone. They don't do that. I *know* they don't.

The doorbell rings again. 'Kate?' calls Rob, confused. 'Are you going to answer it?'

I have no choice. Hands shaking, I wrench it open . . .

It's just the postman.

'Afternoon!' he says cheerfully, inexplicably dressed in huge boots and shorts despite the snow and it being January. He holds out a parcel and something for me to sign. I slowly take the electronic pen and pad.

'Running late today, I'm afraid. It's nothing exciting,' he says. 'And it's for the second-in-command, not you. Boring building bits, most likely.'

I scrawl my name before passing it back.

'Thanking you!' he says, taking it. 'I'll bring you something nice tomorrow instead, shall I?'

'Yes please,' I say automatically. He winks and trudges off down the path, slamming the gate behind him.

I stand there, clutching Rob's parcel.

Right now, tomorrow seems a very, very long way away indeed. Like it may never arrive at all.

A commotion has begun. People are starting to scramble to their feet, and Will can see three heads breaking the surface of the water.

One of them is not moving.

Will's mouth goes dry and he feels the blood drain from his face.

Everyone hastens to help as they move towards the side of the pool, hands reaching out, pulling the flopping limbs of the lifeless body onto the bank. A hush descends as the recently arrived paramedic team swiftly intervenes, but not before Will sees blue skin and cloudy, rolled-back eyes.

Somebody wails – he isn't sure who – and everyone watches open-mouthed as they pump down on the chest of the young man in front of them . . . but it's clear that whatever they're attempting isn't going to have any effect. He hears someone whisper, 'Oh my God.' The man's face appears somehow unreal, like a waxwork. It doesn't look for one second as if he might just open his mouth and say something, like Will has heard people claim about dead relatives in the past. The features are all there, but there is no sum to the parts. 'Oh God,' he hears a female voice repeat.

Rafa's father collapses to his knees in the dirt next

340

to the body, silent tears streaming down his face, and as a stretcher is brought down – voices around them calling needlessly urgent instructions – he reaches out and gently strokes his son's cheek. It feels hideously intrusive to be witnessing such a raw and private moment of grief, and as Will glances at the ground, he sees that he is not the only person respectfully lowering his gaze.

Except, he notices, for the wife of the lawyer. Her eyes are completely dry and she is staring, transfixed, at the body. Her face remains blank, illuminated in the beam of the ambulance lights.

The two divers look exhausted. 'This was with him,' one of them says in English, holding up a slate. 'He was looking for the girl before he died. It's a message telling her to leave the cave. He was wearing a singular aluminium 80, standard open-water gear, had one burned-out light and his mask was on the floor in a side passage. He didn't stand a chance.

'Still no sign of the girl, but when we searched some of the offshoot passages we found particles of silt floating in the water. The freshwater cenote systems here have minimal flow, so whatever disturbed the silt on the floor of the cave did so within the last twelve hours. One of the causes of a silt-out like that would be amateur swimming techniques; untrained divers letting their feet drift towards the cave floor instead of hovering above it. My guess is that's what happened. They kicked up a load of muck, got separated from each other, got lost.

'We're going back to look for her again now, but . . .' He shrugs and trails off.

White as a sheet, Will fumbles for his mobile. This is a call he has been dreading making.

'Kate? I have some news.' He takes a deep breath. 'I'm so sorry. They've found a body.'

Chapter Twenty-Six

Lying on the floor of the bathroom, knees huddled to my chest, I am crying for my sisters, for all of us.

I don't know how to process the news I have just been told. I can't make sense of it. A body. An actual body.

I'm overcome by sheer, numb grief as I see her beautiful smiling face in my mind, all of the best things I know about her flicking through my head at high speed, and yet everything also feels as if it has stopped. I close my eyes and I can feel what it's like to hug her; the warmth of her body, the sound of her laugh. I just want to hold her. And never let go.

I try to remember Anya leaving our house after Christmas. What did I say to her as she walked off down the path, waved back at us cheerily and then disappeared out of sight? What did I do straight afterwards, once I shut the front door quickly to keep the warmth in, not realising the significance of the moment?

I think I told her I loved her. We often say that to each other, finish phone conversations with 'Love you!' I can imagine I would have called it out as she walked away, but it would have been that casual, habit variation rather than the weightier, 'I love you'.

I moan as I picture her being pulled from a pool by strangers; touching her, moving her. She shouldn't be alone, without any of us there. And please – she has to have known how much I love her. Deranged with grief, and although I'm lying on the floor, I reach out into the open space. As I stare at my fingers, my wedding and engagement rings on one side and on the other, the ring that my family gave me for my twenty-first birthday, which I never take off, I see Anya and Emily's hands slipping into mine; imagine holding them like that for ever. But my tears have become so thick that the picture blurs and I can't see it any more.

The door opens quietly and I'm aware of Rob appearing by my side, not saying anything but just sitting down awkwardly on the cold hard floor next to me, gently reaching out and gathering my limp body to him.

And as he puts his arms around me, something gives way like a dam. I begin to sob and sob into his jumper, great yawning sounds of fear and grief that I can't control, an ugly noise. But he lets me do it, doesn't try to soothe or shush me.

'This can't be happening,' I gasp. 'It just can't. She . . . she—' The words disappear away into nothing. 'And all those terrible things I said about that boy. His poor family, they must be so—' I gulp and give a violent shudder. 'I can't think straight Rob, I can't . . .'

'Don't try to.' His voice sounds distant, somehow. 'You're in shock, Kate.'

'Would he have known he was trapped, what was going to happen to him? Do you think that Anya—'

'Don't!' he says, stopping me. 'Don't do this to yourself, Kate.'

'I wasn't there for her!' The guilt knifing into me bursts from my mouth.

'You didn't know, Kate. How could you have done?'

'But don't you see? How could I have not realised that something like that was happening to my sister? Since Sunday . . . I've been just going about my life like, like normal . . . thinking about – other things.' I start to shudder and I see a younger me sitting down at my bedroom mirror in Holly Lodge, carefully applying make-up, excited and nervous. Dabbing subtle perfume to my wrists and then making my way to the wardrobe and reaching for the delicate-as-tissue-paper yet clingy, soft dove-grey dress. A brand-new purchase especially intended to highlight my eyes and hair. Being ready too early and clock-watching eagerly. Jumping in surprise as the doorbell went and thinking, 'It's him!' before rushing to open it.

'I didn't know!' I say brokenly.

'You were on the other side of the world! It's not your *fault*!' Rob says fiercely.

'I told everyone she wouldn't be in there. *That's* my fault! I should never have said anything, I should have just let them do their job. I insisted they take me seriously, they didn't want to, but I phoned that paper – and look what happened!' I am becoming frantic. 'What if that was the difference between them being found and . . .' I can't finish the sentence. 'When

I thought he'd done something to her, that was bad enough, but she was missing, and I didn't know exactly – I couldn't be sure – and so there was a chance, but now . . . I don't see how she can have . . .' I'm choking on my words, stumbling to get them out fast enough to keep up with the jumble in my head. 'And I can't even remember the last thing I said to her Rob, or what she said to me. *I can't remember!*' I start shivering madly.

Rob stays silent, just holds me.

'I have to call my parents, let them know,' I say automatically. At that, I see Emily's face, contorted with fear, picture her screaming, *Anya!* and then I hear my father down a phone line trying to register what I've just blurted out, everything slipping away into expressions of confusion, disbelief and then agony, him saying, 'She can't be dead,' as if somehow there has been a terrible mistake. I see my mother hysterical, shrieking, 'My baby girl. My daughter!'

Over the top of everything, I realise Mathias is crying in his cot. I must have woken him up. Instinctively, I begin to pull away from Rob.

'He'll be OK for a second or two.' Rob doesn't move, but I resist his arms.

'Please,' I beg. 'I can't listen to him needing us, but

not get him. He's too small Rob,' my eyes flood again and tears are running down my face, 'just a baby.' My voice breaks, and hearing myself say those words aloud collapses me from the inside out. I am incapable of getting to my feet.

'I'll go.' Rob stands stiffly, shoots me an anxious look and hurries from the room.

I sit huddled on the floor and stare at the white towel which is hanging from the rail, then fumble for my phone which is on the floor beside me. In my head, I hear Anya saying, 'Hellooo? Kate?' her usual happy greeting when I pick up the phone – I can hear it clear as a bell. I hesitate and then type 'A'. Up comes her name. I start to call, but it doesn't even dial. Someone has switched off my sister's phone and it's going straight to voicemail.

'I can't take your call right now. Leave me a message.'

'I love you.'

Not that she'd be able to understand what I've just said anyway because I'm crying so much; it's barely more than a garbled whisper. Then I realise the lunacy of what I'm doing, hang up, drop my phone and start to cry again. It's not her. It's just an electronic box. She is not there.

Rob appears in the doorway clutching Mathias, who is blinking and looking around him, one hand appearing out of the edge of his blanket and star-fishing slowly. 'I've got to change him,' Rob says. 'I'm so sorry, Kate. We'll be right back, I promise, but . . .'

I reach my arms out. 'I'll do it while you mix up a bottle. He'll be hungry.' I feel dazed. 'I need to phone the police, tell them she's not missing any more.'

'Don't worry about that, I'll take care of it.'

'Thank you.' I struggle to my feet and walk over to take Mathias from him.

He gently lowers him to me, and for once Mathias doesn't make a sound.

In our room, I don't lay Mathias straight down on the changing table. Instead, I wobble over to the edge of our bed, sit down heavily and look down into his curious eyes. He is staring directly back at me and instinctively, despite everything, I automatically make an exaggerated *oooh* sound. He regards me for a second and then his tiny lips draw together. I realise he is trying to copy me. He is so small.

I cling to him with grief, kiss his downy head and watch as his soft dark hair turns into little damp tufts where my fresh tears are falling.

Chapter Twenty-Seven

I have definitely stopped shivering now. That much be good. Much be good? *Must* be good!

I'm not ready. I know that's selfish, because Emily had far less time than I have had . . . but there is still so much I want to do. So much . . .

And Kate will have to organise my funeral, and I can't do that to her, I just can't!

After Emily, our grandparents both died – within six months of each other. We went to both funerals, Kate and I, because Mum had gone to America by then and wasn't there to be upset by our lack of loyalty to her. In fact, we'd started seeing our grandparents again pretty much as soon as she'd gone. It was they who helped Kate when Dad sold Holly Lodge – when Maura decided Dad would find it 'so much more cathartic to be free of the memories'. Because, of course, when you need to be free of memories, you require a luxury penthouse flat in which to exorcise them. *Thank God* Maura was there . . .

My grandmother called her 'that bloody woman'. It made me laugh – I'd never, ever heard Granny swear. She wouldn't want Kate to have to be doing all that funeral stuff again now, either.

I'm drifting again. It's a nice sensation, like I imagine an anaesthetic to be. Something you can't fight. Who would want to? Like floating. Clouds . . . thick clean clouds racing across a brisk summer wash-day sky, but then they look like they might be about to change, become darker, threaten rain. Somehow I am suddenly above them, looking down on the surging, swirling mass . . . and I realise that what I thought were the tops of clouds are in fact the tightly packed bald smooth skulls of people running in a pack, as if on the hunt.

I am behind them, thank God – they haven't seen me yet, but then slowly one head turns, bright yellow eyes look right at me and light up with anticipation.

Tight grey skin pulls into a sinister, hungry smile revealing white, sharp teeth – then, one by one, they all seem to sense a kill, start to swivel their eyes and look at me . . .

No!

Kate!

And there she is in front of me, barely ten, standing at the foot of my bed in Holly Lodge, hair all over the place, patiently shivering in her nightie.

'You had a bad dream, Anya! Do you want me to get Mum or Dad?'

But before I can say yes, suddenly she's Emily, looking lost and saying frantically, *Can you get Mum or Dad?* and I'm holding out my arms to her because she looks so frightened, and she's reaching for me too, but I can't quite get to her.

I hear someone moan in distress. A bad dream. Just a bad dream!

I am actually awake now, aren't I?

I haven't . . . *already* died?

I look around me wildly. There is nothing, and I am unable to move. That would make sense.

But I *can't* be dead! When you're dead all questions are supposed to be answered; things you're not supposed to understand while you're alive – mysteries like 'what was, is, the point of me?' – all suddenly start falling into place.

I wait. But nothing happens.

This waiting is now really bothering me. Niggling. Who was I waiting for? Emily? My grandparents? Must be. I've always wanted them to have been somewhere, continuing – I have missed them very, very much.

And with that, my heart, the whole of me, fills with love for my sister and my grandparents; a totally blissful sense of calm. I see Emily smile, and hear her laughter. It seems to surround me, suffuses all of me. I can feel Kate, too, my mum and my dad, Matty, Rob – Will. *My family*. I have so much love for them all. It warms through me, lights me up from inside – and then I realise the light is somehow in front of me, dazzling my eyes; it's so bright. I'm blinded by it, unable to look away. I'm not frightened, just transfixed. I can hear murmuring voices, they are saying my name.

And I realise *I'm* laughing, because it really is like in the films. How funny! And – predictable! A bright light . . .

I calmly watch it move towards me, feel myself relax – and then, I simply let go.

★   ★   ★

It is as I am staring unseeing through the window, head leaned back on the yellow chair, that something prickles at my skin. Instinctively, I lift my exhausted, red eyes and train them on the still and dark garden – as it would be at one in the morning. The reflection of the fresh snow is making everything more visible than it otherwise would be, and the unspoiled expanse of lawn is an eerily empty stage. Everything feels poised; I expect a fox to emerge from the hedge to trot delicate, precise tracks through the middle of the clearing. But there is nothing, no sign of life. Mathias is in his crib, Rob lying on our bed alongside him, dozing fitfully.

I drop my gaze again. Time isn't even registering any more, one hour simply bleeding into the next . . . The nights I have spent sat slumped on the edge of our bed, mechanically rocking Mathias, have proven good practice for this. When I give up and the movement stops, that's when his eyes flicker open . . . it's all in the timing. Playing the long game. You can't give up . . . I don't *want* to give up. I need to believe that there is still a chance Anya might have survived.

I stare at the puffy, heavily laden branches of the snow-clad fir trees and then up at the clear, quiet sky, but this time, my taut focus snaps as the slightest of movements catches my eye, like someone slipping out of sight behind the summer house over by the back gate. Very alert now, heart thudding, I blink and sit up a bit − fiercely fix my gaze on the snow. There are no marks, there is nothing there . . . but it looked just like a child running to hide! I breathe out slowly. My shattered mind is starting to play very cruel tricks on me.

I'm cautiously leaning back in my chair again when it feels as if the presence is now suddenly behind me; someone has just crept in through the study door. I swear I hear a floorboard creak lightly: they are standing there waiting for me to turn to face them. I grab the arms of the chair and whip round . . . but the room is empty. The computer sits quietly on the desk, the chair is still, the stove cold . . . nothing moves at all.

Only then do I smell it. The study is suddenly full of the scent of apples. I am not imagining it − I'm certain. It's Anya's scent. Unmistakably her. As strong as if she were here, standing right next to me.

I begin to look around wildly, trying to make sense of what's happening − and Rob appears sleepily round the door. Confused, I stare at him. Was it him coming downstairs that I sensed? And as for the smell . . . I am very, very tired. 'Any news?' he says. 'I just woke up. Sorry. I didn't mean to fall . . .' but he pauses mid-sentence and sniffs. 'Apples?' he says, bewildered.

His words freeze me to the spot. He smells it, too? I suck the air in through my nose deeply, desperate to see if . . . But now there is nothing. Now I can't smell it at all!

It – she – has gone.

'*No!*' I shriek, and Rob jumps violently, then looks at me, horrified, as if I am unhinged.

My cry bounces from the walls of the empty room . . . and then the sound dies away completely.

Chapter Twenty-Eight

Her body looks so small and limp as the divers float her to the shore.

The Embassy representative tries to hold him back, but Will breaks free as she is lifted from the water and pushes his way through the small crowd of people who have quickly surrounded her, are pulling at her dive suit and shouting things he doesn't understand. As he stands there in horror, one of the paramedics attempts to lie her flat on the ground and Will watches her arms flop uselessly to one side, and her head slump. Her eyes are closed too, her mouth slightly open. He wants to shove them all aside, grab her and shake her – start shouting at her to look at him, *say* something! He looks wildly around at the medical team. Why are they moving so slowly?

'*Help* her!' he yells, and it makes everyone jump, except for the paramedics, who simply ignore him and carry on with what they are doing, apparently checking her for signs of life, trying to rouse her. One of them calls something out in Spanish, and the lawyer moves quickly to their side and says, 'Anya? Can you hear me? Can you talk to me please, Anya?'

She doesn't respond, and Will gives a low moan of fright, both hands now in his hair, eyes wide and fixed on her grey face.

Someone shoves past him and sinks to the ground with a large piece of kit, from which they start unwrapping paddles. *Oh my God*, he thinks, *they're going to shock her*. It's like watching something from a TV medical drama, only it's happening right in front of him, it's real.

Her body lurches, before slumping again. He hears someone shout another instruction, and her body jerks for a second time. He looks up at the exhausted divers who are looking on quietly, like everyone, waiting for a reaction.

They keep waiting.

The medical team begin to talk urgently among themselves. Again Will can't understand the low hum, can only watch as they start to rush her towards the ambulance. The Embassy representative, who is standing next to them, says something sharply in Spanish and the police start to move everyone else back, as the representative grabs Will's sleeve and pulls. 'Come on! You can go in the ambulance with her.'

They are skilfully preparing Anya to be loaded on, and Will is about to climb in next to her when a woman breaks free from the crowd and rushes up to him. It is the lawyer's wife. 'I didn't know in time!' she bursts out in English. 'That he was taking just her. If I had, I'd have stopped it. Believe me.

'I'd have stopped it,' she repeats, as her husband steps forward in confusion. He speaks to her in Spanish, presumably asking what's going on, but Will doesn't hear the answer over the engine starting up and someone slamming the ambulance doors shut. As they begin to pull sharply away, Will fixes on Anya's motionless face – eyes closed, mouth forced open by a tube. She doesn't even react when the siren gives a singular blast – or when he slowly reaches out and gently touches her cold, pale cheek.

★ ★ ★

My eyes flicker open – and the lights are so bright it hurts. I have no idea where I am, but it feels warm and smells clean. All I can make out are blurry figures buzzing around me. I turn my head groggily at the sound of talking, but can't understand what is being said.

I attempt to sit up, frightened, and one hazy figure moves towards me saying tentatively, in a voice I finally recognise, 'Anya? Don't be scared. It's me.'

Their hand slips into mine, and I know exactly who it is.

It makes me start to cry.

Chapter Twenty-Nine

At first, I can only stare at Will. 'You came all this way for me?'

He nods, and shrugs helplessly. 'How could I not?'

He gives a small smile, but he looks broken: dirty, tired and terrified.

He glances down self-consciously. 'I know, I'm sorry, I look a state.'

'No, you don't,' I say quickly. This must have cost him very dearly, in many ways. 'I am so, so sorry, Will,' I whisper, ashamed. 'I didn't mean—'

'Don't try to talk,' he says quickly. 'There'll be plenty of time for that later.'

There's a long pause, and at the same time we seem to realise we are still holding hands. 'When you're better,' he says, gently removing his, 'and you can come out of hospital, shall I take you back to Kate's?'

Overwhelmed, I only manage to nod again – and silently wipe away a few tears, worried that if I say anything more, I might break down completely.

'Please don't cry!' he begs. 'I promise I will take you, just as soon as they'll let me.'

'Is Kate angry with me?'

'No!' He shakes his head emphatically and moves a little closer. 'She's worried about you, Anya. She just wants you back with her now, that's all – you've been so ill.'

'I have to tell her I'm sorry.' I try to sit up, not realising I am connected to all sorts of wires and a drip.

'OK,' Will says hastily. 'We'll just call her, shall we?' He looks about him, mutters *Sod it* and reaches for his phone. 'We'll do it right now . . . Kate?' He looks at me as he starts to speak, his eyes shining. 'I've got someone here who wants to talk to you . . . Yes, she has, literally just now. Hang on . . .' Smiling, he holds the phone out, and when he sees I can't quite manage to take it, holds it to my ear as I crane my neck up a little.

The room starts to swim as I move, and my head feels very, very heavy. But all I can think about is Kate. I am determined to speak to her.

'Anya?'

And there she is. My sister. I start to weep again. 'Kate, I'm so sorry. I never meant this to . . .'

'Don't, An.' I think she's crying too. It's such a huge, huge relief to hear her voice. 'It doesn't matter, it just doesn't matter. I love you so much! And when you get home, I'm going to . . .'

Her voice begins to sound somehow more distant.

'I'm so sorry,' I say again – and then Will seems to be ducking down, something has clattered to the floor and the colours of the room are fading, the picture in front of me is draining away. Then there are shadows and shapes moving quickly, gentle hands reaching out – I can sense I am being surrounded, can hear someone saying my name. I try very hard to answer over an alarm that has begun to sound about me, but equally, in a moment of clarity realise everything is completely beyond my control, but it's not frightening. Everything is simply melting peacefully away.

I did it. I spoke to her.

Chapter Thirty

Bright shafts of sunlight are picking up flecks of floating dust, and it's warm enough in the small room for the study to feel slightly stuffy.

I'm staring through the window into Kate's garden, nose practically pressed up against the glass. The snow has long since melted away, and it's a glorious summer afternoon. Fat hot-pink rose heads and curls of honeysuckle are contrasted against the blue sky – I can practically smell their old-fashioned sweetness. The trees are in full leaf . . . and there is Kate, carrying a laden tray across the grass towards their shade.

I watch her set it down carefully on the small

wrought-iron table. Teapot, cups, a small milk jug. Side plates too, and a sponge cake. It makes me smile to see her brush her hands briefly on her skirt, surveying everything critically – but satisfied with the spread, she steps away and moves to check on Matty, who is lying on a blanket in the cool. His now chubby little legs are floppily relaxed and his cheeks flushed. He has his tiny mouth slightly open and I imagine he is probably snoring fatly, like a little piglet.

Rob is next to him, also asleep, but with a hand reached out protectively towards his son. Kate pauses and stares at them – and her face completely relaxes. She is positively bathing them in love. It brings a lump to my throat, and tearfully, I turn my gaze instead to Will, who is reclining a little farther away on a lounger. He has his eyes closed, face turned up to the sun. I can see his freckles starting to appear. He twitches slightly, my scrutiny perhaps disturbing him, like someone gently stroking your hair when you weren't expecting it. He changes position slightly and folds his arms, but then resettles happily.

I can't stop staring at them all. It's a sight that once seemed so very far away from me as to be impossible.

'Anya?' There is a cough, and I turn back to the woman who is sitting in the cream chair, waiting for me.

'Sorry,' I apologise, 'I lost myself there for a moment.'

'It's fine. We're nearly done for today.'

'Where did we get up to?'

'Your rescuer's torches coming up through the water towards you—'

'—that I thought were angels,' I say, embarrassed. 'I was very confused.'

'Confused . . .' Claire repeats, sounding almost amused. 'Anya, doing research for this, I found out about an incident that happened in South Africa about twenty years ago. A student who had never dived a cave before went into the Sterkfontein system, a series of underwater chambers and lakes. He became separated from his dive partners who got out and raised the alarm. But because of "adverse conditions" and unexplained police delays,' she pauses and looks at me pointedly, 'not only did they not search for him properly, they did what amounted to about five hours across five weeks. Eventually they found his body, which was on a small beach in an air dome they hadn't realised was there. When they conducted the post-mortem, they found that he'd got three weeks' worth of beard growth and a body-mass loss of twenty kilos. He had been trapped, alive, waiting to be rescued, for *three weeks* before he died. He left messages to his family – scrawled in the beach shingle, I think.'

I look down at the floor.

'So I would say, thinking you were seeing angels probably wasn't far off from reality, if you know what I mean,' she says sardonically. 'If the police had stuck to their guns and not let the divers in to look for you again . . . On the other hand, if my colleague hadn't called that lawyer in the first place . . .'

'It wouldn't have made any difference,' I say quietly, thinking of Rafa as I say that. 'We didn't have enough air to get out. I know now that cave divers work on a rule of thirds. You keep at least an extra third of your air supply in reserve in case of an emergency. Neither of us had done that. Your colleague wasn't to blame.'

'But I'm his boss.' She corrects me subtly and then shrugs with a sigh. 'I thought he was up to something, but I didn't stop to check. I should have. That's why, when I found out the whole story, I had to contact you guys afterwards to put things right . . . come and talk to you in person.'

Not that she saw a potentially lucrative opportunity, then? Perhaps I'm a little more cynical than I used to be. Although it's OK, I suppose, we all have something we want to come out of this.

'Thank God you found that air space. And,' she continues, gaining momentum, 'what if that little girl hadn't seen the truck on the Tuesday and reported it? Imagine that . . . Rafa really wasn't the expert instructor after all, was he?'

I glance away. Maybe I will let her think that's how it happened. This 'real-life' memoir she's so enthused about writing and having published doesn't need to be the whole truth. Haven't enough people already been hurt without anyone needing to know exactly what happened once Rafa and I went under the water?

Chapter Thirty-One

As we began our descent, despite trying to tell myself it was all in my mind and Rafa didn't really mean me any harm, my fear had begun to blow up into a full panic attack.

Rafa looked at me quizzically through his mask – he could see from the bubbles that I was breathing fast. *Are you OK?* he signalled, and I signed back that yes, I was, as I tried to calm myself and not think about the stories I'd been told about perfectly rational people suddenly feeling compelled to rip their mask off at depth, despite the obvious dangers.

Not that I'd ever had a problem diving before, it

was simply because I was with him. What was he going to do once we were out of the water? I could feel his eyes on me again as we drifted towards the cave entrance. Even though we were passing serene fronds, floating elegantly in the sunlight that was streaming into the water from above, I felt nothing but a mounting sense of dread. I wanted to get away from him.

The dark, wide seam in the rock loomed out towards me and my heart thudded. What was I going to do? *What was I going to do?*

Several small fish darted out of our way, making plain their intention to avoid us and the cave completely, as Rafa, who was ahead of me, turned, stopped and gestured towards the entrance.

I hesitated. If we didn't go into the cave, in mere minutes we'd be climbing out of the water . . . and intuitively I knew that only meant danger for me. There was no doubt in my mind. Attempting to think clearly, and trying to stall, I followed him into the edge of the mouth and we peered in. He shone his torch into the darkness. The light picked up the edges of a sign – on which there was a skull and crossbones. Dear God, he hadn't been joking. He motioned for me to follow him over to the board for a closer look, and I shook my head. I couldn't have done it even if I'd wanted to. Again he beckoned me. Again I refused.

He moved so fast, I barely realised what was happening until it was too late.

Blocking my exit with his body, he reached down for his dive knife and whipped the blade right up, inches in front of my terrified face. He paused for a moment, then jerked towards me. Instinctively I pulled back, away from him.

Closer still he came – he was forcing me into the cave. The darkness enveloped us as he moved us away from the comparatively radiant patch of turquoise blue that led straight to the surface. I felt something dig into my back. It was the sign. We were in.

Incredulously, I then watched him lower his blade and give me a delighted thumbs-up, before gesturing around us.

Was he fucking *serious*? He actually thought that was a reasonable way to 'help' me into the cave? Barely breathing, I let the tension in my arms relax slightly, only for him to reach out and grab my torch from my unsuspecting hand. I felt my stomach jolt with sick fear as I spun in the water to watch him bolting off past the sign, almost playfully, much deeper into the cave.

I didn't even stop to think about it. So petrified was I of being left alone in the dark, I made the second-biggest snap decision of my life. I followed him.

The thin dual beams of torchlight illuminated the monster's garden around us as Rafa forced us on. Weird, misshapen rock formations like oversized sculptures were everywhere, icicle-like speleothems looming out of the darkness, the like of which I'd only ever seen before in pictures. The ceiling looked as if it belonged in a crazed gothic ice church – the creation of someone on narcotics – with hundreds of rock conicals coming down to sharp points, in places nearly meeting their counterparts growing from the ground up. I might have found it spectacular, had I not been desperate to get out.

Dead ahead of us was what looked like an under-water runaway-train mineshaft entrance, only with two rocks either side of it rather than the archetypal wooden sleepers. The water was so clear, I could also see the start of a fixed line someone before us had left behind, disappearing out of sight through the 'doorway'.

Oh God, he wasn't going to go in there, was he?

Sure enough, he picked up pace and darted through

the gateway. My chest tight with the effort of keeping up, I attempted to stay right behind him.

The main passage had tunnels leading off it, like a windpipe branching into a pair of lungs. The guide-line was on my right, and as he selected the left-hand branch, I quickly calculated that to get back out again, I'd have to turn 180 degrees and then at the intersection turn right, and the guideline would be on my left.

Blood pounding in my head, I rounded a bend and drew up short as there he was, waiting for me. To my astonishment, he gave me another delighted thumbs-up and passed me back my light, like what had just happened was no big deal. Grabbing at it shakily, I barely paid attention to his motioning that we would do just five more minutes, clearly under the impression he'd broken my fear. After a second or two, as I tried frantically to gather myself, I signed my agreement, waited until he'd turned to swim on and then swung round on the spot. I was getting out of here *right now*.

But as I moved, inexplicably the water went from clear to zero visibility. It took just seconds. I could see nothing but dense floating particles; it was as if someone had shaken out a giant Hoover bag.

Trying to swallow my new panic, I remembered what I had been told during my open-water training about emergencies. *Keep calm. Stop.* I waited for the water to settle.

But it didn't.

I had no idea what had happened, why it was suddenly like this – I literally couldn't see my hand in front of my face. I couldn't see my console, and had no way of telling how much air I had. I needed to leave the cramped passageway, move to where surely the visibility would be better.

So I very carefully turned the 180 degrees that I knew would retrace my steps, and allowed myself to drift back down the tunnel. I was going to be *fine*. I felt myself reach the intersection; turned right.

It was going to be OK.

I put my left hand out.

But the line wasn't there.

I felt my heart flutter. Had I turned too far, gone in a complete circle? I couldn't have . . . I wasn't coming back on myself, was I? I looked around. Where the hell was the line? And where was Rafa?

I tried to reason it out. It didn't feel like I'd turned *that* much. I'd not done more than half a circle. I must have gone in the right direction, surely? I turned and retraced my movements. But the water wasn't clouded when I returned. Had it settled, or was this a different chamber?

I stopped. Did another 180 degrees, came back for my second go – but still nothing. No line, no large room ahead, ready to open out to safety.

I started to think about the other offshoot passages, and turned cold. Had I gone down one of them by mistake? Now completely disorientated, I looked around myself frantically. I reached up, and my fingers made contact with the rock ceiling just a little way above my head.

I began to breathe faster and had to make a huge effort to force myself to stay calm. Rafa was still in here somewhere . . . I checked my console, and realised it wasn't working properly, displaying information I *knew* was wrong . . . Perhaps the wireless signal was confused in the cave? I waved my arm to see if that would help, and immediately smashed the screen into a rock, breaking it completely. I knew the danger that alone placed me in. I had to get out immediately, without any more delay.

The next few moments spent blundering blindly around in the tunnels count as some of the most frightening of my life. I realised there was every chance I was simply going deeper and deeper underground, but I didn't know what else to do. I didn't recognise anything at all . . . when, thank God, the passageway began to widen.

My heart lifted with hope, and I was so sure I'd found my way back; but when I turned and shone my light behind me, there were no two stones either side of the gateway and no line. It wasn't the same entry point.

I was lost. I had no idea where I was.

Em, Kate, Mum and Dad appeared in my head . . . and I tried very hard not to think about how it might feel to run out of air, and if it was going to hurt.

I swam back in to the narrower section – I had no choice, I had to find the exit point . . . faster and faster I went down the Swiss-cheese passages, began to chant the Lord's Prayer through in my head as my fear mounted with every turn that didn't take me to the line, or the magical patch of light blue that led to the surface and safety.

This way and that; my movements became more and more frenzied, I could hear my breathing escalating, becoming panicked gasps – as the battery power of my light started to fade. Without a torch I had no hope, no hope at all. I would be in pitch-black, unable to see a thing – incapable of swimming to safety. It began to dwindle even more, dimmed further still . . . and then expired completely. I was plunged into darkness.

A scream burst inside my head as I groped forwards, my hands out in front of me, barely moving even inches in the black. The rocks I'd admired earlier were now liabilities, able to cut or catch me to them. Blindly trying to feel my way through the water, fingers scrabbling, I felt the tunnel lift slightly: I'd just gone uphill.

Then, just as suddenly *I* lifted, as if I had risen above the water. I distinctly felt my head come clean out of it. I unsteadily put my hand down beneath me and felt a large rock. I wasn't able to stand, and there was no floor below my feet, but I was able to half lean myself against it. I ripped back my mask, removed my regulator – and took a damp gulp. I was *breathing*!

Instinctively I laughed, giddily, and then just as quickly began to weep with the relief.

Miraculously, I'd found air, completely by accident. I was the luckiest, luckiest girl in the world.

It took a moment or two, but my initial sense of

release was such that I was able, comparatively rationally, to work out that because there was no light at all, there wouldn't be an immediately obvious seam or crack in the rock leading to the ground above, despite the fact that I was able to breathe. I knew these underwater systems were shallow – Rafa and I had discussed depths – but there was no obvious dry exit point here. Was it more likely that the dome I was in had resulted at some stage – probably years ago – from a partial ceiling collapse, which would explain the rock beneath me? I carefully adjusted my leaning position on it, upper body like an encumbered, half-beached mermaid, legs still dangling in the water. Did that also mean the air was, at some point, going to run out? I swallowed. It was so dark I had no way of knowing how large or small a space it was.

The hideous irony that my only hope of escape was Rafa, looming out of the darkness, was not lost on me.

Now of course I know that he tried. That in fact he died looking for me.

He *did* end up knowing a secret – it was not simply a dive that went wrong because he led me

382

to believe he was properly trained when he wasn't; although that is what everyone thinks. When asked, I told the authorities that we swam into the cave and we became separated. I tried to escape and found the air dome, where I waited to be rescued. Which is true, if not the whole story.

How would it help his family to know that I was afraid for my life? That, whatever his reasons, Rafa had forced me into that cave and I became lost trying to escape *him*? Their son, maybe someone's brother, will still be dead. Isn't it better that he is allowed to be a hero to them, and that they believe he died honourably, looking for me?

I thought a lot about his girlfriend afterwards, too, given she was under the impression that her boyfriend had been cheating on her when he died.

So I contacted her. Maybe it was survivor's guilt, or shame for my part in Rafa's plot to make her jealous. I wanted to make it better for her.

I called her at the dive shop, pretending to be enquiring about an excursion, but then confessed who I was and told her that she should know nothing had happened between Rafa and me at all. He had been in love with *her*. He was just a guy trying to make his girlfriend jealous.

'He told you I was his girlfriend?' There was a silence down the phone. 'Do you always believe things that men tell you when you have only just met them?'

I was totally taken aback, and only managed a foolish, stumbled 'Um, I don't know, really.' Then I realised Rafa hadn't told me anything, not to start with. I had assumed they were together when I saw them arguing in the shop.

'What else did he say?' she demanded.

'That he wanted you to leave your husband,' I stammered.

She said nothing for a moment, but then, her voice shivering with energy, she said, 'You have no idea. No idea at all. Let me guess about *you* and Rafa. He said you were special, that he was lucky to have met you.'

Shocked, I gripped the phone a little tighter. Said baldly out of context like that, the sentiment sounded so throwaway and cheap.

'Did he also say he was going to change your life for ever? Did you let down your guard? He was very charming. Girls didn't often say no to him. And let me assure you, he didn't like it if you tried to. He didn't like it at all.'

Then I remembered him tightly holding her wrist, and her trying to struggle free.

'You were a fool.' Her voice thickened and I realised she was near to tears. 'But you got to fly home, safe, away from here. Consider yourself very lucky.' And then she hung up.

Perhaps it was only to be expected that she was angry – and hostile. If some strange woman who knew I'd been having an affair rang *me* out of the blue, and I thought there was a chance my husband might find out – wouldn't I say something, *anything*, to get rid of her? And if Esther had been involved with Rafa, and knew I was the last woman to spend time with him, time that she would never believe wasn't intimate, wouldn't she hate me and want to say something to hurt me?

But equally I wondered exactly what she had been alluding to. Had she just confirmed that my instinct about Rafa had been right?

There was still no actual evidence of any wrongdoing, bar his waving the knife around, which could simply have been a very misguided attempt to, as he said, 'help' me. And when Kate haltingly confessed about her having called the newspapers, doing criminal-record searches on Rafa – which Claire subsequently discovered related to a different man altogether – I saw once again how powerful and destructive unanswered questions can be.

I don't want to place doubt in the minds of his family, leave them forever wondering 'what if'. So isn't it better that I say nothing?

Even though I will never know if I made the right choice to swim away from him. If I had stayed with him, would we have both survived?

Shaking slightly, I lean over to let in some air, glancing at Kate's picture of Emily as I do so. The room has suddenly become very oppressive.

I simply followed my instinct. It was all I had.

The sound of children playing in nearby gardens carries over to us, and it's a relief to hear happy, normal noise.

I open the window, making Will, who has woken up, glance over. At first he smiles happily at me, but then he frowns, presumably at the sight of my expression, and says something to Kate I don't catch. He has already risen to his feet, and she in turn is looking anxious. They begin to make their way to the back door and before I can say anything, they appear in the room with us.

'Are you all right?' Will says in concern. 'You looked upset.'

'I'm fine.' I smile at him. 'I think we're done now anyway, aren't we?'

Claire nods. 'Unless you can think of anything we've missed?'

I hesitate. 'If I do, I'll let you know.'

'OK, well, I'm going to get writing,' she says excitedly. 'I'll have a first draft of the manuscript to you soon, I hope. Structurally I thought maybe I'd start with you, Kate, then tell Anya's side of the story, intersperse it with Will's experiences.'

'Have you contacted Ramiro Garza yet?' Will says.

'The police chief guy? Don't worry.' Claire smiles briefly. 'I've got it covered.'

'And you'll also be sure to put the charity contact details in at the end?' I ask. 'So people can donate to the voluntary rescue organisation?'

She nods. 'I promise. This won't have all been in vain, Anya,' she adds earnestly.

Evidently she thinks this is my attempt to make good, to serve up a warning to other travellers – even seasoned ones like me – not to let your guard down, not to relax *too* much.

Perhaps I did allow myself to become complacent,

and distracted. Esther was right. I am very lucky –
because if my experience has stripped me of some
of my exuberance, it has still not left my new world
wanting. I look at Kate – and then Will. Rather, my
eyes are now opening to new possibilities. But I don't
want to talk about what happened any more, and I
can't help a tired tear sliding down my face.

Kate is too quick even for Will, crossing the room
to wrap me in a tight hug. 'Don't cry,' she whispers,
as she strokes my hair. 'It's over. You're home now.'

Donations to the fund for international cave rescues can be made at www.littlesisterfund.co.uk